AFTER GLADYS

Helen Ryan

Copyright © 2022 Helen Ryan

All rights reserved, including the right to reproduce this book, or portions thereof in any form. No part of this text may be reproduced, transmitted, downloaded, decompiled, reverse engineered, or stored, in any form or introduced into any information storage and retrieval system, in any form or by any means, whether electronic or mechanical without the express written permission of the author.

This is a work of fiction. Names and characters are the product of the author's imagination and any resemblance to actual persons, living or dead, is entirely coincidental.

The views expressed in this work are solely those of the author and do not necessarily reflect the views of the publisher, and the publisher hereby disclaims any responsibility for them.

ISBN: 9798356420573

PublishNation
www.publishnation.co.uk

"It isn't possible to love and to part. You will wish that it was. You can transmute love, ignore it, muddle it, but you can never pull it out of you. I know from experience that the poets are right: love is eternal."

E.M. Forster

Previously...
{The Demise of Gladys King}

Having done the bidding of little old lady Gladys King – sordid though it was – Jane reaped the reward she'd been promised and become a millionaire on Gladys' death. Gladys' two nieces, her only living heirs, had suspected foul play but failed to produce any evidence to that effect and the case was settled.

Jane was keen to leave her safe, comfortable life in Guildford and move to a rural retreat in the Cotswolds with husband, Larry. Larry was much less eager to do so but felt unable to resist his strong-willed wife.

Shortly after moving into her beautiful, converted barn, Jane is desperate to show off her property to a group of their close friends and has a New Year's Eve party. The following day, on Jane's insistence, despite the dense fog which has settled over the fields and roads and the sciatica which he's developed after all the household tasks assigned to him, Larry provides one of the guests, Debbie, with a lift to the railway station. On his way home, he swerves to avoid a cyclist. His car turns over and he is killed instantly.

This is what happens afterwards...

CHAPTER 1

A vapour trail of sorrow

When Debbie went to see Jane, she found herself standing in the same room she herself had occupied only months previously. Except now it was January, the blinds were down and there was a heaviness in the air-tight room which spoke of grief.

She had closed the door quietly, shutting out the memory of visiting her dying father on a similar grey afternoon in winter, years ago. Although longing to snap up the blinds and allow access to what pitiful amount of light there was available, she'd held back, whispering instead to the figure lying across the bed, face down.

"Jane, it's me, Debbie."

Stella had called her on her way to work the day before, to relay the news about Larry. Her first thoughts had been about her own role in the tragedy. Had she kept stock of time she would have called for a cab instead of relying on Larry's kindness. But Stella had anticipated this response and was prepared.

"Don't torment yourself, Debbie. This was an accident. A horrible, tragic accident."

She'd wept then, standing on Firth Street, amongst the early bird shoppers and office workers, sweeping around and past her, clutching their coffee cups and shouting into their phones. She'd wondered briefly whether to retreat home, but she was almost at the deli and they would struggle without her. She stood in front of a book shop, wiped her eyes and popped a mint in her mouth. Staring at her reflection in the window, the cover of a book on display came slowly into focus. *Don't Look Down*, a memoir by someone she'd never heard of, showed the back of a man clinging to a sheer face of rock while a blizzard raged about him. Given the plight of the lone climber, however experienced he might be, the advice seemed somewhat inadequate.

Stella had told her of Jane's call, received in the dead of night, and how Bob had not heard her vibrating mobile and thus slept on, unaware. She'd left the bedroom, unable, initially, to absorb the news while prone. It was only when she was on her feet, her blood circulating, that she realised who was calling her and why.

Debbie had hoped for more detail, had wanted to detain Stella a little longer – anything so that she wasn't about to be left alone with the appalling news that Larry lived less than ten minutes after she had pecked him on the cheek, his warm cheek, in the station carpark only the day before.

She had thought him preoccupied on their drive. He'd seemed tense. She mentioned the fog and, once, on a tight bend, had gripped the sides of the passenger seat. He'd murmured an apology and said something about the adverse weather conditions but hadn't spoken again apart, ironically, from wishing her 'a safe trip' when they drew up at the station. She'd been glad when the journey was over, hoping to disguise her relief by smiling broadly and saying how grateful she was. But he didn't look back when she turned around on the station steps to wave to him. She watched as he did a rapid three-point turn and sped off, back into the unyielding fog, to his death. And then she'd heard an announcement regarding the arrival of her train and had only made it aboard because one of the guards had seen her scuttling across the footbridge and waited before dinging his bell.

Stella had called Debbie from her car, on her way to collect Jane and bring her back to stay with them. She'd left Bob, reeling from the news, to ensure the boys got up before noon and attempted some homework, now that the new school term was looming. The boys were perfectly capable of fending for themselves, but Stella still preferred one of them to be there, casting a parental eye over their antics. Luckily, Bob was working from home that week. He hadn't offered to come with her. They both knew, without any discussion, that Jane would prefer just Stella's company. So, despite the rush hour – which was much less because the schools were yet to go back – she had left the house by eight o'clock.

Before she rang off, Stella assured Debbie that she'd call again that evening and let her know how Jane was – as if either of them would need a description to appreciate the immensity of her loss. Debbie was on her way to bed when her mobile rang. Although she could hear the exhaustion in Stella's voice, she also recognized that Stella wanted to talk and process what she'd been through during that long day; off load it all before attempting to sleep.

"She's holding it together very well. In fact, so much so, that I fear for her."

"She's a very practical person, isn't she? It probably comes in useful in such times."

"Yes. She'd already told Larry's brother, Michael. They were close, I understand. In fact, Bob and I have met him a couple of times. I think he lives somewhere in south-west London. Anyway, he's coming over the day after tomorrow so that they can arrange the funeral."

"Where will it take place? Larry's friends and colleagues all live around here."

"I'm presuming it will be local to here. But I don't know. I suppose they'll work out the details over the next few days."

"Where's Larry now? If you see what I mean."

"In a chapel of rest in Cirencester."

"Oh. I'd have thought Jane would have wanted to remain where she was so that she could visit him. Or is that just me?"

"I don't think she wanted to be on her own. Can you imagine what it must have felt like to be so alone in that strange, unfamiliar place on such a night?"

But Debbie's intuition proved correct.

Jane had sat up with a start on hearing Debbie's whisper.

"Sorry," said Debbie. "I should have knocked."

"Debbie," said Jane. She was wearing plain trousers and a tee shirt. A jumper was slung over the leather chair and a holdall was open on the coffee table. Debbie reached over to her, smoothing down her tangled hair as if she were a child rudely awoken from a dream.

"I'm so, so sorry," she said.

Jane nodded, pressing both her hands into her shoulders and massaging the back of her neck.

"My neck aches like hell," she said, closing her eyes and looking up towards the ceiling, as she worked her muscles.

"You poor thing. You must feel absolutely wretched."

Debbie stood up.

"Shall I open the blinds?"

Jane nodded again.

"I lived in here for a couple of months, if not longer," Debbie said. "It seems so strange to be back."

They looked at each other as the weak afternoon light gradually entered the room. There were bluish circles under Jane's eyes.

"I don't suppose you thought for a minute you would be."

Jane reached over to the chair for her jumper, bringing it over her head. Debbie recognised it as the pink cashmere she'd worn the day she'd told them all about the new house in the Cotswolds. She couldn't remember the details of Jane's conversation with Jill, but she did recall the way she'd brushed the crumbs from her jumper in a clear expression of her irritation. Why did they both continue with the pretence of friendship, she wondered?

"Stella told me you'd been in touch with Larry's brother. It must have been terribly difficult to relay such news."

"Awful. But there was some tiny comfort in sharing it. And he's taken over a lot of the other calls I needed to make. So…" she trailed off, her voice breaking a little.

Debbie went back over and sat down next to her on the bed, taking her hand.

"Be kind to yourself, Jane."

There was silence between them as Jane pressed a tissue into the corners of her eyes.

"I don't know what I'm doing here," she said.

Debbie squeezed her hand. She knew precisely what she meant.

"I understand."

"Do you think Stella and Bob would think me mad if I said I wanted to go back? To be near him."

"No," said Debbie, her own eyes filling on hearing Jane's words. "They would think that whatever helps you is what you should do."

They sat on for a long while, only speaking occasionally.

Outside, the wintry light leaked away leaving just the glow of a halo around the moon.

~ ~ ~

Michael collected Jane the following evening and they drove back to *The Old Byre*. He was younger than Larry by a few years and although the brothers shared some physical characteristics – same colouring, height and build – they were very different in other ways. From an early age, Michael had rejected any idea of a conventional working life inside an office. He'd held a variety of jobs where he worked in the open air, eventually settling on the life of a tree surgeon – albeit in the suburbs of London. In the prime areas of the capital, he maintained, there was always an abundance of work from wealthy householders prepared to pay high prices to keep their wisteria in check and their hedges maintained. It had its risks. On many an occasion, Larry had shaken his head in disbelief when learning of his brother's latest adventure with a chainsaw thirty feet above ground.

"He'll come a cropper one of these days," was one of their mother's familiar observations on her younger son's choice of career. "It'll be his arm or his leg," she would add, dourly. "Why couldn't he have chosen something safe like Larry? Larry doesn't have to hang from a rope at the top of trees to earn a good living."

It was as well she was no longer alive to experience the bitter irony of Larry's fate.

Michael was married with three children, all adult and well on their way to full independence. None of his offspring had chosen 'safe' pursuits. His two sons had gone from skateboarding to *Parkour*. One of them now worked full time for his father and was likely to take over the business. The other ran a diving school in Spain and his daughter, the youngest, had been a gymnast and was looking into joining a circus as a tightrope walker. How their mother, Lilly, ever slept at night had baffled Larry.

Michael said he would stay until after Larry's funeral. In January his workload was much less burdensome and what jobs there were in the diary, he could postpone or leave to his son to deal with. He was entranced by the house and its land, saying he could see what had drawn Jane to want to purchase it.

"This place is exactly where I'd like to end my days," he assured her, when she disclosed that Larry would not have chosen the property.

"I scoffed at his misgivings if I listened at all. I was so intent in getting what I thought I wanted – fulfilling some childhood fantasy. You can imagine how that feels now."

Jane's candour surprised Michael. He hadn't discerned any such reluctance from Larry, just assumed that they were both keen to embrace the country life. He and Lilly had talked about visiting them for a weekend in their new abode but nothing had been fixed. Indeed, he hadn't seen Larry for some months, although they were frequently in contact by email and on the phone.

Being with someone in the house brought some routine for Jane. There were walks together and meals were shared, although neither of them had much appetite. They would watch each other pushing the food around their plates and wonder why they just didn't agree to have a boiled egg and a piece of toast. In the evenings, Michael was in his room, skyping his family or watching the news on his laptop. Occasionally, they'd meet in the kitchen in the early hours of the morning, confessing that they were unable to sleep and hoping a cup of tea might help them settle. They'd shared some memories of Larry too, usually out walking when the feel of the cold air in their lungs and the sight of the frost in the fields made their grief more bearable.

"But there'll be no real memories of him in this house, will there?" she observed to Michael. They were having a drink together in front of the log burner which Michael had been keen to get going. Alcohol had not played much of a role since Larry's death. But that evening, as Larry's funeral loomed, Jane had suggested they share some wine before 'pretending to eat something.'

"Although, now the fire's going, I do have some vivid memories of him lugging logs backwards and forwards on new year's eve, not to mention grappling with the controls."

"He wasn't a particularly practical man," said Michael, noting that Jane had just smiled, and he couldn't recall seeing her do so before. "Although he had the upper hand with me on the internal combustion engine."

A little later, Jane went out to the kitchen to get their meal underway. When she returned, Michael was on his knees in front of the fire and she knew from his gently heaving shoulders, that he was crying. She'd known Larry around twenty-five years. He'd known him for the entirety of his life, she thought. Twice as long.

She returned to the kitchen grateful she'd taken her wine with her. Downing its contents in two greedy gulps, she took the bottle from the fridge and refilled her glass.

Michael spoke at the funeral. A testament to Larry's popularity, it was a packed affair in a crematorium unfamiliar to Jane. They'd arranged a lunch afterwards at a local hotel. Bob and Stella had driven up with Debbie. They'd offered to stay with Jane afterwards, as Michael was returning to London with Lilly and the children that same afternoon. She had declined, reassuring them that her parents were staying for a few days so she wouldn't be alone. Tabby and Mark had, very kindly, brought them in their car.

"Is it too soon to ask you if you have any plans?" asked Stella, when they found themselves together in the Ladies' room at the hotel, post lunch.

Stella had remarked to Bob that she thought Jane would survive her loss, 'more or less intact.' Looking at her, even in the harsh light of the fluorescent beam above them, Stella was even more convinced of this. Jane had clearly rejected the conventional image of the grieving widow. Concealer had been applied, Tabby-style, to the shadows beneath her eyes. She looked stunning in a red dress – apparently one of Larry's favourites – although walking behind his coffin the dress had not been in evidence. Jane had chosen to wear a long black woollen coat with a fur collar, reminiscent of a character from a Russian novel. Instead of a veil and hat, a large pair of sunglasses hid her eyes from the rest of the mourners. A light snowfall would have added to the drama of the scene but instead, a watery sun popped in and out of the clouds. Although Debbie and Stella had exchanged knowing glances when seeing how Jane had chosen to present herself, they had been cognizant of the occasion and avoided comment.

"I'm going to try to stay in the house," she said, applying a ruby coloured lipstick. She brought out a tissue and pressed it between her lips. "Being there with Michael, I realised how much I like it. It's a wonderful place and, yes, I know, it's too big and too expensive to run –" she laughed suddenly. "And I'm going to have to get a job! I can't really manage on what we have left having blown all the money on the house. Me, that is. I blew all the money. Doesn't it all just serve me right?"

"Jane…" Stella murmured, about to offer Jane a hug and then seeing the lipstick, decided against it. She patted her instead.

Jane blinked away her tears with a fierce shake of her head.

"No, it's true, Stella. I miss him. I miss his smile and ready laugh and no one will ever love me as he did. I let him go – and I will never forgive myself."

And then she laughed again, just briefly, before a tear rolled down her cheek.

"I got what I deserved. And it's to my shame that Larry didn't."

Jane dabbed the tear away, glancing at herself in the mirror. What a terrible burden beauty is, thought Stella. She wasn't sure she fully understood Jane's last comment about Larry. What she did understand was that guilt so often hooks up with grief to make the whole process just that bit more difficult for the bereaved to bear their loss.

"Jane," she said, recalling that this was just what she'd said to Debbie, "What happened to Larry was an accident. *An accident.*"

Someone should have got up from their seat at the service and shouted it out loudly, she decided.

"Anyway," sighed Jane. "My parents will stay with me for a while and that will distract me. I can concentrate on *their* welfare – instead of my own. Mum, particularly, is devasted about Larry. She adored him."

"We all did, Jane."

Jane nodded.

"We'd better get back. They'll be wondering if the wailing widow has topped herself."

So Jane, thought Stella, smiling at the remark. Whatever her faults, her vanity, she has such spirit.

"You only need to ask and I'll come down to stay or you can visit us – whenever you want."

"Thank you, Stella. You and Bob couldn't have been kinder. I feel very lucky to have you."

They went back out to join the rest of the mourners, most of whom were now heading back home. Michael had been looking for Jane, anxious to check on her before leaving. In the corner of the room, by a large window overlooking the hotel garden, she saw her parents. Her mother staring around her, her gloved hands twisting together, looked so tiny and isolated that Jane had to fight the desire to rush over and gather her in her arms. Her father was standing with his back to the room, his hands in his pockets. *I must get them home*, Jane thought, *they're exhausted.*

"Keep in touch," said Michael, hugging Jane to him. The words caught in his throat and he pulled away without looking at her.

Jane called after him. When he turned around, his expression was so like Larry's that it felt like she'd been winded. She grabbed the nearest chair to steady herself as a wave of longing swept over her. How would she ever survive never seeing him again?

"Michael. Thank you. Thank you for everything."

He nodded and made his way to the door, leaving a vapour trail of sorrow behind him.

CHAPTER 2

The clack of the letter box

Jane's parents were thrilled with *The Old Byre*. As they entered the lounge with its picture window, looking out over the courtyard, she saw her father bring his handkerchief out of his pocket to blow his nose.

"Larry must have loved this room," he said, his eyes inflamed with the tears he'd fought so valiantly against since he'd arrived at the crematorium that morning. "And just look at that. A wood burner. Oh, this place has everything, Jane. I'm not surprised you both fell in love with it."

"I'm not sure Larry felt quite the same as I did," Jane admitted.

"Probably because it will require quite a bit of upkeep, I imagine. That might have worried him."

Jane's stomach had been churning ever since they'd arrived back at the house. She kept reminding herself that she was shattered, that the day had been the worst of her life, that how else would she be feeling after saying farewell to the most significant person she knew. For all the brave words she spewed out to Stella, they were, ultimately, just that. Words. *Fighting talk*, as her father might have called them; designed to galvanise the army when their ammunition ran out and they faced annihilation.

"You'll feel better after a good night's sleep," said her mother, predictably, surveying her daughter's face now stripped of the mask she'd worn at the funeral.

"A good night's sleep?" Jane said, smiling. "What's that?"

The three of them were sitting in the kitchen, having opted for toast and jam before bed. They'd eaten at the hotel and needed nothing more substantial. The tortured passion of Chopin's Sonata in B flat minor occupied the room like an additional presence, removing the need for conversation.

As it happened, she did sleep that night. Somehow, her parents' presence during the evening, the love she felt flowing in her direction every time she might look at one of them, brought a calm to her she had not expected.

In the morning, some welcome news arrived in the post. Alex Snow had written informing her that there'd been an overpayment of inheritance tax and he was transferring the sum of £18784.32 into her account. It would keep her solvent for most of the year and enable her to take her time in finding another job. The letter also reminded her that she needed to get in touch with him about Larry's estate.

Despite her parents' advancing years, they were energetic people and, after a few days of living with them, Jane concluded that they spent less time than she did sitting around. Her mother would usually announce at the breakfast table what job she had lined up for the day.

"I'm going through the house with a duster today, Jane," she'd say.

Her father would be just as eager to show they were there as much for practical reasons as emotional ones.

"And I thought I'd sort out the log store. You'll need to order some more before too long. And, forgive me darling, but have you thought what you're going to do about Larry's cars? Would you like me to look into disposing of them to some collector? The last thing you want is them rusting in the drive over the winter."

"That would be so helpful, Dad. Although the Alfa is in quite a state, isn't it? Will anyone want it?"

The local garage had towed it back to the house after Larry's accident. It sat there, in the drive, the physical embodiment of Jane's loss. Every day she told herself that she would try to drive it into one of the garages but, when it came to it, she couldn't bear the idea of sitting in the seat where Larry had breathed his last moments. *Give yourself time,* she thought, wishing she'd asked Michael to do it when he'd stayed with her.

"Well, we'll find out, won't we?" said her father, gently. "But I'll need the receipts so see if you can dig them out. I expect Larry kept them in a file somewhere. You may as well get the benefit of the money." And then he'd stopped speaking and patted her hand. "Not that money is important at this time."

You don't know the half of it, thought Jane.

"Yes, Larry was well organised. I'll look for them as soon as I've finished my coffee and you can make a start."

So, in the week her parents stayed, there was not as much grief on display as Jane had expected. In fact, they appeared by their actions to be leading by example rather than delivering trite lectures about 'keeping busy' and 'staying positive.'

On their last evening together, they ate in the dining room, Jane unable to quell her anguish when she remembered the last time there had been a gathering around the table. There were candles and wine.

"I've appreciated everything you've done this week," she said to her parents, tears flooding her eyes. Fleetingly, she'd wondered about asking if they wanted to move in permanently with her, but she had the foresight to realise that such offers should not be made when emotions were running so high. Anyway, they had their own life back where they lived in their tatty little bungalow, on the edge of town. Her father still played bridge and supported the local football team. Her mother had three close friends she met up with on a regular basis. There were trips to historic houses and galleries, gardens and museums. They wouldn't be so stupid as to live in the middle of nowhere, dependent on Jane driving them places, miles away from the GP and the supermarket.

Jane's sadness was too much for her mother, who picked up her serviette and wiped her own tears away.

"Don't cry, mum," Jane said with a hiccough. "I'll be ok."

She looked at them both – their familiar expressions of concern – and added, "in the end."

~ ~ ~

Alex Snow was surprised to hear from his receptionist that Jane Sedgefield was on the phone and looking to make an appointment with him. He looked after his own diary, experience having taught him that allowing others any authority to manage his daily schedule ended in chaos. There would be three appointments listed in as many hours, barely allowing him to follow up immediately on his client's instructions. He liked to stay on top of his caseload rather than always chasing his tail, avoiding calls from clients or, even worse, lying to them about the progress he'd made.

Jane had decided not to email him with the news about Larry. Even though she was tempted, she felt it would dishonour Larry to do so.

"Mrs Sedgefield," he said when the call was transferred to him. "How's country life? Have you adapted yet?"

She was sure that she had given Mr Snow permission to use her first name but he appeared unable to step over the boundary into such dangerous territory. Larry had laughed at his adherence to formality.

"He's so obviously old school," he'd observed. "No doubt he was taught that maintaining a professional distance from clients is essential. Not that calling someone by their first name means that you're blurring the lines between business and pleasure."

Noting that Larry appeared a little jealous of her regard for her solicitor, Jane found the characteristic oddly endearing. You knew where you were with Alex Snow, she decided. His integrity was indisputable.

Rapidly, her words falling over each other in an effort to deliver the news about Larry in as succinct a form as possible, Jane told him that he had another probate matter on his hands.

"Although I assume it will be much less complicated this time," she finished off.

Jane's phlegmatic tone did not fool Mr Snow. He's seen it before. In order to maintain a sense of normality in a life shattered by sudden death, she was seeking order where she could find it. Sorting out Larry's affairs was one way in which she could pretend she was in control – even though the very experience of losing him had taught her a different lesson.

He offered his condolences, imagining her face as she spoke into her phone, no doubt standing in that magnificent kitchen – he'd seen the brochure – alone. Then he concentrated on the formalities of the process until the end of their conversation.

"Will you stay, Mrs Sedgefield? Stay where you are?"

"Jane, please. Please call me Jane. And yes, for the time being, I think I will." She laughed, suddenly, startling him. "However ridiculous that might appear."

"Why ridiculous? I don't see that."

"Because it was a shared dream, I suppose, and now it's not. And on a practical level, it's a large house. For one middle aged lady."

What a vacuous way of describing myself, she thought.

"There's nothing wrong in giving it a go. In fact, I admire you." And then he added, "Jane".

Jane imagined him blushing as he uttered her name. He would not find it comfortable to break with one of his rules even to accommodate her in her grief. She noted the brief silence and then, by way of ending their conversation, said she'd post the documents to him in the next couple of days.

Later, Alex Snow thought he should have advised her that she was undoubtedly capable of obtaining probate without instructing him to do so. This was as simple a matter as there could be. From what she'd said, there were no separate assets and they held the house as joint tenants. There was a will. There would be no inheritance tax implications. Although not wanting, in such an uncertain world, to reject new instructions, his fees for handling the estate of Gladys King had been substantial and the firm's conveyancing department had also benefitted. Rather than lose her as a client, however, he decided that he would undertake the matter but not bill her. It seemed entirely right in light of their history and, of course, the appalling blow Larry's sudden death must have dealt her.

After ringing off, Jane went back to the sorting out of Larry's clothes. It wasn't that she wanted to be rid of all trace of him. It was just something which needed doing, however painful, and she had neither the energy nor the heart to think up a more imaginative task for the day. And, having just moved, much of what 'needed doing' had been simplified for her. They'd both had a clear out of their wardrobes prior to moving day and most of their documentation had been neatly filed in the bureau in the hall. She'd found the receipts for Larry's cars within minutes of her father's request and he'd returned home with them, saying he'd sort it out and confirm the details with her. It would be difficult to watch the cars being collected: bits of Larry being driven away, never to be seen again. And what about his two sets of golf clubs? She should find a good home for them, too.

Both Stella and Debbie had been in touch in the last twenty-four hours, as if they'd made a note of the date when her parents would leave. Debbie was coming for the weekend, doing only a half day at the refuge on the Friday so that she could travel up to Cirencester in the afternoon. She'd been due some leave from the deli, she told Jane, so she could stay until Monday morning. In fact, she'd had to plead hard to have the Saturday *and* the Monday off work. In the end, reluctantly, she'd resorted to telling them what had happened over the new year and her boss had relented. But the tussle had annoyed Debbie. Given how badly paid she was, despite her competence, she'd not expected to be treated so disparagingly.

At the refuge, she was supporting Halina, who was originally from Poland and had a daughter, Alicja, aged fifteen. Halina was in her mid-thirties, a thin and unsmiling woman, often on edge, Debbie had struggled to make any sort of relationship with her. Halina had no problem with the language as Debbie had suspected when first meeting her. She just didn't appear to want anyone meddling in her affairs, despite having – apparently – fled to the refuge from an abusive relationship with a man, not Alicja's father. She said she'd been given an ultimatum by social services. Get away from him or we'll take your daughter. Debbie questioned whether it had been framed in such a harsh, unfeeling manner. After all, support had been offered, such as re-housing when something suitable became available, but that's how Halina eventually described it to Debbie.

"I wanted to stay. It was our home. He would have left me alone in the end. Probably. But they did not listen to me. I was not given time. Just threats."

"But couldn't you have got a lawyer," asked Debbie. "We have a list of local solicitors here. You could get an injunction and get him out."

Halina had dismissed this idea with a wave of her hand and cast a pitying look at Debbie. "You don't understand," she said.

And Debbie had shaken her head and admitted she didn't. Later she learned that Halina's situation was more complicated. She was, in fact, a sex worker and occasionally knocked about by a variety of men. Debbie was shocked. Halina didn't look like a prostitute. Not that Debbie had ever met one – so far as she knew. She was basing her prejudices on films she'd seen – young girls in mini-skirts and stockings hanging around on street corners, smoking. And as on many an occasion mentoring some of the women in the refuge, she was struck by the narrowness of her previous existence, her shameful ignorance of others' worlds and the way in which poverty informs choice.

The school had expressed concerns about Alicja and her 'living conditions'. When a social worker visited the flat around 7 one evening, Halina was not there and although Alicja did her best to concoct reasons for her absence, the social worker waited, doggedly, until ten pm. When it was apparent to them both that Halina had not 'just dashed out to the supermarket for milk and cereal for the next day's breakfast,' Alicja was deposited with the parents of one of her school friends for the night. They had a flat in the same block and seemed to be used to Alicja coming around for meals and company. At a crisis meeting with social services the following afternoon, Halina presented with a bruised eye and a cut lip. Other investigations had been undertaken in the meantime and Halina's occupation had been clarified. A senior social worker present noted that Alicja appeared to be more embarrassed than surprised by her mother's injuries.

Although Debbie did her best to talk to Halina, it was evident that her attention was unwelcome. But her experience with Alicja was completely different. Curled up in an armchair in the corner of the communal lounge, Alicja would frequently answer for her mother when Debbie tried to engage her. Halina did not appreciate this, snapping at her daughter to 'shut up' or 'get on with your schoolwork'. It pained Debbie to watch this interaction. Alicja was a tall, well developed young woman with blonde hair and an attractive, ready smile. In the top sets for every subject, she was particularly keen on the environment and eager to become an *eco-warrior*, she told Debbie. A newspaper cutting featuring Greta Thunberg was stuck above her bed at the refuge.

"She is my heroine," she announced proudly to Debbie. "In fact, she is the world's heroine."

The friendship between Debbie and Alicja began when Halina gave her permission for Debbie to take her daughter to the nature reserve one Sunday. When Debbie collected her, she was humbled by Alicja's excitement, the shine in her eyes. She'd prepared a packed lunch for them both, saying she hoped Debbie liked *Oscypek*, a Polish smoked cheese made of salted sheep milk. Halina was outside, smoking, when they left, looking so gloomy that Debbie wondered if she shouldn't be asking if she wanted to come as well. But she knew from her discussions with the staff at the refuge that Alicja needed a world of her own.

They were lucky. Despite it being the most wretched time of the year, soggy paths, dripping trees, low-lying clouds which kept out the light, the day they'd chosen was something of an exception. There was a couple of hours of sunshine and they were able to use the binoculars when Debbie espied a flock of Whooper swans flying overhead. They lunched in the bird-hide and then went for hot chocolate in a nearby café on their way home. When they parted, Alicja said she would have something to talk about at school the following day and even though Debbie had next to no experience of teenagers, the thought crossed her mind that Alicja's peers were unlikely to be impressed by her account of a ramble in the countryside. But the girl's enthusiasm for the natural world had given Debbie an idea and she looked forward to raising it with Jane that coming weekend.

After over a week by herself, Jane was desperate for some company. She'd thought she would benefit from some time by herself, able to discharge her misery without having to consider who else she was upsetting in the process. But her introspection bored her after a couple of days. She drove into Cirencester and wandered around the town, choosing a different car park to the one she and Larry had used on the day of their argument. It was a lonely trip brim full of painful memories. At one point, on the way home, her vision blurred by tears, she pulled onto the grass verge and gave vent to her anguish. Perched on the five barred gate leading to an empty, unploughed field, a couple of black crows peered at her, pitilessly. *The earth is dead*, they cawed.

Distraction arrived the following morning. Sitting in the kitchen drinking her second coffee of the day, she heard the clack of the letter box.

There was no envelope. It was just a sheet of notepaper, folded in two with Jane's name, handwritten, on one side. Before reading the note, she opened the front door, hoping to catch a glimpse of the messenger. In the distance, just about to turn left out of the drive was a man on a bike but, unfortunately, before she was able to get a good look at him, he'd disappeared.

CHAPTER 3

'He wants to meet me'

Jane was trying to concentrate on what Debbie was saying. Having mentioned to Jane that, for confidentiality reasons, she needed to be careful about disclosing names, it was difficult to be entirely sure just who they were discussing. But she managed to glean that Debbie wanted to bring a Polish girl for a visit to *The Old Byre*. She explained that she doubted that the teenager had ever visited the English countryside and how much she would appreciate the freedom after being cooped up with her difficult mother for the last few weeks – and, probably, for many more weeks to come.

Debbie had arrived by cab that afternoon, having insisted that Jane should not collect her from the station. She couldn't cope with travelling the same road with her – albeit in the opposite direction – that she had travelled with Larry only a few weeks ago. Having hoped for the same cabbie she'd met on her last visit, this time he was a much younger man and as silent as her previous driver had been loquacious.

They were sitting in the kitchen, watching the shadows lengthen in the courtyard as the January darkness closed in.

Realising that Debbie had now finished her account of the goings-on in the Refuge and had been hoping for a response, Jane re-focused.

"Yes, of course you can bring her – Helena, was it– stay the night too if you wish. It's quite a distance to travel in one day."

"Alicja. Halina – not Helena – is her mother. Thank you. Obviously, I've no idea what steps I'll have to go through to get the necessary permission."

A few minutes later, they decanted to the living room.

"It's so atmospheric here," Debbie commented, as Jane put on the side lights. "It's magical."

Kneeling down in front of the wood-burner, Jane put a match to the little stack of kindling she'd arranged earlier.

"I'm becoming expert at this," she said. "Tending a fire is very therapeutic."

"I know it's very early days," said Debbie, "but you seem to be adapting. Or am I talking nonsense?"

Jane remained on the floor, shuffling over to rest her back against one of the sofas. She usually started out by sitting close to the fire, before being driven back by its fierce heat.

"Oh, who knows?" she replied, with a sigh. "To be honest, I just feel I hobble my way through the days. Like some injured animal, driven by instinct to keep going rather than lying down and dying in a ditch at the side of the road. And the nights? Let's not talk about them. They're long and hellish."

Jane stopped talking, twisting a lock of hair around her fingers.

"Christ," she went on, "that sounds bleak - sorry. Look, it's great to have you here."

"Don't apologise."

"My life lacks purpose. I know that."

"Give yourself some time, Jane, for Heaven's sake."

"Mmm. I think *time* is the problem. I feel this tremendous urge to be consumed by something outside myself. Anything, really, which might interrupt my thoughts for a few hours. You know, if there was an earthquake or a tsunami – or maybe, just a flood – and I could rush around helping people, saving lives. Doing something useful. A reminder that bad things happen all the time. Why should I be immune from tragedy?"

Debbie didn't respond. She went into the kitchen and selected a bottle of wine from the fridge. Holding it up to Jane, she smiled.

"I know it's no substitute for a tsunami – and, by the way, I think it's an unlikely event. But you might get a flood."

When Jane returned her smile, she went back to fetch a couple of glasses.

"Talk if you want – or we can just sit here," Debbie reassured Jane. "I don't want to put any pressure on you."

There was a short silence in which they both focused on the humming of the wood-burner eating its way through a regular supply of logs. The room was becoming a sauna.

"I am reliving our marriage," said Jane, eventually. "And it's not just terribly painful, it's exhausting. I wish I could slow my mind down – regulate the memories so that I only have to deal with a few a day. But it doesn't work like that. On some days there's just one or two and it only rains a little bit and then at other times, I'm inundated with them and in a raging storm with thunder and lightning and I think I'll go mad. Not just because of thinking back to all we did together but because a lot of what *I* did brought me to the place I'm now in. He didn't get killed coming back one night from the golf club to where we used to live. He got killed because I'd nagged him to drive you on a foggy day – when his back was giving him pain – and he was navigating unfamiliar roads to and from a house he hadn't *actually* wanted to live in in the first place."

Looking into her wineglass, Jane stopped talking.

"Sorry, that was crass of me. Sounds as if I'm implicating you in the story. I'm not, of course."

"I know," said Debbie, gently. "But blaming yourself doesn't lead anywhere. It's futile."

"Futile or not, I can't help the responsibility I feel. Because, at the heart of it, I believe I *do* bear some responsibility and I can't just shrug that off."

"Look," said Debbie. She was reminded of her own grief when Kev had died – equally suddenly although in different circumstances. Her experience enabled her to be braver with Jane than she might have been had she not known a similar loss. "After Kev died, I became obsessed with trying to recall when I'd last been kind to him, shown him the affection he deserved – said I loved him, slept with him. I desperately wanted to believe that he had felt himself loved while he was alive. But we can't live like that – behaving as if every day could be last for the person we live with – or our own, for that matter. Life would be too intense and we'd never say the things we need to say to each other. Wouldn't it just mean that honesty would disappear from our lives?"

"I forget. You've lived through this."

"You couldn't have foreseen what happened to Larry, Jane. You didn't know there was going to be a cyclist at a critical moment on Larry's drive home. It was a series of events which combined and resulted in a tragic outcome. You're talking as if you *caused* it. You didn't."

During their evening, Debbie would watch Jane drifting off somewhere inside herself. She assumed it was part of the processing of memories which she'd so vividly described; images from the past passing, uninvited, through her mind. But, in fact, it was the note which preoccupied Jane that evening. After her second glass of wine and with the excuse of nipping to the toilet, she went back into her bedroom, opening the bedside drawer to look yet again at what had fluttered down on to the mat only hours earlier. She already knew the contents off by heart but each time she went over the handwritten words, she hoped it would bring some enlightenment. How did he know where she lived? What was he trying to achieve? Did she want any part of it?

Jane didn't reveal anything to Debbie, deciding that she couldn't cope with yet more intense discussion. After they'd eaten, they watched a film. Debbie saw it through to the end. Jane barely got past the opening scenes – a typical French *place*, fringed with bustling bars and cafés and stone troughs overflowing with lavender – before falling asleep.

~ ~ ~

It was Monday afternoon. Debbie had caught an early train and Jane was now alone again. She had told herself that morning, upon waking, that she should at least try to give some thought to her future. As she had declared boldly to Debbie, she needed purpose.

She tried to think back to the plans she'd had when they decided to move. But the truth was, albeit reluctantly acknowledged, that she hadn't really had any; just vague fantasies such as becoming a potter and keeping a horse. The vagueness hadn't concerned her. There was excitement enough in moving from their 'suburban rut', as she described it to Larry when he'd displayed cold feet about their adventure, to pastures green and lush. Only now, instead of verdant meadows, there was just a stony dirt track in a bleak landscape stretching as far as she could see. Her belief that it was feasible to remain where she was and construct a life for herself might be deluded after all. It was only a matter of time until someone challenged her and suggested, gently or otherwise, that she pack up and head back to reality.

There were also financial considerations. She might well be able to remain where she was for the next twelve to eighteen months, but it wasn't a long-term strategy. It was either move – or get a job. And a job which paid would involve a commute, possibly of a couple of hours a day. And she wasn't certain there was any purpose in hanging on to the house if that were the case.

She stood at the kitchen window looking out past the courtyard to the field they'd acquired and wondering whether there was any money to be had from leasing it to a nearby farmer. She remembered something being said to this effect by the estate agent on their first visit to the property. She recalled her reply as well – "No, that won't be necessary. I've got big plans for that field!" What she would benefit from was some 'local' knowledge but she'd barely exchanged more than a greeting or two with those encountered when out walking. It was precisely what Stella had warned her about when she sought her view on any prospective purchase – "too remote – you'll be getting into the car every day to go anywhere." But she hadn't listened to the old adage that *location* is key; hence her current predicament. She could fall dangerously ill and no one would know until, a week later, her decomposing body was found on the floor of one of her many bathrooms. *Recluse discovered dead in remote farmhouse* it would say in the local paper – if there was still one circulating. The thought brought her neatly back to the fate of Gladys King, dying alone on a bedroom floor and being found – like a twisted puppet whose strings had been severed – by the housekeeper. She pushed Gladys away and returned to her quandary regarding the note. Whoever wrote it was, quite clearly, local. Perhaps, on a pragmatic basis alone, she should respond to him.

Jane had been on the brink of telling Debbie about it when they'd had breakfast before her departure, but it had seemed perverse to bring it up at the last minute when she'd had the whole of Debbie's visit to do so. So, she'd stuck to the inconsequential and then regretted doing so when she waved her off in the cab at the door. Given the misgivings she had about her own judgement, it might be wise to seek someone else's view.

"Hi Stella. It's me. Have you got a few moments?"

"Hi Jane. Good to hear from you. Did you have a good weekend with Debbie? What did you get up to?"

"Yes. It was great although I'm not sure I was the most joyful of company."

"You're always good company, Jane. I bet it was great. I thought of you both on Saturday night and wished I was there, sitting in front of that lovely fire, quaffing the Chardonnay! At least January is almost finished. The evenings lighten a little in February and perhaps we'll have a glorious spring. Let's hope so. Anyway, enough of my waxing lyrical, can I help in any way?"

Already feeling more composed at the sound of the warmth in Stella's voice, Jane reflected on Stella's natural talent for not just knowing what to say, but *how* to say it too.

"Well, it's a bit weird. But on Friday morning I received a note. A handwritten note. Like something from the end of the nineteenth century. It was from the cyclist whom Larry swerved to avoid. He wants to meet me."

CHAPTER 4

A *'Ted Hughes type of man'*

Richard Marks had never believed that he was responsible for the accident and there had been no suggestion from the police or their accident investigators to the contrary. Larry's death, while assisted by hazardous weather conditions, had been brought about by Larry himself. Richard's role was limited to that of witness. Accordingly, there was nothing resembling an apology in his note. Gratitude for his own life being spared wasn't expressed either. There was simply regret that a man had died on the same stretch of road as he too had been travelling at that minute on that day.

Richard was aware of these omissions and the entirely understandable scepticism which might arise in the mind of Jane Sedgefield. If he bore no responsibility, what exactly was the point of the note? But, he decided, some healing for them both might emerge from making such a connection with her. And for that connection to have true meaning, he was certain that they needed to meet, face to face. Anyone could write a note; anyone could say anything in a note. But eyes and mouths and balled fists and sweating brows often told a more authentic story. And there was no purpose in taking such action if it lacked authenticity. He was as sure as he could be about that.

An examination of the contents of his wastepaper basket would testify to the difficulties Richard experienced in penning his missive. His address was deliberately omitted. Should she take umbrage at his unsolicited approach, he didn't want a posse of over-protective relatives turning up at his gate to brick in his windows or, worse, beat him to a pulp. He left her his mobile number, which was still a risk but one he felt able to live with.

On new year's day, Richard knew he was not being sensible when he told his two daughters that he was going out for a bike ride.

"In this, Dad?" said Cressie, looking out though the living room window at the wall of white beyond. "Don't be stupid. It's terrible out there. A pea- souper. Isn't that what they used to call these dense fogs?"

"That was prior to the Clean Air Act," said Richard, already putting on his high-viz top and searching around in the dresser for some batteries for his bike lights. "The pollution pouring into the atmosphere from factories and chimneys and coal fires made conditions worse back then. We don't have those type of fogs anymore. Anyway, it's probably not as bad as it looks. I'll just do a quick thirty minutes and then be back in time for...."

He didn't finish the sentence. Time for what? Cressie and Phoebe had been with him nearly a week and he could never have predicted just how difficult he had found the experience. Twenty-two and twenty-four respectively, their priorities were just different to his, ranging from the issue of the etiquette of a shared kitchen to what constituted a good film for inter-generational viewing. They were miles apart, he'd concluded and, much as he loved them, he now couldn't wait until the miles were – once again – a physical reality as well as a cultural one. Their mother, Miranda, whom he'd now been separated from for over a decade, had questioned her daughters closely when they announced they were going to spend the new year with their father 'in the countryside'. She wondered initially if he were suffering from some degenerative, or even terminal, illness and wanted to spend time with them while still the father they recognized. Richard Marks was not known for his ability to tolerate any house guest for more than a night or two. She could still remember the lengths he'd go to avoid any prolonged human contact, whether they were at a social function or one of the exhibition openings they had regularly attended. His general distrust of people was tinged with contempt. 'Most people have no interest in examining their own lives and motives', he maintained when they'd first met, 'they don't realise that to live a meaningful life, one has to live with focus and purpose.'

There was a warning in that statement, Miranda realised. Too late, of course. She fell hard for a man whose faith in his own beliefs – a type of academic arrogance – was matched by such good looks. A 'Ted Hughes type of man' she'd said to her mother – who, recalling the fate of Sylvia Plath, was a little startled by the comparison – intense and attractive in a wild way with his thick black hair, usually uncombed, the fierceness of his stare still apparent behind black framed glasses. Cressie and Phoebe may not have inherited their father's academic brilliance, or passion, but his looks had been passed down. They had both been able to acquire reasonable incomes by the utilisation of their 'erotic capital' – as they laughingly put it. Neither had any intention of following their father into the academic life. They ruffled his hair as they went past him in the evening and made comments about his reading material.

"Ever actually read anything solely for the purpose of enjoyment, Dad?"

"Tell me, dear father, what *do* you do for fun?"

Richard was an art historian, specialising in medieval sculpture, a national expert – if not a world one – on international Gothic style sculpture. His field of study had sent him around Europe giving lectures or on book promotions. Few holidays had been enjoyed by the family which didn't include a trip to a vast draughty cathedral or museum so that Richard could study the iconography or altarpiece. After their parents had separated, the girls enjoyed holidays by the beach, jet-skiing and theme parks, Phoebe maintaining that she had been 'scarred for life' by the endless scenes of the dying Jesus she'd endured in the first ten years of her life.

"And if it's not Jesus, it's some other rotting corpse" she'd tell her friends, embellishing her most famous anecdote when they'd gone to a museum in Avignon and spent a full hour looking at the withered corpse of Cardinal Jean de La Grange who'd died in 1402. "Funerary art! Can you imagine spending moments of your precious holiday looking at death?" And just about everyone, of those who were still listening to her, would query the adjective – *funerary*. "Part of my vocabulary at aged eleven," she'd explain, rolling her eyes. "Is it any wonder I decided to study fashion?"

Cressie too, although less affected, had longed for colour and life and noise as she emerged from of a childhood with stark memories of standing on cold marble floors in dark interiors, being told to whisper and not run around. She was now doing an internship with a musical producer. Rarely still, even as an adult she devoted some minutes of each day standing on her head or cartwheeling around the local park near her mother's home in north London. Her father's terraced cottage was confining and a little claustrophobic although the garden was large and, had it been summer, she could have discharged her excess energy by climbing one of the trees. When Richard had first moved there, after he'd retired from his academic post to concentrate on his research and writing, she'd clambered up an old magnolia tree. Richard, sitting at his desk in his study, had looked out of the window to see Cressie perched on a branch, waving at him through a tangle of leaves. Most parents would have grabbed their mobile phones and taken pictures, sending them round to their contacts – *Cressida up to her usual tricks*! – but Richard just waved back and returned to his books. But what he also *didn't* do was mouth at her 'be careful', or 'come down before you fall, for God's sake.' He wasn't the sort of parent who displayed his own neuroticism, denting a child's confidence in the process.

That particular afternoon he should have heeded his daughters' reservations. The fog looked set in for the remainder of the day. Looking right and then left as he emerged onto the road, wheeling his bike, there was little visibility in either direction. But now he was out, he felt unable to consider changing his mind. He'd had no exercise in the last forty-eight hours and that was highly unusual for him. Normally, he went out on his bike every single day, come rain or shine. It was less a habit than a form of addiction. It never really occurred to him that he might endanger another's life. After all, it was cars that killed cyclists, not the other way around: the statistics were there to prove it. He strapped on his helmet – which even had an additional light on it – wrapped his scarf around his mouth and climbed onto his bike.

The accident happened around nineteen minutes into his ride. He was already on his way home, keeping to his promise to be back within the half hour. The local roads were well known to him since he'd been cycling them for the last six years. He knew when to hug the bend and when he needed to be especially wary because oncoming cars frequently veered over the white line. He despised a minority of car drivers as much as they loathed him; a mutual animosity which now appeared ingrained into the national psyche. On this occasion, he hadn't chance to mutter under his breath *'fucking idiot.'* He heard the squeal of tyres *behind* him as the Alpha Romeo went into its swerve and then saw the car turn over several times in *front* of him, before sliding for ten yards and landing on its side.

Richard's first thought was that traffic in either direction was now at risk of colliding with Larry's car. He had his mobile with him – *"well if you must go, Dad, make sure you've got your mobile with you"* – and he'd alerted the emergency services within the minute. He was told not to approach the vehicle under any circumstances and to remain in a safe place nearby. The latter instruction wasn't that easy as there wasn't anywhere along that fateful stretch of road. But, once he mobilised his thoughts, he recalled having just passed the entrance to a farm. Wheeling his bike back in that direction, he wondered if the driver was dead. An image of the car exploding as he approached it overrode his instinct to run over and see if he could pull the driver from the wreckage.

He remained where he was for fifteen minutes, flagging down two cars which passed, to warn them of the blockage ahead. The fog lay like a cloak over the fields around him, immoveable and malign. It needed wind to disperse it and the atmosphere was eerily still. The cold penetrated his trainers and lodged in his toes. He heard the wail of a siren for some minutes before the police vehicle rolled towards him. Noting that he was beginning to shiver, whether from cold or shock or both, the two officers told him to get into the van. One of them got out and helped him stow his bike in the back. He protested, but only mildly. The ambulance was five minutes away, they said, its progress slowed by the fog.

At the scene of the crash, Richard was told to stay where he was as the policemen undertook a preliminary investigation. He watched them, peering into the upturned vehicle, the older man shaking his head. They walked slowly back to him, talking.

"What happened?" one of them asked.

"He came from behind me," Richard explained. "Swerved, I think, and then went into a spin."

"Swerved to avoid you."

"Or lost control in overtaking me, I didn't see. I only saw what occurred in front of me."

The policeman nodded. He wasn't going to proffer an opinion, but he'd already formed the view that Larry was driving recklessly given the conditions. The skid marks told some of the story.

"You were lucky," he added. He'd noted the lights on Richard's bike, his high visibility jacket and his helmet. He didn't question why he was out in the fog, gambling with his life. If Richard hadn't appreciated the risks before the accident, he most certainly would now.

"Not a good start to someone's new year," muttered his colleague.

~ ~ ~

Richard hadn't thought to contact his daughters to let them know the reason for his delay. The distraction of their phones and Facebook meant that they hadn't noticed that time was ticking away. It was the swirling yellow light of the police vehicle, suffusing the front room, which made them both look up from their devices.

"Christ," breathed Cressie.

Phoebe dashed to the window.

"It's ok, it's ok. Dad's there. He looks alright."

They ushered their father inside, Cressie taking his bike from him and Phoebe leading him to the lounge. He was hit by the warmth. The central heating had been on almost permanently since they arrived with him on Boxing Day. He'd given up asking them to wear more clothes, turning down the thermostat instead to limit the cost.

Struggling out of his jacket and pulling off his shoes, he slumped down into an armchair before taking off his glasses and rubbing them with the edge of his jumper.

"What happened?" asked Cressie. Her heartbeat sounded in her ears, like waves against the sea wall.

"Do you want tea, Dad – or brandy – or anything?" asked Phoebe, generally the more practically minded of the two. And then noting how cold he looked – "how about a hot water bottle? That always warms me up quickly."

Richard managed a faint smile. His daughters' solicitous comments moved him. As if he was seeing them again after a long, long time, he was suddenly aware of how precious they were. What he'd just witnessed, the speed with which a human life can be extinguished, the random nature of the universe with its ice and fog, brought about a fleeting recalibration. How could he, possibly, have wished them gone? He was – had become – after years of living with only himself to consider, a selfish man.

"Brandy. Good idea."

Following his brief account of the accident, the evening was spent together. Richard didn't disappear to his study immediately after they'd eaten. The girls put their phones away at the dinner table. Phoebe cooked a Spanish omelette and Cressie cleaned up the kitchen afterwards, bringing them all coffee as they settled down to watch a Hollywood comedy. Richard didn't complain and even laughed out loud during one of the more slapstick moments. Cressie stole a look at Phoebe and smiled before flinging her arm around her father's shoulders and ruffling his hair.

They left in the morning, with their copious amounts of luggage piled onto the back seat of Phoebe's Mini Cooper and Cressie waving dramatically to her father as they drove off. Instead of uttering the familiar parental stricture to *drive sensibly*, he called after them *I'll miss you*. And as he stood under a patchy blue sky, tilting his face upwards to enjoy the feel of the cold air against his skin, he meant it.

He learnt the identity of the driver a few days later when he gave a statement to the police. Larry Sedgefield, fifty-three, had left a widow, Jane, they said and, to add to the tragedy, the couple had only just moved into the area. When, one afternoon towards the end of January, one of Richard's neighbours – a forty something single woman with time on her hands whom Richard usually tried to avoid – discovered that Richard had been involved in the accident, she revealed that a friend of hers had shown the couple around *The Old Byre* back in September.

He knew her name and now he knew her address. Was he inviting unnecessary complexity into his safe, ordered life to contact her and express his remorse at her husband's death? Or was the act of acknowledging loss just what any decent human being should do in the circumstances?

After several attempts, he decided on a rather cursory form of words.

> *Dear Mrs Sedgefield*
> *Forgive this intrusion.*
> *I was the cyclist who was present when your husband's car overturned.*
> *I write to express my deepest sympathy for your sudden loss and, although you may have no wish to meet me, I would welcome such a meeting to express my condolences in person.*
> *You can contact me on my mobile (07881 – 343414) but <u>please</u> do not feel any obligation to do so.*
> *Richard Marks*

Since it meant his daily bike ride had a purpose, he decided to deliver his missive to The Old Byre rather than use the post. In one fluid action, he managed to cycle up the drive and barely alight from his bike before stuffing the note through the letter box. He peddled away at speed, not looking over his shoulder when he thought he heard the click of the front door opening.

Whether Jane Sedgefield responded to his suggestion was almost a matter of indifference to him. He'd done what he felt was appropriate. In the days following, when he struggled to pin down his motive for writing the note in the first place, he had to concede that guilt probably did play a part.

It arose from the fact that he was alive and Larry Sedgefield was dead; a form of survivor guilt, he supposed.

CHAPTER 5

Visual poetry

February began with a cold snap. In the first week, the temperature barely rose above freezing point. This exacerbated the influenza epidemic which had been raging since late December. Hospitals were bulging with elderly patients whether with complications from the 'flu virus or broken bones because they'd slipped on the ice.

Debbie's neighbour, Betty, was in her eighties and frail. With one dodgy hip already, she couldn't afford another fall. Debbie had collected a list from her and was out shopping when she received a call from a social worker about Alicja. They hadn't been back to the nature reserve. Debbie said she was waiting for better weather, when the first signs of Spring might be in evidence. The week before they'd met in town instead and had lunch together. As before, Debbie had felt humbled seeing Alicja's excitement as they sat in the window of a café awaiting that day's special – lamb hotpot. Evidently, such ordinary events were not a feature of Alicja's life. Debbie watched her sipping a diet coke, looking out of the window at the Sunday shoppers. She was wondering how to approach the issue of Alicja's jacket.

She wanted to be sensitive about it. She'd already observed, in the short time she'd spent at the Refuge, that many of the women held on tightly to their pride and dignity; that she should think carefully before offering advice in accordance with her own cultural values. Her values might have been arrived at after thoughtful consideration – other than simply inherited – but they weren't universal. And there were different definitions of *kindness* besides her own, too.

When she and Alicja had met that morning, outside Boots, she'd asked her how long she'd been there because her usually bright face looked pinched with cold. She had no scarf, no gloves and her jacket was a thin summer one.

"Would you like to go shopping after lunch?" Debbie said, eventually.

"Sure, I can come with you. I've only my homework to go back to," Alicja replied. Her usual radiance had returned in the warmth of the café and with the input of food.

"For you, I mean. Not me."

Alicja's large blue eyes widened with surprise.

"Me? I don't have any money."

"I'd like to buy you something. Something special. Just for you."

Alicja smiled.

"Ok. But you don't have to do that. This lunch is enough for me."

Debbie smiled back.

"I know. But I'd like to. Do you think your mother would mind?"

"Mind? I doubt it. She wouldn't need to know, anyway."

"She might," said Debbie, hoping she wasn't about to ruin their friendship for ever. "If she saw you wearing it. I'd like to buy you a coat. A warm one. Would you like that?"

"But that's expensive," she said, before adding hastily "Although it needn't be. I can get something cheap. Maybe there's a market we can go to."

There were a few high street fashion shops for them to visit and browse. To begin with, Alicja was hesitant, clearly worried that she might seem presumptuous choosing an item with a price tag of over £19.99. But when Debbie picked out coats with higher prices, she looked more at ease and started looking in earnest along the racks of winter jackets before choosing a classic three-quarter black woollen coat. With her blonde shoulder length hair, the colour suited her. A couple of teenage girls turned around to look at her as she stood in front of the mirror. Noticing them staring, Debbie nodded at her.

"See. You look amazing. A model!"

As they queued up to pay, Debbie picked out a pair of woollen gloves and a black scarf from the rack next to them. Popping them into the basket, she grinned at Alicja.

"Vital accessories," she whispered.

Alicja flushed with pleasure as the shop assistant placed their purchases in a large carrier bag and handed it to her.

Outside on the street, she hugged the bag to her chest.

"Thank you," she said, kissing Debbie on the cheek. "I've had the best day ever."

A few days later, Debbie was back on the high street with Betty's shopping list. There was marmalade, bread, jacket potatoes, sausages and milk. It was as she was looking at the cakes, wondering whether Betty might prefer a Victoria Sponge to a lemon drizzle cake – a little gift from Debbie to brighten her day – when her mobile rang.

Alicja's social worker said she wanted to set up a 'safeguarding' meeting with Alicja and when she'd asked if she would like anyone else to be present for support, Alicja had asked for Debbie.

"I haven't known her for any length of time but we've struck up a good relationship, I think," Debbie explained.

"She obviously trusts you," said the social worker. "Is it ok with you?"

"What does her mother say? I've been supporting them both, you see. Or trying to, in the case of Halina."

"It's up to Alicja. She's deemed mature enough to provide her own views."

"I see. Well, then it's fine with me."

"Great! I'll be in touch."

Debbie carried on with Betty's shopping, wishing she'd been more specific about the sort of sausages she wanted. Betty didn't have a mobile and Debbie wasn't sure her query justified Betty heaving up from her chair and hobbling to answer the telephone on the hall table. She made a mental note to ask Betty if she'd like an extension installed in her living room. Betty said she was pleased with the Victoria sponge but then insisted on Debbie taking half of it home with her – like a child returning from a birthday party – which made Debbie wonder if the pleasure was feigned.

The meeting at social services took place in their offices the following Friday morning when Debbie would usually have been at the Refuge. The three of them were squashed together in a room not much bigger than a broom cupboard. Debbie had to rest her feet on the vacuum cleaner as there was no space for them on the floor. The social worker, Barbara Todd, kindly, in her early fifties had the demeanour of someone permanently under siege. Initially she forgot to switch off her mobile and when it rang five minutes into the meeting, she jumped visibly, startling Debbie and making Alicja giggle. Every now and again, after making some point which might touch a nerve with Alicja, she would smile nervously; a woman used to her words acting as lit matches being cast onto the combustible human in front of her.

Alicja came across as a confident girl on the cusp of womanhood. She was clear in what she wanted.

"No, I don't feel safe with my mother. I don't want to return to live with her."

Debbie recalled the brusque manner in which Halina spoke to her daughter. She'd never seen her show Alicja affection and, tellingly, Alicja didn't seem to expect any either. But Barbara Todd had not anticipated this response.

"Oh, I see. Can you say particularly why you don't feel safe?"

Debbie was flabbergasted at this question. She wanted to interject – "For God's sake, why did they come to the refuge in the first place? What don't you understand about her mother's profession and the inherent risks involved?"

Alicja went into some detail about the hours her mother kept, the comings and goings at the flat and the bruises she'd seen from time to time on her mother's arms. Barbara Todd scribbled down notes as she talked.

"Anyway, my mother will be glad to get rid of me," she went on. "There's no.... no place for me in her life."

It wasn't an expression of self-pity; just a fact.

How had she turned out so well balanced, thought Debbie? How is it that some of us thrive whatever life hurls at us as children while others, who appear to have been loved and cherished, struggle to live well?

"Is there a relative you'd like to live with?"

Alicja shook her head.

"Not that I know of. My Dad went back to Poland when I was little and I never hear from him. There are cousins there too but none that I'm in touch with. I'd hate to go back there."

"We can find a foster placement for you. But I can't guarantee where that will be, I'm afraid."

A brief silence followed as the three of them considered this piece of information, even though it was the logical extension of Alicja's refusal to return to live with her mother.

"I'll have to change schools?" Alicja asked. Having displayed little outward emotion during the meeting, a frown in the shape of two furrows appeared between her eyebrows. She looked over at Debbie as if about to say something to her. But then changed her mind and gave a shrug instead, flattening her lips in an expression of resignation.

"Possibly," said Barbara, accompanying her reply with one of her nervous smiles. "But we'll do our best to limit the disruption for you. So, let's see."

Afterwards, Debbie took Alicja to a nearby cafe even though she had assured Barbara that she'd drive her back to school straightaway.

"That was tough, Alicja," she said as she placed a hot chocolate and a croissant down in front of her. "You did well."

Alicja picked up her drink and asked if Debbie wanted some of the croissant.

"No, it's for you."

Alicja ate for a while, looking around her as she always did when they were out, enjoying the novelty of being in a busy café particularly on a school day. As she brushed the flecks of pastry from around her mouth, she smiled at Debbie.

"Things will be fine," she said. "Don't worry about me, Debbie."

The shine in her clear blue eyes and the brightness of her smile suggested she meant it too. Debbie had to turn away quickly so that Alicja didn't notice that the hope embedded in those words brought her close to tears.

~ ~ ~

Jane was still trying to establish some pattern to her daily life. Larry had been dead almost two months and still her world held no shape. The wound left by his absence bled as much as it had on the day it happened. If, after a few hours of sleep the sight of the morning light eased its flow, it haemorrhaged again as darkness descended in early evening. The unrelenting quality to her misery frightened her. Perhaps she should have locked up the house and stayed with Bob and Stella until something approaching equilibrium had returned.

At the end of February, Michael and Lilly came to stay for a few days. Lilly was a bright lively woman who had been a drama teacher at a private school specialising in the arts but had left her job some years ago to develop an interior design business. It had arisen from a trip to Japan which she and Michael had made to celebrate a wedding anniversary. After visiting a number of galleries, Lilly had become fascinated with Japanese woodblock printing; *visual poetry*, as she described it to her clients when asking whether they were seeking 'landscapes, nature or warriors' in the wallpapers which she would have specially printed at huge cost. She was petite with spiky blonde hair and large brown eyes. Used to bossing everyone around, including her own husband and children, Lilly was adamant that Jane needed to get out of the house regularly and that she should consider taking up some voluntary activity until she'd decided on whether to look for paid employment in the area.

"Jesus, Jane. You'll go mad sitting around this house for weeks on end. You need to do something! Anything to get you out for a few hours."

"Hey, Lil, go steady on her," Michael said, laughing.

Even his laugh reminds me of Larry, Jane thought, before conceding that Lilly was right.

"It's ok, Michael. She's dead right. I need someone to give me a good shake."

Lilly went over to her and pretended to shake her. She then kissed her on both cheeks and suggested they take a trip out somewhere. Despite it being ten o'clock in the morning, all the house lights were on. Nevertheless, three heads turned to look out of the kitchen window at the same time. Heavy grey clouds threatened rain.

"Mmm," said Michael. "Looks set in for the day to me. What did you have in mind, Lil? A hike in the hills? Or, perhaps, a drive to the seaside?"

"Don't be so negative," said Lilly. "What about Oxford? Plenty to see and do there. Always a good exhibition on. Yes, it's a bit of a drive but we've got all day. We can have lunch or dinner or both out. Save us having to cook."

Michael glanced at Jane for her reaction.

"Sounds great," said Jane. "Honestly. I'd love to do that. But isn't it a bit far for a day trip?"

"I can drive there. And Mike can drive back," declared Lilly, leaving no room for objection.

On the way over, Lilly confessed that she was keen to visit The Ashmolean Museum to see a new exhibition of early nineteenth century Japanese print making. The rain, coupled with roadworks, meant that what should have been an hour's drive turned into almost two. Parking wasn't easy either. Some stress was evident by the time they emerged, in their waterproofs, onto Beaumont Street.

"I think I'll hole up in a pub for the day," said Michael. "And give the plum blossom a miss."

"Oh no you won't! Anyway, you're driving back so you can forget any of that nonsense. Let's head straight to the museum, shall we?" said Lilly. "If you don't want to see the Japanese prints, there's more than enough to occupy you in their permanent collections. A *fantastic* place to spend the day *and* we can eat there too, if we don't fancy venturing much further. I'm sure there will be a warming soup of the day to revive us."

"Mmmm. Irresistible."

Lilly ignored him and, pulling up her hood, walked briskly in the direction of the museum as if she'd lived in the city all her life. Michael gave Jane a doleful glance and linked arms with her.

"Our mistress has spoken."

If only this was Larry, Jane thought, feeling the pressure of Michael's arm against her own. When had we last linked arms, I don't remember? I don't even remember the last time we made love. Amidst the memories which assaulted her, arrows piercing her flesh, the intimate ones seemed to be missing. And when she tried to unearth them, scrabbling through the tangled threads of her mind, she failed. It is my own unique method of punishing myself, she decided. *I don't find them because I can't bear what they will do to me.*

On reaching the museum, Michael went off on his own to track down Guy Fawkes' Lantern – which, apparently, lit Fawkes' path as he stole along the cellars beneath the Houses of Parliament on the night he was captured – it being noted, by Lilly, that it just happened to be on the same level as the café.

Jane followed Lilly into the Japanese *Surimono* prints exhibition. She learned that these prints had not been made for commercial purposes but were commissioned privately between friends, the majority by members of private poetry clubs, in the late 18th and early 19th century. The verses incorporated into the prints were called *kyoka – wild poetry* – a 31 syllable form. First came the words, often decided upon through a competition, which were then passed to a professional artist for illustration. There was no just drifting past quickly since many of the prints were small and needed concentration.

There was one print which Jane returned to. Entitled *An arhat with a tiger* it depicted a buddha like figure with a sleepy, contented tiger wrapped around him. In fact, it was difficult not to see the two figures as one because there was no space between them. Jane wondered if this meant that the mystical *arhat* had tamed his demons in accordance with Buddhist ideology. One of the verses on the print read "*Living in the mountain, just let the year advance entirely as it likes.*" Perhaps, that's what I should do, she decided, before smiling to herself at the idea of suddenly adopting a Zen-like approach to the coming months. She imagined Debbie's expression when, during her next visit, she discovered Jane sitting cross-legged in the courtyard; eyes closed and chanting.

By the time she and Lilly headed for the café in search of sustenance, it was gone 2 p.m. Michael had texted Lilly to say he had 'gone off for a wander around the town' and to let him know when they had finished.

"Extraordinary," was Lilly's clipped description of the exhibition, before proceeding to talk about her own conversion to Japanese art through the work of *Hiroshige* and his *One hundred views of Edo* – ancient Tokyo.

"Whistler, the American artist, was influenced by him. His painting of *Caprice in Purple and Gold* shows a golden screen behind her which, incidentally, was the inspiration for designing my own screens. They've brought me lots of headaches but proved very popular with my more cultured – and wealthy – clientele."

The immediate effect of her immersion into that intimate fusion of colour and emotion, wrought in such exquisite detail, was to bring about a state of tranquillity for Jane, for the first time since she had lost Larry. She could not trust that it would last beyond that day and nor did she choose to articulate it to Lilly as they sat together, eating lunch. But Lilly knew the power of art. She believed in it.

"Goethe said that there is no surer way of evading the world than by Art; and no surer way of uniting with it than by Art."

She reached over and squeezed Jane's hand.

"It's like oxygen," she said. "It heals."

Lilly laughed as she saw the look on Jane's face.

"Yes. I'm a bit mad, I know. It's a good job Mike's not here. He'd add pretentious to that description."

CHAPTER 6

Two can be bold

The words in the *arhat* print remained with Jane in the days following the visit to Oxford. Whether they motivated her – take a chance, see what happens, stop trying to control everything – to call Richard Marks, she was never sure. If it were the case, her behaviour might be considered bizarre, if not unhinged; like the novel where the protagonist decides to base every decision in his life on the fall of the dice.

"Or, perhaps," as she said to Richard, only minutes after meeting him, "I was simply intrigued by receiving a note from a stranger. Anyway, Mr Marks, I think the question should be reversed. What motivated *you* to write to me."

As they smiled at each other, over their coffee at a café tucked away in the pretty backstreets of Cirencester, it occurred to them both simultaneously that an onlooker, aware of the facts behind their meeting, may think their light heartedness inappropriate.

Jane, in her best white woollen coat, had walked past the café twice before summoning up the courage to enter. On doing so, she had immediately spotted Richard, sitting in a corner – as he said he would be – reading a book – *an actual book*, his text read, *I am in my fifties with black hair and glasses.* Jane had not sent any description, just confirmed the time and venue and said she would find him. He had stood up to greet her, average height, solidly built, a wide, fleeting smile showing good teeth. With his black turtle necked jumper, he had the bearing of the academic he was.

People noticed them: he, dark and rugged, she blonde and pale. Was it business or pleasure, they wondered?

"It's good of you to come," he said. "Let me get you something. What would like to drink?"

"It's ok, I can get it," said Jane.

"No, please, sit."

She obeyed, unbuttoning her coat, hit by the stifling warmth of the room. It was busy and noisy.

They plunged into a conversation, like divers into the cold sea, hoping that whatever lay beneath would be worth the discomfort of the moment.

"Please, call me Richard," he said, in answer to her question. "May I call you Jane?"

She laughed suddenly, self-consciously.

"I'm sorry. It's just such an odd situation. I suppose I'm nervous."

"I just wanted to meet you in person and say how sorry I am about your husband. It's probably presumptuous of me, to request this meeting. Perhaps even selfish. But you're here. And I'm glad. I can only imagine what you have been through during these last few weeks. Really, I am so very sorry."

He kept his eyes on her as he spoke and she was struck, first, by his sincerity and then by his attractiveness. But she didn't give herself an inward shake. She continued to enjoy his gaze.

"Do you want to know anything more about the day?" he asked. "If so, ask. I'm told it helps – some people – occasionally – to know the details of their loved one's last moments. It can help to fill in the bits they find themselves endlessly ruminating upon. I have no idea if it would help you."

His words were exact and measured, she decided.

She didn't want to know. Any such knowledge could go either way, in her opinion, and she hadn't 'endlessly ruminated upon' Larry's last minutes on earth anyway. She had focussed on their last moments together and her insistence that *he* drive Debbie, rather than she. That indisputable fact overrode everything else and she could not conceive of a time when it would not do so.

"You sound as if you have personal experience of something similar," Jane said.

"No," said Richard. "I haven't. I've been lucky. Just like I was lucky on January the first. And your husband wasn't."

She looked down into her coffee cup and then shook her head.

"No. I don't want any details, thank you. I learned quite a bit from the police at the time. It's enough. But I appreciate the…. the gesture on your part. It's brave of you."

Richard wanted to challenge her use of the word 'gesture': it suggested his words were not heartfelt. He frequently irritated friends and colleagues with his pedantry. But, since he had only just met her, he bit his lip, painful though it was.

"How are you managing? If that doesn't sound a disingenuous question. It must still be so raw for you."

"They say grief is a journey without destination," she replied. "So it's too early to say."

And then she added. "I know that wasn't an answer. I don't have one."

"I understand, from a busy-body neighbour of mine, by the way, that you and your husband had only just moved into the area."

"Yes. Seeking a change of lifestyle. Well, I was anyway."

Jane went on to talk about where they'd come from in Surrey and what had attracted her to *The Old Byre*. She referred to her fantasies about country life and having a horse, wondering why she was revealing so much to a stranger. He reciprocated with a brief description of his terraced house in which he had lived alone for many years.

"I think I just wanted a complete change," she said. "To see what it was like to live a different life."

"A re-invention?"

"Yes, perhaps. I hadn't bargained for such a radical one."

"Will you stay around here?"

She shrugged.

"Everyone asks me that. I have no idea. On some days it seems likely, feasible, and then on others it seems to be utterly stupid. Rattling around that big house on my own, going slowly mad."

Gladys King popped into her head again. This time, it was the image of her at her bedroom window that night. A headless figure: abandoned. And now, like Larry, dead.

"You don't seem like a woman going mad, slowly or otherwise, if I may be frank," Richard said. Jane looked at his eyes behind the dark frames of his glasses. They were an intense blue, beneath heavy eyebrows. There was a confidence to him which fascinated her.

"And you can tell after spending ten minutes with me?" *Two can be bold*, she thought.

"I can," he said. "And people who are going mad do not usually recognize it or acknowledge it – from what I've observed in my fifty years, which is, admittedly, limited."

He looked over her head, breaking eye contact for the first time since he'd placed her coffee in front of her.

"You look and speak like someone who knows very well what they're feeling. And why."

She wasn't entirely sure what he meant by the remark.

They sat without talking for a few moments. Suddenly aware of the level of noise in the café – the chatter, the clink of glasses and plates, the shouts from the counter announcing food to be collected – Jane wanted to put her hands over her ears.

"Let's get out of here, shall we?" he said, surprising her. "It's served its purpose."

Jane stood up and reached for her coat which she'd placed on the back of her chair. But he was there before her and held it as she placed her arms within the sleeves. She flicked her hair out from under the collar and murmured her thanks.

The cafe dwellers looked on. *Obviously pleasure*, after all, was the general opinion – unvoiced, of course.

Out in the street, they faced one another. It was a fine morning in the first week of March, a day on which to imagine the lighter nights and the feel of the spring to come. It was a hopeful sort of a day, Jane thought, looking at Richard as he pulled a sweatshirt over his head.

"You came by car?" he asked.

"Yes. And you by bike?"

He explained that it was his only mode of transport. He didn't bother with a car.

"I'm glad we've met," he said.

Jane nodded, smiling at him, suddenly hating the idea of being on her own again. And so, now confident of the water she'd dived into, she plunged a bit deeper.

"Would you like to come over for lunch one day? See the place."

"I'd like that," he said. "You've got my mobile. Text me."

He turned and walked away, raising his hand up as he did so. Jane was left, standing outside the bow window of the café. Inside the onlookers had hoped for something a little more exciting than a brief wave.

Jane went straight back to her car and headed for home. She looked at herself in the driver's mirror as she switched on the ignition, as if checking her thoughts were not on display in a bubble above her head. There were no tears in her eyes. They were clear.

As she exited the village, she passed him. To begin with, she wasn't sure. He was cycling furiously, his head down. But she recognized the red and grey sweatshirt. She slowed and pulled over some thirty yards down the road, her hazard lights flashing. As he went by, he reduced his frantic pace and stopped. She rolled down her window.

"Come now," she said. "Follow me."

He was sweating under his helmet and he drew a hand across his mouth.

"Ok."

~ ~ ~

In the weeks which followed the meeting with social services, Debbie started to have some concerns for Alicja. On her usual Fridays at the Refuge, she always waited for her to return from school so that they could catch up with each other and arrange a trip out for the forthcoming Sunday. On the last two Fridays, Alicja had not returned at the usual time and Debbie had eventually given up and left. It seemed uncharacteristic of her to be hanging around shopping malls or coffee shops, but Halina merely shrugged when Debbie was brave enough to make some tentative enquiries of her daughter's whereabouts.

"Of course, she's growing up," Debbie observed to one of the permanent staff, Tanya. "Why on earth would she not start wanting to develop friendships with kids her own age? It's only natural."

"The relationship between her and her mother has deteriorated recently," said Tanya. "They spend their time avoiding one another. If Halina is in the lounge or kitchen, Alicja goes to their bedroom. I've barely heard them exchange more than a couple of words with one another. Recently we had a half-hearted discussion about offering them some form of mediation. But none of us believe that Halina would accept what she would perceive as interference."

Debbie presumed that Halina had been informed of Alicja's wish to live separately from her. It made her more determined to arrange some time with Alicja on her own. She rang the social worker and asked her what steps were required to take Alicja away for a weekend, describing Jane's place 'in the country' and how much she thought Alicja would gain from a break there.

It seemed largely a matter for Halina, from what Barbara Todd said. As far as she, Barbara, was concerned, provided Debbie left full details of where they were going – address, Jane's full name – she could see no reason why the overnight visit should not go ahead. Debbie had been through a rigorous process to become a volunteer at the Refuge. There had been a police check and references from two independent sources.

"Supposing Halina does not agree?" asked Debbie, recalling how spiteful she could be towards Alicja.

"Difficult," was Barbara's, less than clear, response.

After a few missed calls, Alicja answered and, although she wanted to, Debbie didn't enquire why she appeared to be avoiding her. Such a conversation would be better had face to face. They agreed to meet at a café in town that forthcoming Sunday morning

In the event, Alicja was late and, since there was a cold wind, Debbie decided to find a table inside the café and then text her. Before she could, however, Alicja was there, wearing her old thin jacket, hair scraped back from her face and tied roughly at her neck. There was a pallid look to her skin and her eyes had none of their usual sparkle. She smells of smoke, thought Debbie, as Alicja muttered an apology for being late and, leaving her hands in her pockets, slid down into the chair.

Debbie asked her what she would like to drink and whether she wanted something to eat.

"No. I'm ok, thanks. I can't stay long. I've homework to complete before tomorrow." The words were spoken without looking at Debbie.

"What's going on, Alicja?"

"What do you mean?"

"You're not yourself. You can tell me. We're friends, aren't we?"

She watched as Alicja's eyes brimmed with tears and then put her hand gently over Alicja's, feeling the young, tender skin under her own.

"Tell me."

A few tears escaped onto her cheeks and, brushing them away, she swallowed.

"It's that place. The refuge. I hate it. I'm sick of sharing a bedroom with Mum. She's on the phone to everyone she knows, complaining about me, saying I'm an ungrateful bitch and she can't wait to get rid of me."

Each word produced a hiccough or a few more tears. Debbie scrabbled in her handbag until she'd found a tissue.

"Do you want to go?" she asked, handing her the tissue. "Let's walk around for a while as we talk."

Alicja didn't need to be persuaded. She jumped up and headed for the door as if making a bolt for freedom. Debbie grabbed her belongings and hurried after her, hoping she'd not have to endure the ignominy of chasing a teenager through crowds of Sunday shoppers.

She was relieved to see Alicja standing with her back to the street, staring into a charity shop window some yards away. She'd stopped crying and smiled weakly as Debbie joined her.

They walked without talking to a small park nearby and found an empty bench. Pigeons pecked and jostled each other around their feet, expecting food.

"Have you spoken to Barbara about how things are between you and your mother?" Debbie asked. She took out her trusty stock of mints from her coat pocket and offered them to Alicja.

"No," she answered, slipping a mint into her mouth and immediately crunching it.

Since they'd met up, Debbie had wanted to ask why she wasn't wearing her black coat but divined that it would not be politic to do so. She didn't want to sound like another nagging parent – although Halina appeared to prefer insults to nagging.

"Would you like me to speak to her?"

Alicja turned to look at her.

"Would you?"

"Of course," said Debbie. "I'll ask her to hurry up with finding a ….." She hesitated, uncertain whether to call it what it was – a foster placement. But Alicja surprised her.

"Foster parents. I know. My mother says they only do it for the money and not to expect to be happy. But you've made your bed now, she says. *You'll learn the hard way.*" She'd imitated her mother's accent so accurately that Debbie had to suppress a smile.

"That's nonsense," exclaimed Debbie. And so cruel, she thought. "They're thoroughly checked out. I bet you'll be fine."

"Will you stay in touch with me," Alicja asked, in a small voice. A surge of anger shot through Debbie. How quickly and effectively her mother had stolen her bloom and confidence.

"You bet I bloody well will!" she said, fiercely. "You'll not get rid of me so easily." A look of confusion spread over Alicja's face.

"I don't want to get rid of you," she said.

Debbie laughed. "It's just a silly expression," she explained. "I know you don't."

Alicja smiled at her.

"Now," said Debbie, "I wanted to meet up with you to ask if you'd like a trip to the countryside one weekend. I've got a friend with the most wonderful house in the world. There's a bedroom for you and a field and garden for you to explore and we can birdwatch and even go on a bat hunt when it's dark."

What am I talking about, Debbie asked herself? I've absolutely no idea whether there are any bats around at *The Old Byre*.

"Really? A holiday?" asked Alicja. The wind had brought some colour to her cheeks. She took the band out of her hair and shook it loose.

Debbie nodded.

"Yes, a little one. We could go down on a Friday after school and stay until the Sunday afternoon. Although I'll have to ask your mother."

"Oh, she won't care," Alicja retorted. "She'll like having the bedroom to herself." She imitated her mother's voice again. "*You're welcome to her!*"

Debbie laughed.

49

"Great, I'll get my friend, Jane, to give me some dates and we'll set something up really soon. Something to look forward to, hey?"

She nudged Alicja with her elbow, grinning at her.

"Jane, your friend, what's she like?"

"Oooh. Jane. My age. Good fun. Pretty laid back. But she's been through a lot recently."

Debbie went on to explain about Larry's death although omitted her own part in the tragedy.

"I'm sure she'll welcome the company. I think she gets lonely all on her own. And she doesn't really know anyone in the area."

Alicja frowned.

"Why did she move there when she didn't know anybody?"

"Good question," Debbie replied. "But I can't really answer it. Perhaps she was searching for adventure."

Alicja looked thoughtful.

"Searching for adventure," she repeated. "I'm going to do that one day."

Debbie insisted on going back to The Refuge with Alicja despite it being a long bus ride in the opposite direction to her own home. As they approached the house, a large Victorian one, formerly a vicarage Debbie had been told, they saw Halina leaning against the front door, smoking. She gave a smirk as they approached her.

"Darling mama is here to greet me," murmured Alicja.

Debbie noticed that Halina was wearing Alicja's black woollen coat. She couldn't help herself.

"Hello, Halina, you look smart! Been shopping?"

Beside her, Alicja was blushing with the embarrassment, fearful that Debbie would think she had given the coat to her mother.

As she punched in the entry code, Debbie whispered to her.

"Don't worry, Alicja. We'll find a way of getting it back. I promise."

And she meant it. With every fibre of her being. She would return the damned coat to its rightful owner even if she had to rip it from Halina's back herself.

CHAPTER 7

Let grief return another day

Jane was brushing her teeth, musing as she awaited the little buzz on her electric toothbrush to inform her that she had been at it for the requisite two minutes. She was considering what had occurred that afternoon and how unlikely it would have been had she not been living a considerable distance away from anyone who knew her. She acknowledged too that it was much easier to behave as you wished with no close neighbours; nobody spying on you. What does that say about the lives most of us live, she wondered? All kept in check because of what society expects of us. Social control imposed, in no short measure, simply by our physical proximity to others?

Richard was lying in bed in the room adjacent. She could see his long legs outstretched when she stood back from the sink to check that he was still there. Initially, she hadn't wanted him to stay the night. It seemed a step too far. But his presence next to her, when they'd awoken from their post coital nap, was of such comfort that she later confessed to him – much later – that she couldn't bear the idea of spending the night alone. She'd opened her eyes, remembered, and then looked across at him. He was lying on his side staring at her. She pulled the duvet up further to cover her breasts and he'd smiled at this.

"Bit late now, Jane Sedgefield," he said. "Anyway, I can't see much, I need my glasses. Any idea where they are?"

"Over on the dressing table, I think," she said. "Do you want me to get them for you?"

"Actually, I'm starving. Have you got anything to eat or was that offer just a ruse to get me here?"

That conversation was around two o'clock in the afternoon, less than two hours since they'd arrived back from Cirencester. Very few words had been exchanged. She made a pretence of showing him around the house and he responded by pretending to be interested. When they arrived in the, mis-termed, master bedroom which, by no coincidence, was the last room on the tour, neither of them hesitated. Sex with a stranger – the most exciting sex in the world, although rarely the most satisfying. Richard contemplated this theory, if such it was, as he peeled his body away from Jane's after his orgasm. Was it too quick, not quick enough, should he have enquired more – *'is this ok?'*, *'is it here?' 'or here?'* His instinct was against turning passion into a game of twenty questions. And looking at her now, smiling at him, stretching, then laughing, he guessed her instinct was much the same.

Afterwards, they showered together, playfully, adopting roles neither of them really believed in. It was just a simpler way to smooth the transition from the intimacy of the bedroom back to ordinary life – eating, drinking and conversation. What do you do for a living? How long were you married? Why have you plonked yourself in the countryside to live the life of a semi-hermit? Did you ever want children? Would you like smoked salmon and soda bread?

That part of meeting someone new also had its own excitement; those days of discovery, when one or other lover deems it vital to establish whether there is any prospect of their lustful union developing into something resembling a 'relationship'.

They shared a platter of smoked salmon for lunch and then went out for a long walk. Richard looked up the bridleways and public footpaths local to the house on his mobile before they left, saying he was more familiar with where he lived – the other side of Cirencester – but there would be some overlap if they ventured far enough. The weather favoured them in the sense that there was no rain. It was a blustery, March day with lots of cloud and little sun. They hopped over stiles and squeezed between kissing-gates, but they didn't touch or kiss.

They'd ended up at the pub before realising that neither of them had any money or cards on them. Richard's wallet lay on the bedside table back at *The Old Byre* and Jane hadn't thought to bring anything out with her. Richard said he'd jog back alone with the keys and pick up some cash but then they'd rethought the plan, apologising to the bar staff, and plodded home.

Richard elected to search the fridge for ingredients with which to concoct an evening meal while Jane sat on one of the leather stools and watched him, drinking in his graceful movements along with the wine. *My lover*, she thought.

Over dinner, Richard spoke of his daughters, bringing out his mobile at one point to show Jane some photographs. One showed Phoebe's face on the front cover of a teenage girls' magazine – *Our guide to the natural look* – long dark hair, perfect skin and the intense blue eyes inherited from her father. Cressie was dark too but wore her hair short and had a mischievous look about her. She had the height for a model whereas Phoebe didn't, he explained. She'd done a bit when she was younger but didn't have the patience for it whereas Phoebe had struck lucky with her agency and still got regular work. It meant she could rent a decent flat in London.

"But compared to what you do, what you've done with your life, they're so different," Jane observed, recalling the detail in which he'd described the flourishing of Gothic style sculpture throughout Europe in the decades following 1400. Jane knew nothing of what he spoke about, feeling uncomfortable in her ignorance. She'd made some comment about seeing *The Burghers of Calais* in the *Ca' Pesaro museum* in Venice and how impressed she'd been with the realism Rodin had achieved in sculpting the hands and feet of the six men. When Richard did not respond, she realised she may have committed a *faux pas*. Making reference to a piece of sculpture so as to prove she had some appreciation of the art form was akin to saying to a Shakespearean scholar that once she'd read a play written by Rattigan. It had no relevance; merely emphasised that she had no knowledge of the subject matter apart from that of the common tourist. She'd been put in her place when he'd said a few minutes later that he'd never been in a gallery or museum without there being some specific purpose to his visit. 'Wandering around aimlessly' as he put it, was a waste of time – 'focus is imperative.'

"I didn't expect, or want for that matter, my daughters to be carbon copies of me," Richard said in answer to her comment about Phoebe and Cressie. "Anyway, they're young. You're not stuck with career choices nowadays in quite the same way we were."

Jane had wanted to explore Richard's choice of specialism. Wasn't it a bit narrow? Twenty-five years of life devoted to the study of just a few decades of sculpture. But, she supposed, that was the essence of the life of the academic. 'Study for study's sake' might define it – but it was not a theory she felt confident to voice. There would be time for that.

Richard Marks was not a man for small talk. This became apparent as the evening wore on. He became restless after dinner, sitting in the living room in front of a fire. Every now and again, he'd get up and walk around, standing at the picture window and staring out into the night.

He sat apart from her. There was no cuddling up on the sofa, gazing into the orange flames of the fire. Jane had suggested she put some music on and asked if he had any preference.

"Rock or jazz or classical?"

"I tend to listen to music rather than just have it on in the background," he said.

"Well, we can listen," she'd retorted, mildly irritated at this judgmental reply.

"Ok, have you any Bruckner? His seventh symphony is my favourite."

Jane wondered whether she could pick that up on *Spotify*. She had heard of the composer but could not have provided one single fact about him. She might have a stab at his nationality: German? (She learnt later, from Richard of course, that he was Austrian.) When her play list appeared and she saw the Chopin sonata, which she had played almost incessantly since the night of Larry's funeral, she opted for that instead. Richard glanced at her, almost sharply, as Arthur Rubenstein's magic filled the room.

She shrugged. "Sorry, I've been obsessed with this piece of music for weeks. It popped up of its own accord."

He smiled and came to sit next to her. He's a man who needs standing up to, she thought. Far too used to being pandered to because of his superior intellect.

"You know," he started to say. His expression was serious behind the heavy black frame of his glasses.

She turned expectantly towards him, placing her hand on his knee, moving a little closer.

"The burghers you mentioned."

Jesus, Jane said to herself, suppressing a smile. *He's going to give me a lecture on the burghers of Calais.*

"Cheese or beef?" she quipped.

"Seriously," he replied. Her internal conversation continued. *And suppose I don't want to be serious, not tonight.* "Their story –"

Before he could continue, she interrupted again.

"God, yes. What an amazing story of sacrifice!"

Twitching with enthusiasm at the prospect of puncturing another myth harboured by the ignorant, he spoke rapidly.

"Well, that's where you're wrong, you see. A French professor called Moeglin," – Jane noted that Richard's French accent was perfect – "has reinterpreted the whole episode after studying other sources from that particular period. 1347 – during the Hundred Years' War. The burghers were not at any point at risk of being executed by King Edward. The third, I think. A pardon for the people of Calais had already been negotiated and they were merely performing a rite or ritual."

Jane decided to cut the lecture short.

"Fascinating," Jane said. "But what a pity you've destroyed the romance attached to that glorious sculpture! Cruel beyond belief!"

Richard's response to this bit of teasing was to put his head back against the sofa and close his eyes.

"Yes, I thought you said we had to *listen* to the music," she said.

"Touché," he murmured. "I'll shut up now."

She leant over and kissed him lightly on the lips.

They sat, silently, until the Chopin had finished.

"Magnificent," Richard said. "You have impeccable taste."

Jane had felt tears pricking her eyes as she listened. Larry had arrived in the room: *invited* in by her, in fact. Had she done it as an act of punishment? How dare I sit in here with my lover, in the same space last occupied by him, a mere two months since his death.

As she swallowed back her emotion, Richard looked at her.

"Are you already regretting this?" he asked. "If so, don't worry. I'll go."

"No, please don't. Please stay," she said.

"Stay the night? Are you sure? I didn't bring my lights out with me so it wouldn't be advisable to cycle back now. But I could call a cab. Honestly, it's no problem. It's probably too much for you – too soon – for me to stay. I understand."

"Would you mind staying? I would like you to. I don't want to be alone tonight. I'm not sure why."

But she did know why. At some point she would need to address precisely what she'd done in the last twenty-four hours and she'd prefer to face that in the daylight, not during the interminable hours of a sleepless night.

"I'll stay," he said. "But I'll leave early, if that's ok."

"Of course. Christ, I don't want you to think of me as some needy, weak thing that's going to stalk you for the rest of your life."

"I don't. I don't have any such illusions about myself, for a start," he said.

Now that was settled, Jane felt less emotional. Tomorrow could wait until tomorrow.

She made coffee and located the Bruckner. And they sat, relaxed, though the whole of the seventh symphony with only the screech of an owl triggering a short exchange of words.

Later, in bed, they heard it again.

"It's definitely a barn owl," said Richard.

"I thought owls went to-whit-to-woo," she said.

"That's the tawny owl," he explained. "And the cry combines the male and female answering each other. There are six types of owl indigenous to the United Kingdom. Although I've only ever spotted three types around where I live. Do you know what the collective noun is for wise old owls?"

"No, tell me."

"A parliament. It's a wonderful term, isn't it? Like a collection of crows – a murder. A group of ravens – a conspiracy or unkindness. The history of birds is steeped in rural myth and legend."

Jane was too sleepy to chat further about the nomenclature given to flocks of birdlife. She already felt her general knowledge had improved sufficiently in the last twenty-four hours to consider entering the local pub quiz. Imagine asking Richard if he wanted to make up a two-person team with her – his horror! Stifling a giggle, she turned away from his hot breath and went to sleep.

~ ~ ~

Jane slept that night. It was the first refreshing sleep she'd had since Larry had died. It was the sex or the long walk, she decided. Or it was the knowledge of having someone next to her; not being alone. Richard was a strong physical presence, muscular *and* virile. Loathe though she was to admit it, she'd felt vulnerable in the house at night. She'd toyed with the idea of getting a dog even though she'd never been a domestic animal enthusiast. She was too house proud. A dog's claws would scratch the wood flooring and its hairs would plug the gaps along the skirting boards and coat the sofas. It would take up occupation in front of the log burner and refuse to move. How did you know whether you'd have one that barked all day long and who would look after it in your absence? On car journeys she might be forced to take the beast along with her and you couldn't restrain it with a seat belt. It would be jumping around in the back seat, licking your ear to distract you, farting and whining. She'd be forced to drive off the motor way for it to pee or worse, evacuate its bowels onto some grass verge whereupon she'd feel obliged to scoop it up into one of those colourful little bags and chuck it into the boot. The smell would linger for days afterwards, embarrassing her should she have a passenger. It was no good, the prospect was an intolerable one. Enduring loneliness was preferable.

Richard left early as he said he would, having coffee with her but refusing breakfast. She watched him ride off on his bike, wondering if he was relieved to be away from her and her neediness. He hadn't kissed her goodbye or said he'd be in touch, just mentioned, as they were drinking their coffee, that he was working 'on a paper' and was keen to make progress. Someone in Barcelona was awaiting a call from him. She didn't seek any further details. Whatever it was he was working on, she'd be unlikely to make any sensible contribution to the subject.

He hadn't asked what she had planned for the day either and she was left with the impression that for Richard Marks, out of sight was out of mind. He was content with his world although, she was confident enough to suspect, she'd been a welcome diversion in his routine.

Jane knew now, now she was alone, that she'd be forced to think of Larry and whether her fling with Richard was shameful and despoiled his memory. And, anyway, if it did, wasn't it a little late to be having any such crisis of conscience? Being a widow, whether for ten years or ten weeks, didn't demand celibacy, she decided. Larry been her beloved husband. She'd been faithful to him when he was alive. Fidelity after his death was meaningless. She'd taken a lover, or whatever the phrase was, and derived comfort from his company and his touch. It didn't need justification or confession. Her *dalliance* had lifted her melancholia in a manner she'd thought inconceivable only twenty-four hours previously. Let grief return another day – as it surely would.

Regret was not an emotion which surfaced on that fine morning in early March. In the garden, the sun battled with the clouds for its place in the sky. Spring announced its arrival in the yellow primula and purple crocus already in flower at the base of the wisteria tree in the courtyard.

There were buds on the hawthorn at the boundary of the field and a mild breeze carried the scent of wild garlic in its wake.

CHAPTER 8

Like a bell ringing; intermittently, hopefully

Alex Snow had dealt with only two cases of 'undue influence' in his professional life. Sometimes the possibility of *coercion* was raised – a conversation usually generated by the disappointment felt by the aggrieved that their inheritance had fallen short of their entitlement, rather than a mind unhinged by the loss of a loved one. But it rarely proceeded to litigation or, even, serious negotiations as it had done in the case of Gladys King's estate. Alex had become proficient at shutting down the lines of suspicion before it all got out of hand, even though less scrupulous practitioners may have sniffed money and encouraged their client's sense of grievance.

But a third case had now landed in his lap and it had the capacity to go 'all the way' – as he described it to one of his fellow partners.

"Not only has my client got an *entirely* valid case, watertight, it has the facts more normally found in the plot of a best seller – or in an examination question."

"Watertight?" queried his colleague. "That sounds very certain from one such as you, Alex. But don't enlighten me now. I've got a new client waiting to see me about the terms in a commercial lease and I've hardly glanced at the bloody thing."

Back in his office, Alex turned back to the case of the usurper and the usurped.

Veronica Stern was a woman in her late forties. She was thin – in almost every respect: narrow lips, a straight mouth on a pinched face attached to a curve-less body. She had a chest flatter than most men and favoured shapeless skirts, seemingly designed to hang below the knees. Occasionally she might exchange her brogues for some court shoes, worn with 30 dernier tights possibly inherited from her mother.

Alex wasn't a man who thought judging a woman on their attractiveness, or otherwise, was a practice to be indulged in. But he wasn't impervious to beauty either. Thus, he was ashamed, when Veronica sat opposite him at their first meeting of how often he thought of Jane Sedgefield. It was like comparing two different species, he decided. Should they be seated side by side, it would be a fine example of the huge variation there was in the human form – and not a little cruel either.

He was appalled too that when she outlined the nature of her relationship with the deceased, Tim Blake, his immediate response was one of disbelief that any man might find her remotely attractive. How did you make love, convincingly, to one so lacking in the most basic of female characteristics? He was intrigued to know what Tim had looked like. He must be equally lacking in the looks department, he decided, before giving himself a firm mental shake at the vacuity of his thoughts.

Tim Blake had left his wife for Veronica; abandoned her, after fifteen years of marriage, together with their twelve-year old son, Bradley, to shack up with the will o' wisp Veronica in her 1930s stockings. It was hard to imagine what had motivated him. Perhaps Veronica was kind and supportive and his wife had been a nag and a bully. But he'd left his son too and that must have involved the most terrible of decisions.

"Tim was denied access to Bradley after their separation. Initially, there were amicable arrangements for contact but once she learned of my existence, she became bitter and did what she could to poison Bradley's mind against his father," Veronica explained at their first meeting, her legs wrapped around each other so tightly as to risk the formation of clots in her veins. "Tim was devastated by this. He tried – *we* tried – everything to make her change her mind. Tim gave her their main residence outright and only retained their weekend cottage, which is where we lived together. But she never relented and, eventually, Bradley stopped coming for the weekends, always making excuses about football matches and homework."

Alex nodded, avoided interrupting, making notes of her account on his computer. Occasionally, when she stopped talking, he'd look up to see her struggling to speak as the force of recounting Tim's misery overtook her.

"I'm sorry," she said and, each time and always, Alex smiled his gentle smile, reassuring her that they had plenty of time and she should not feel the necessity to apologise. He was only too aware what it must cost his clients to sit in front of a stranger and reveal the most intimate areas of their lives; encapsulate their darkest moments in an hour and a half's consultation.

When he suggested a break, Veronica appeared grateful and asked for some herbal tea as caffeine didn't agree with her. As they sipped their drinks, Alex asked her about herself. Did he detect a northern accent? Did she work?

He hadn't been prepared for Veronica to reveal that she was a biographer and had a back list which included some notable women: an American astronaut, a British primatologist and a Russian journalist. She was currently working on a biography of a female geneticist but declined to reveal her identity to Alex, saying her publisher had forbidden her from doing so. It was a competitive industry, she explained. You didn't want two biographies of the same person being released in the same year. She spoke authoritatively and enthusiastically about her work, looking less like a person who cannot trust the world enough even to smile and more like someone at home in her own skin. In turn, Alex did a quick reappraisal of his client, reprimanding himself for his prejudice.

When they returned to the business in hand, Veronica seemed more relaxed and trusting. She had already decided that she liked Alex Snow rather a lot. Not only was he handsome with his tidy moustache and slim physique, he was kind and respectful. She admired his smart, dark suit, wondering when she'd last seen a man sport a waistcoat. His office was ordered but attractive. She'd noted the huge print behind him, at odds with the man in front of her, she decided. It was a joyful abstract, full of complexity in its lines and colour. Having also harboured her preconceptions of him – a lawyer, little heart, no soul – she'd have expected something more conventional. He saw her studying it and enlightened her.

"Yes, a fabulous painting, isn't it? Kandinsky's first love was music and it inspired a lot of his compositions. I never tire of looking at it – although it's usually my clients who get to do so!"

She liked him even more after that, glancing at his left hand to see if he wore a wedding ring. He didn't.

"So how long were you and Tim together before his death?" asked Alex.

"Just over fifteen years. He made a new will when he realised his cancer was terminal, leaving the house to me. Since it was held in his sole name, we just decided it was easier to do a will rather than mess around transferring the house into our joint names. There were savings too."

"And then Bradley came back on the scene?"

"It was me," said Veronica, her hands twisting in her lap. "*I* contacted him. *I* tracked him down, believing that they should reconcile before Tim died. I know that's what Tim wanted and I thought it was something I could do for him. There was precious little else – in the circumstances."

Alex nodded.

"Over what period of time before Tim died did Bradley see him?"

"Oh, about seven to eight weeks. Not long. He visited him a lot in that time, though. More than I thought was necessary and it became a bone of contention between us, actually."

"Between whom?"

Veronica swallowed.

"Tim and me. They became very close, very quickly. I felt side-lined."

Veronica pinched the bridge of her nose with her thumb and index finger.

"I was being driven out. And I soon had my suspicions about Bradley's true motives."

"Tell me a little more about him. How old is he? Where is he living?"

"He's 27, not in any relationship – so far as I know. Works in a benefits office, I think, in some form of administrative role. Somewhere in London – Greenford, I seem to remember. Rents a flat with friends."

"You say you had your suspicions? What were those?"

"Even from the beginning, he wasn't friendly towards me. He seemed intent in keeping his distance, often asking me to leave Tim's bedroom so that he could have time with his father alone. During Tim's last two weeks, when he was coming to the end, he insisted on moving into the house so that he could be at his father's bedside when he died. When I objected, Tim became distressed and begged me to allow Bradley to stay. It was during that period that Tim changed his will."

"How did that come about? Did you know about it?"

"Not until after it was done. Tim never told me as, by then, he was too weak to talk. I went to London for just the day, to see my agent. I think I was only gone about six hours. Bradley had just moved in with us, said I shouldn't worry, he was more than capable of coping with his father. I worked out that he took that opportunity to call one of those Wills companies and someone, apparently, came over immediately. They took Tim's instructions and then sent the will a few days' afterwards. Bradley intercepted it. Well, you know the rest, you've seen it – got it witnessed – a stroke of luck for him – by asking the gardeners working in the big house three doors down if they'd pop in for a minute while I was out doing the weekly shop. I know that was the case because I visited the people who live there, checking on the dates."

"Extraordinary," Alex murmured.

"And now he's got the lot," Veronica finished off. "I have no home. That's all that I wanted, really. To remain living there. I didn't need his savings. I have my own income, always have had. But I can't afford to buy him out. You know what property prices are like around here and it's a beautiful place, if small."

Alex sat back in his chair.

"You've got more than one method of legal redress, Miss Stern," he said. "But everything you've told me suggests a pretty clear case of undue influence. I expect you've heard of that. I advise we contest the will on that basis. Our first step is to let Bradley know out intentions and then enter a caveat in the Probate Registry which will prevent a grant of probate being obtained."

Veronica's face lightened as she absorbed his advice.
"There's hope then?"

"Absolutely. The whole scenario smacks of coercion. Why else would he have arranged the will change when you were absent from the home? Why else would he not have mentioned it to you? Why else would he have had the will witnessed when you were – yet again – out of the way? Because he knew you'd speak to Tim and object. The facts speak for themselves. What other hypothesis is there?"

"That's such a relief," she said, sighing.

Alex wondered then if he hadn't gone a bit too far with his – virtual – guarantee of success. There were no guarantees in litigation. Perhaps, he'd been too keen to reassure sad, maltreated Veronica that she would not lose her home after all. It would, however, be an interesting piece of litigation and he had to admit to a frisson of excitement at the prospect.

After some discussion, always delicate, concerning the issue of costs, Alex said he'd write confirming his advice and terms of business, and to request formally the payment of a sizeable sum on account. He was a little surprised that Veronica appeared taken aback by this.

"Oh, I see," she replied, her face assuming the rather distrustful expression she'd displayed when first entering his office. "I assumed I'd get charged after the job was done. Not beforehand."

"Payment on account of costs is standard in the profession," he replied. "If this proceeds to a trial, I'll be seeking much more from you."

"And will I recover those costs if we win? I assume I will."

Alex hesitated.

"You should, but not necessarily. Except in very specific circumstances, costs lie in the discretion of the court."

Veronica looked perplexed.

"It sounds very risky. And very expensive."

After his earlier, premature words regarding the merits of her case, Alex was glad of the opportunity to wholeheartedly agree with her – in terms of both risk and costs.

~ ~ ~

That same afternoon, Jane called Alex to enquire about his progress concerning Larry. She and her father had realised that they were unable to sell Larry's cars, both registered in his name, without the necessary grant of probate. There was also the matter of Larry's life insurance which Jane hadn't known about prior to his death. This amounted to a reasonable sum of money and meant Jane was more financially secure than she had originally thought.

Considering it quite some coincidence that only hours before he had been thinking of her, Alex said he was making excellent progress and should have the matter finalised before the end of the month.

"How are things with you, Jane?" he asked, wanting to prolong their conversation.

"I'm feeling more positive," she said, wondering if he would ask her why. *Oh, I've taken a lover – yes, I know – it's not really socially acceptable is it, after such a short period of time? And with the man who played a role in Larry's death, too. Scandalous!*

"I'm pleased to hear that," was Alex's polite, respectful response. Had she wished to expand on her statement, she would have done so.

"And you, Alex? Any more trips to Scotland to look forward to as spring approaches?"

"No. I'm very busy at the moment. But hoping to book something up for June so I should get a move on. It's a popular time to go to the mountains."

He was sure she had no interest whatsoever in his holiday arrangements.

"I'll be in touch shortly," he said, as a prelude to ending the call.

"Ok, Alex, thank you. Do let me know if I owe you anything at this stage."

Alex went on to explain that he would only be seeking repayment of the disbursements from her. His actual work had been minimal. He was happy, in view of their past business, not to charge her.

"That's so kind. But it's not necessary – really."

"It's fine, Jane. You've been though a lot. I'm pleased to be able to help a little, that's all. Allow me to do that."

"I will. But only if *you'll* allow me to take you to lunch one day to say thank you."

She sensed his hesitation: a moral man who would never take advantage, she thought.

Alex imagined her standing in reception, waiting for him, and then walking to the restaurant together, sitting opposite him.

"Yes. I think I could accept such an invitation," he said, immediately regretting the formality embedded in his words. He'd meant to sound funny, to make her laugh, to expel any idea she might harbour that he was a dull pedant of a man, who walked alone in the hills with just his binoculars for company. Instead, he decided, she now knew for sure. He was awkward and stiff with not a spark of spontaneity in his being.

"I'll look forward to it," said Jane. And then she added "You're a bit of an enigma to me, Alex Snow."

Those words lingered in Alex's mind for the next few days, like a bell ringing – intermittently; hopefully.

CHAPTER 9

The solemn, sculpted images of dead people

Alex had never married. He could say that he'd never quite got around to it. There was some truth in that. He'd met women whom he liked but, certainly when he was younger, failed to cherish. Relationships needed cultivating: new plants to be bedded in, watered, nourished, to ensure firm roots. But events either conspired against him – or he allowed them to.

"You've got an issue with commitment," said his last lady friend, as she stood in his bathroom watching him shower. The noise created by the pump combined with the jets of water cascading over his head meant he hadn't caught her meaning, initially.

"Sorry?" he'd shouted, peering at her though the steam, his hair and moustache a sticky, soapy mess.

She'd yelled then, bellowed at him with irritation, repeating her criticism. Emerging eventually, he'd padded through the flat looking for her. He'd half slipped on the tiled kitchen floor, banging his foot, before realising she'd left. Instead of feeling miserable, he was elated. It was a Saturday morning. He had the whole weekend to himself without having to accommodate her. The shopping trip she'd suggested the night before, when they were having dinner, had filled him with a dread he could barely articulate. He proceeded to wait half an hour, to ensure she'd left the immediate area, and then went to one of the better places on the high street for a full English breakfast. The silence as he ate was bliss.

His route into the legal profession had been a conventional one. University followed by a training contract in a high street practice, before leaving to set up his own practice with two colleagues, Julia Temple and David Jackson. The firm had built up a good local reputation and they were now, after nearly two decades, well established. But it was tough. There'd been a squabble over who should be the managing partner – or, more specifically, who should *not* be. Dealing with staff matters, the accountants, keeping an eye on the bookkeeper, liaising with banks, handling complaints, were not additional burdens to their fee-paying work which any of the three partners wanted to assume. In the end, to keep the peace, as was often the role adopted by Alex Snow, he'd agreed to it.

He'd bought a duplex flat with a wrap-around balcony a fifteen-minute walk from the office. His two partners had told him firmly that living so near to his client base was a very bad idea.

"Christ, Alex, why do you think Julia and I live miles out of town? The last thing you want is to bump into a client every time you set foot out of your door," David remarked, when Alex asked him to undertake the conveyancing on his new property.

"Well, for one thing, I don't relish your daily commute and anyway, I don't mind seeing clients out and about. It's good for business. Not to mention how convenient it will be when the burglar alarm goes off in the middle of the night."

David and Julia had looked a little shame-faced then. Alex was always the key holder. Not only did he live close by, he didn't have kids. And, thus, he didn't have the school run, was expected to take his holidays in term time, could cover when one or other of them was off work with a sick child. A childless adult was always deemed to be *available*. In the past, Julia had brought her twin toddlers into the office, assuming everyone found them as charming as she did as they rampaged through reception, throwing the magazines around, switching the television on and off repeatedly and spilling their drinks all over the newly laid carpet. And the noise they made! Eventually, on the pretext he'd an important phone call to make, Alex had shut his door against them. Every time he looked up, one or other would be pressing a food-smeared little face against one of the glass panels, shouting "hello" at him and knocking until Julia deigned to lift her eyes from her computer screen to remonstrate with them.

A demanding career, together with the occasional love interest, had been enough for him – until recently anyway. In the last few years, he saw his enthusiasm waning. He was forty-nine. Was he going to go on as he had done for another twenty years? Holidaying alone in various parts of Europe, usually mountainous regions where he could walk, was beginning to lose its attraction. An unencumbered life is fine when you're young, with supple limbs, a strong heart and a hunger to explore. Now, for perhaps the first time, he wondered what it would be like to have a companion to share those long winter evenings, leafing through holiday brochures, discussing the news.

Ultimately, you just get weary of your own company.

~ ~ ~

Jane didn't have to wait too long before Richard contacted her again. She'd thought of making the first move by suggesting a walk and a pub lunch but however she worded her message, it hinted at desperation. And one matter she felt certain about, even after less than twenty-four hours in his company, was his abhorrence of anyone pestering him. She imagined most of his social and business interactions were on his terms alone.

She didn't respond to him immediately, waiting a full four hours before saying, yes, she'd love to pop over for lunch at his place. She was interested to see how he lived, the paintings on his walls, his study, the books on his shelves and whether he bothered with any photos of the two exquisite looking daughters. As she was contemplating this on her drive over the following day, she wondered if he had looked for a photo of Larry and what he'd concluded, if anything, when he hadn't found one. Jane hadn't got around to placing Larry in a frame and displaying him on her bedside table which, given the lustful spectacle of the previous week, was just as well. Larry's eyes following their progress, on a mattress they'd had throughout their marriage and which probably still bore the imprint of his body, would have dampened their ardour – like a bucket of cold water being thrown over them.

As before, lunch didn't happen until the middle of the afternoon. They attended to their more important appetites before Richard produced some olives, cheese and crackers, barely apologising for throwing together something so much less substantial than had been promised. There was no wine either. Richard didn't drink during the day as it interfered with his work for which he needed 'absolute concentration'. When Jane suggested a walk, he declined.

"I've been out on my bike already today, so if you don't mind, I'll pass on that."

As they drank their tea, Jane could see he was already eager to get shot of her.

"So, what have you planned for the rest of the day?" he enquired. It was hardly subtle, Jane thought, particularly as there wasn't that much of 'the day' left.

Her response was sarcastic. "Oh, I've got a dinner party tonight with twelve guests arriving. Before then, I want to wallpaper one of the bedrooms *and* I'm in the middle of a novel I'm reading in the original French. How about you – still working on that paper you mentioned when we last met?"

She cocked her head, challenging him with a direct stare. Richard reddened. He stood up and began clearing away their cups, even though she'd hadn't finished. But he said nothing.

Jane rose too and, adopting a resolute air, she left the room running up the stairs to retrieve her coat and bag from where they'd been abandoned, recklessly, on the floor of Richard's bedroom.

He was waiting for her at the bottom of the stairs when she came down them.

"Don't leave in a huff," he said, trying to catch her arm as she made for the front door.

"Enjoy the rest of your day," she said, banging the door behind her.

She crashed the gears as she attempted to drive away quickly and hadn't gone more than a few yards before acknowledging that she'd behaved exactly as she had been determined not to – a pathetic, clingy, needy woman, demanding more, or expecting more, than she had any right to. No doubt he was pleased she'd shown her true colours so early on. It would save a lot of discomfort in the long run.

His cottage was much as she had expected. There were a few miniature sculptures scattered around and two large prints in the living room; architectural drawings of buildings she didn't recognize. The bedrooms, of which there were two, were unadorned, painted in neutral colours. A twin-bedded room for the girls and a much larger bedroom with a double bed for himself. There was no bath, just a walk-in shower. Downstairs, the living room was a decent size with an open fire and the dining room had been made into a study. She had asked to see the study. He'd given her a quizzical look but flung open the door for her before going to the kitchen to prepare their meagre repast.

"Don't disturb anything," he warned, as if she were a child. "It looks chaotic in there, but it's not."

As she looked around, she thought back to Gladys' study and the bird skeleton with which she'd become so obsessed. This was a tiny room in comparison, unable to contain Richard's extensive library. Books overflowed from the shelves, onto the floor, along the windowsills and, even, under the desk. A rectangular mahogany table provided an extension to the desk and had a large stack of papers in each corner. She looked at the top document on each of the piles, hoping to discern something of Richard's inner life and what preoccupied him. One was entitled "The Revival of Portraiture in the Fourteenth Century" and another concerned "The Great Neapolitan tombs." She wondered why he might think she – or, indeed, anyone – would wish to delve further into either of these subjects. The idea that he may later discover her curled up in a corner of the living room immersed in a biography of *Philip the Bold*, was ridiculous. Perhaps it was the comment she'd made, as she picked at the black olives with a cocktail stick, which had dissuaded him from spending further time with her that day.

"I'm surprised anyone can spend a quarter of a century on such a short period of history and still remain fascinated with it. Do you never want to, you know...."

Richard's expression prevented her from continuing with her idle thoughts.

She laughed.

"Ooops! Sorry, was that a crass and ignorant comment?"

He didn't answer her directly.

"You're not the first to voice that sentiment. I've become used to hearing it."

He pushed the plate of cheese over to her, almost aggressively.

"Forgive me if I don't indulge you with an answer," he said.

"That's a trifle harsh, isn't it?" she said. *For God's sake, man*, she thought, *rise to the challenge and defend your work.*

She noticed that he'd been buttering the same cracker for the equivalent amount of time it would take to mortar a line of bricks.

"You'll be asking me what's the point next. What's the purpose behind any academic study?"

"Well, that's a legitimate question, isn't it? History affords us – or so I understand – the knowledge to avoid making the same mistakes again. But how do we benefit by knowing about the development of sculpture in the fourteenth century? I'm not being rude. I'm actually interested."

"It *is* history," he said, his voice rising a little. "*Art* history is about interpreting cultures and events. Why does this sculpture look this way? What's its social relevance? What religious beliefs are embodied within it?"

His cracker was now ready for its cheese. He waffled on for a few minutes, citing examples of those pieces which had inspired him as a young man.

"Anyway, it's quite a complex subject to debate over a plate of olives," he finished off.

"And especially with someone like me?"

"I didn't say that. Why are you sparring with me anyway?"

"Sparring! I hadn't realised I was."

There was contempt in the look he cast at Jane, then, she decided, so his unsubtle hint that she should take her leave was not unexpected.

On her drive home, Jane questioned why she had voiced her opinion of his life's work in such a mocking manner. They could have had a perfectly reasonable discussion without her being offensive. His response *was* defensive, but she had provoked it. Did it suggest she felt inferior to him, intellectually, and was anxious to show she didn't care? If so, the exchange had proved the opposite. An apology was warranted.

She didn't need to compose one. As she was putting on her trainers to go out for a walk before dinner, a text came in from Richard. He said he was sorry that they had 'parted on bad terms' and he hoped they could still see each other. Next time, he would make her a proper lunch. His lack of effort, he said, was 'unforgivable'. Having decided she'd played enough games for one day, she texted straight back –

I will expect caviar and smoked salmon and champagne!

Adding, a few seconds later – *after our usual first course, naturally.*

Richard didn't respond with an emoji. A thumbs up or a smiley face were not elements in his vocabulary. His text comprised one word – *Great.*

No doubt now hunched over his desk studying the solemn sculpted images of dead people, he was missing a wonderful sunny late afternoon, she thought. The hour was about to go forward and the earth was opening up after its winter slumber. There were fat buds poking out from glossy green leaves on the Camellia bushes by the front door. As she strode out in the direction of the public footpath, accessed via the field adjoining her own, she stood for a few moments watching the new-born lambs skipping alongside their mothers.

The camellias were going to produce an abundance of pink flowers. She imagined their beautiful waxy petals as she placed her key in the lock on her return, hoping it might distract her from the sight of Larry's cars which were still lined up on the forecourt; the headlamps suggestive of two pairs of eyes desperately seeking their owner. No matter how many lights she switched on throughout the house as the evening gathered, how loud she played music, how brightly the stove burned, she could never quite shake off the melancholy which descended on her at that hour of the day. It was a like a homeless acquaintance whom you hoped would find another place to stay but, whether invited to or not, always seemed to end up sleeping on your sofa.

CHAPTER 10

For the time being, undisclosed

As Jane made up the beds in the two rooms which Debbie and Alicja would sleep in that weekend, she contemplated the recent developments in her life and whether it was appropriate to disclose them. She now harboured two secrets – if one wished to refer to them in such child-like terms. It smacked of weakness, on the part of a woman of fifty plus, to be reticent about revealing the decisions she'd taken to enable her to survive the cataclysmic shift in her inner, and outer, landscape, post Larry.

That morning, a Friday in the first week in April, she'd been for an interview for a job in an interior design shop in Cheltenham and was waiting to hear if she'd be offered the post. Initially, on hearing about the opportunity from Lilly, she'd thought it too far to travel but when she learned it was for only three days a week – although one of the days was Saturday – the forty-five-minute car journey there and back seemed less of an obstacle.

Jane had no commercial experience in interior design, as she pointed out to Lilly when she called her.

"I was a PA in my last job," she said. "I have no knowledge of the subject whatsoever, let alone any actual *retail* experience."

"You mean using a till?" asked Lilly, barely able to keep the scorn from her tone. "Are you asking me to believe you might struggle with that?"

"No. But it's likely to be a significant omission in my CV that I've never worked in any shop, ever. And that's before we get on to the skills necessary to advise people on their own interiors. Fabrics, flooring, lighting."

"Come on, Jane, you've got an eye for things. And you look so good. That's what they want. Attractive, well-spoken members of staff. Not bored fine art graduates who'd prefer to be a curator in a gallery. If you got offered it, would you be interested?"

"Yes. I'd give it a go, certainly. I've nothing to lose. It should be interesting. And I need something different." As she spouted these words, Jane wondered which one of them she was trying to convince.

"I'll give you a reference if you need one. You can mention me. Say you've done the odd bit of work for me and show them my web site."

"Lilly! But I haven't."

"Oh, who gives a toss," said Lilly. "Do you think they'll be inundated with candidates of your calibre? Take a risk. You said yourself, what have you got to lose? And Cheltenham is a great city. *Loads* going on there. *Lots* of money swishing around. *Lovely* architecture with interiors which need refurbishing."

"You make it sound like a dream job! Yes, I'll give it a try. Thanks."

"Brilliant. Now look, you've got some homework to do before your interview. You need to study their website. Look at their stock, how they present it. Try to find out a bit about them. Say what you're particularly interested in or passionate about."

Jane interrupted her. "Like what?"

"Oh, just make it up, for God's sake. Fabrics, for instance. Look up a few designers and mention them – just to make yourself sound knowledgeable. Fake it, Jane. Men do it all the time! You know, men apply for roles they want whether they've got the competency to do the job or not. Whereas women always think it's necessary to be qualified or experienced before they can even apply for a similar role."

Jane laughed. "Are you sure you're happy to give a false reference for me?"

"Don't be so proper. Of course I am. There's nothing wrong with a bit of nepotism. If that's what it is. Anyway, when you get the job, you can steer customers in my direction if you get the chance. I'd like an opening in Cheltenham."

"Aha!" said Jane. "So that's your motive!"

"Oh, there's rarely such a thing as a pure motive, I find," said Lilly. "Oh yes, and one last piece of advice, if you get an interview, make a visit to Cheltenham beforehand to take a look around at the various buildings and areas in the town. You need to know your client base and be aware of the various styles of houses they're living in."

"Can't I just look it up on the net?"

"No!" Lilly retorted. "Absolutely not. You can't possibly get a feel for a place without exploring its streets and smelling its air. What else have you got to do anyway?"

Jane thought of Richard. It occurred to her that whatever Lilly may think about her frolics – and she doubted that Lilly would be censorious – Michael may not have such a casual response to how quickly Jane had taken a new lover.

Fired up by Lilly's faith in her and eager for her days to have some solid purpose, she applied for the job the same afternoon she'd learned of the vacancy. An email had come back two days later, inviting her for an interview that Friday at 11am. It gave her the Thursday to explore Cheltenham in accordance with Lilly's robust advice. That morning, her first thought when she woke up – early, it was only 6am – was not, as it almost invariably was, Larry; it was whether she should call Richard and ask if he fancied lunch in Cheltenham. Surely, he was just the person to explore the town with. No doubt he knew the history of every significant building. It would be like having your own personal tour guide. Might as well make the most of his talents.

She rang him just after eight. There was no answer. He's probably out on his bike, she decided. He likes an early morning ride and it means he can devote the rest of the day to his work without interruption. Well, he'd have to reappraise his day when she called.

He rang back before 9. "What's up?" were his first words, as if she was one of his daughters who only called at that hour if there was a problem.

She outlined the purpose of her trip out for lunch and suggested she join him.

"A job? I hadn't realised you were interested in interior design," he said, adding quickly "Perhaps I should listen more," as if he suddenly recalled their last conversation. He didn't sound overcome with enthusiasm.

"There'll be no shopping involved, if that's your concern," said Jane. "Don't worry, I wouldn't dream of taking any man shopping. It's the perfect way to spoil a day out. And I don't mean from the man's point of view, either."

"Yes, ok. What time will you be round? After midday would at least allow me to finish off some stuff."

Before she set off, Jane researched Cheltenham on the net, knowing she needed to have some rudimentary knowledge of its history now that Richard was coming. Otherwise, it would be just another opportunity for her to display her ignorance.

She had a vague recollection of Cheltenham being a Regency town with many fine examples of the period but recalled little from the brief visit she'd made twenty years ago. Her search suggested that *Pittville Circus* would be a good starting point for their little tour and they needed to take in the Royal Crescent too. Delighted to discover that the town's Art Gallery and Museum was home to an important collection of the British Arts and Crafts movement, inspired by William Morris, she added it to their itinerary. Morris' prints, fabrics and wallpapers never seemed to go out of fashion so time spent there, soaking up the principles Morris espoused – functional designs using nature as your guide – would be useful for her interview.

Richard didn't like being driven. Clearly, he'd grown unused to it, as he seemed unable to stay still. He squirmed and fidgeted during the journey like an anxious child, distracting her to the point of annoyance.

"What *is* the matter?" she asked, eventually, after half an hour of enduring his restlessness.

Richard appeared unaware of his behaviour. "What do you mean?" he said.

"You seem on edge. You're not relaxed. Is it my driving?"

"No, of course not. Sorry, I'm just not a good passenger. Well, if I'm honest, I'm not good at doing nothing."

"You're bored," Jane declared.

Since he neither confirmed nor denied her diagnosis, she decided to engage him. He was happiest, she knew, when imparting knowledge.

"Tell me about William Morris."

"What makes you think I know anything about William Morris? I find his designs fussy. They're not for me."

"You don't think they're beautiful evocations of the natural world?" said Jane, repeating what she'd read earlier.

"No, frankly. I do know one fact about him, though, which people forget," said Richard. His fidgeting had stopped. "He founded the Society for Protection of Ancient Buildings in the 1870s. As far as I know, it's still going today. Although I don't appreciate much of his craft, I think he was quite remarkable. Certainly, a man who left a considerable legacy."

"Oh, I must remember that about the Society. What was the name of it again?"

Richard repeated it, slowly and then added, "*SPAB* – was its abbreviated form. That should help you."

Jane smiled. Richard appeared unable to discuss anything without affecting the air of the lecturer – a superior one. She wondered what his students must have thought of him. Whether the boys were all irritated by his manner and most of the girls in love with him.

"What subject did you teach? Was it your speciality or broader than that?"

It's what she should have asked when they'd had lunch the previous week, instead of being so rude.

"Oh, much broader. I've taught a number of different modules in my time but, usually, I covered Renaissance Art which spans almost four centuries. I often focused on sculpture but the syllabus itself covered all the visual arts."

Richard continued with the topic, outlining a typical syllabus in Renaissance Art. He started with a brief reference to thirteenth century humanism which Jane found much more accessible than the titbits about Gothic sculpture which she'd picked up from him. They were occupied with *Donatello* and the introduction of 'free-standing statues' when they arrived in Cheltenham.

After they'd walked and spent an hour or so in the gallery, Jane asked if they could go and visit the shop she'd applied to before heading back.

"I don't want to go in," she said. "If I'm noticed, that will just feel embarrassing tomorrow."

"Why?" queried Richard. "Surely they'd expect you to have visited a store you've expressed a wish to work for?"

So, they ended up inside *Magnifique* with its rows of wallpaper rolls and bolts of fabrics and artfully placed pieces of furniture. There was even a room mocked up with that season's newest paints and wallpaper. It was a jumble of geometric shapes in pinks and purples.

"Christ, this would give me a headache," murmured Richard. "It's an assault on your senses. And not in a good way."

"Keep you buzzing, awake and alive!" whispered Jane.

"I can see you will be a perfect fit for the place," remarked Richard. "Just don't get any ideas about selling me anything."

"Wouldn't dream of it," said Jane, suppressing a giggle at the thought of Richard leafing through books of swatches of curtain material, making notes as he did so.

~ ~ ~

Jane was out in the courtyard with Alicja and Debbie when her mobile rang. She'd placed a little bistro table and chairs under the wisteria and they were having a drink before dinner. It was a bit chilly and they all had their coats on but there was still some light in the sky.

"Hey, do you mind if I take this?" she asked, looking at Debbie. Debbie nodded as she sipped her wine.

Jane wandered away from the table but was back a minute later, beaming.

"Good news?" asked Debbie. She'd already noticed that Jane appeared brighter than on her last visit although, timing wise, that was hardly surprising. She seemed more at home in the house. There were little touches suggesting some permanence which hadn't been in evidence before. Perhaps Jane was beginning to adapt to life alone, she decided.

"I have a job!" she declared to them both and then, holding up her glass to Debbie, "following your example and encouraged – or, perhaps, bullied would be a more precise word – by my brother-in-law's wife, I decided on a complete change."

She provided a brief description of her role at *Magnifique*, describing herself as 'a glorified shop assistant, really' but "I will be expected to advise customers on the shop's products and, down the line, hopefully, be allowed to visit clients in their own homes to help plan their interiors".

Debbie's eyes widened. "Jane, that's such brilliant news. Such a change for you after the stresses of your last job."

"Yes, three days should be tolerable although Saturdays could be a bit of a drag if I want to get away for a weekend."

"Same as me in that respect. I just take leave occasionally – like this weekend. Never very popular. I trust your employers will be more understanding than mine."

Jane felt Alicja's eyes on her. "Have you any idea what you'd like to do when you leave school or university, Alicja?"

Alicja flushed as Debbie and Jane awaited her response.

"Oh, not really. I like the outdoors, nature, conservation. Something in that area."

Her blonde hair tucked into the collar, Alicja was wearing her black woollen coat. Jane had admired it when they were introduced.

"There's quite a history to that coat," said Debbie, smiling, before realising that the story of her confrontation with Halina was hardly the subject for entertainment. "But that's for another time, perhaps," she added.

Alicja had come back from school earlier than expected that afternoon. She'd entered the bedroom to find Halina and Debbie engaged in a full and frank exchange about Alicja's coat.

"I didn't invite you in here. *Please* get out," Halina was saying. In fact, Debbie had knocked and Halina, assuming she was staff, had shouted for her to 'come in'. Her face had assumed its stony look as soon as she saw who it was.

Debbie did not try to smooth the ground between them. It was futile. Halina had no interest in a friendly relationship with her.

"I'm taking Alicja away this weekend, as you know. She'll need her coat. I've come to ensure she gets it. I bought it for her, not you."

When Halina did not reply, Debbie repeated herself, knowing that, as a mere volunteer, she was overstepping the mark. Alicja's eyes darted between them, wide with anxiety.

Halina picked up her cigarettes and lighter from the table and left the room, pushing roughly past her daughter.

Alicja went over and sat down on her bed.

"I'm sorry, Alicja," said Debbie. "It's not the best start to our weekend. But she needs to be told. She can't treat you like this and expect me – or anyone – to stand by and witness it, without challenge."

"You, not anyone else," Alicja murmured, looking down at her hands.

"Sorry, what do you mean?"

"*You* tell her. No-one else does. They just sit about here and let her say anything she wants. I hate it. I hate her. Wherever I go will be better than here."

Debbie went over and sat next to her, putting her arm around her shoulders. "Have you heard anything, yet?"

Alicja shook her head.

"Look," said Debbie brightly. "Forget all this just for the next couple of days. We're going to have a great time. I promise! But we need to get going quickly. I'm being very brave and driving there but it's a Friday and the traffic is already building up. It's past three and it will take us at least two and half hours, I reckon."

Alicja jumped up and went over to a chest of drawers. "Will I need jumpers?"

"Yes, a couple only and an extra pair of jeans or jogging bottoms. Trainers or boots as we'll do lots of walking and it may be muddy. Have you got any spare ones?"

Alicja was busy stuffing clothes into her school rucksack. "Only my school shoes and trainers."

"No worries. I've bought some spare boots and I bet we're similar sizes. We'll manage. Now where is that wretched coat?"

Alicja looked over towards the wardrobe in the corner.

Debbie marched over, pulling at the door so vigorously the whole cupboard wobbled.

"Yikes!" she exclaimed, wincing at the stench of cigarette smoke which assailed her. Inside were a jumble of clothes, none of them on hangers except the treasured coat. She held it up to Alicja.

"Could do with an airing," she said, shaking and beating it as you would a Persian rug. "We'll hang it up in the back of the car and keep the window open."

Alicja smiled broadly at her.

"Let's go, shall we?" said Debbie. "Have you got your toothbrush?"

"In the bathroom, I think," said Alicja. She scurried off, returning seconds later with the most threadbare of brushes Debbie had ever seen. There was no wash bag, no flannel, no sanitary protection. Debbie assumed she had a hairbrush in her bag but, later, as she settled Alicja into her room at Jane's, all she saw – laid out almost proudly in the adjoining bathroom – was the new toothbrush and toothpaste she'd bought when they stopped at a motorway service station and a plastic comb. She wanted to say 'if we visit Cirencester tomorrow, we can get you a hairbrush and anything else you need' but she didn't want to patronise the girl; nor did she want to be continually pointing out the extent of her mother's neglect.

The drive to Jane's had been much as Debbie had expected, full of delays caused by roadworks, general Friday afternoon congestion and, just in the last stretch of the journey, a broken-down car. But they'd made it for just after 6 which Debbie declared 'miraculous'.

"What would you like to do tomorrow?" asked Jane, directing her question at Alicja.

"I'm happy with anything," she said. "It's a beautiful area. I love it. And you have a lovely house too."

"I hope you enjoy it so much that you want to come back again," said Jane. "It's a big house and it's nice to have company. I'm afraid I don't have any pets. I thought about a pony or a donkey but, now I've got a job, I think I'll have to shelve that plan for the time being."

Debbie looked over at her and smiled, gratefully.

"I think a long walk and a pub lunch, don't you, Alicja?" said Debbie. "If it's nice we could have a picnic but I'm not sure it'll be warm enough."

"Oh, please," said Alicja, her face pink with pleasure, "*Please* let's have a picnic! I don't mind the weather – if you two don't."

She's probably imagining something out of an old children's story book, thought Jane. She wasn't sure she could conjure up anything so magical – rugs and picnic baskets, platters of fruit, chicken legs and scotch eggs.

Debbie looked over at Jane. "Well, I'm game if you are, Jane? To hell with the weather. We'll have to build a den if it rains!"

They had their picnic – sandwiches, chocolate biscuits and cartons of apple juice, all of which Alicja insisted on carrying in her rucksack – sitting on a stone wall. The grass was too damp to sit on as it had been drizzling ever since they'd set foot outside the house. Following a trail which Debbie had discovered on the net before setting out, they were all ravenous by the time they decided that the weather showed no sign of improving.

"This is a typical English picnic," declared Debbie to Alicja. "Drizzle down the back of your neck is an essential part of the experience."

But nothing could dampen Alicja's enthusiasm. She pelted across fields, peering over fences, leaping over stiles, staring back at the cows and cooing over the lambs, leaving her two companions far behind.

"She doesn't really behave like a girl of fifteen, does she? She seems younger," observed Jane.

"Oh, sometimes she seems much older than her years, believe me," Debbie replied, as she squeezed herself through a gate. "But I think for the moment, here, she is making up for a lost childhood. From what she's told me, she's never seen the real countryside before. It's a foreign land to her. I get the impression that she can be herself with me, doesn't have to assume the responsibility she's shouldered living with her mother. Her mother is very critical of her, as if she's jealous for some ridiculous reason. It's great to be able to give her this weekend."

Debbie stopped walking and turned to face Jane. Her hood had slipped off and her face glistened with rain.

"And thanks so much for inviting us. It's very good of you to be so welcoming."

"God, it's me who should thank you!" said Jane, reaching over and pulling Debbie's hood back on her head. "A weekend without company can be a very lonely one."

"Yes, I remember," said Debbie, tying her hood strings in a double bow beneath her chin.

"Of course you do," said Jane.

They walked on together, Debbie suggesting they increased their pace before they lost sight of Alicja.

"I'm in charge of her, remember. Alicja!" shouted Debbie. "Wait for us!"

Jane wondered for a moment, as they were alone, whether she should mention Richard. Was she being dishonest in suggesting she spent most of her waking hours alone, pining for Larry?

But the moment passed.

Jane's relationship with Richard remained, for the time being, undisclosed.

CHAPTER 11

Genitals swinging

Alicja didn't like looking back. Although she'd kept a diary once, when she was around twelve, she no longer did so. She'd found that beautiful little diary in a charity shop when accompanying her mother on one of their periodic hunts for cheap clothing. It was perfect because it wasn't for any particular year, just the days of each week were missing. She wasn't given any pocket money and had to plead with Halina to buy it for her. Since her mother was pleased because she'd found some leather trousers which fitted her, she grudgingly handed the diary over at the till.

"The money would be better spent on a jumper for you," she hissed at Alicja as they stood at the counter. The male shop assistant had looked over at Alicja and winked at her. It was a kind gesture, designed to alleviate Alicja's embarrassment at her mother's hurtful remark.

Alicja had spent the rest of the day painstakingly writing each day of the week against its date for that year. There were old black and white photographs on every page, of men and women at work – whether in the fields or fishing, washing clothes by the river or at machines in a factory. They fascinated her. She had few possessions, no books of her own and no recourse to a computer, save at school and the library. It put her at a disadvantage where her studies were concerned but she'd discovered early that they'd barely money for rent and food. There was no surplus and, even if there were, it would not be spent on her.

Occasionally, Alicja would wonder about her father and why he never contacted her. She knew that he had returned to Poland when Alicja was two or three, but she had little recollection of him. What few memories she had did not bring her any comfort. If he cared, he would have been in touch. Her mother had drilled that sad fact into her over the years. Even as a young child, she had seen disappointment in her mother's eyes whenever the past was referred to, so she stopped asking about life in Poland. She'd stroke her mother's long thick hair and speak to her in soothing whispers and back then, when Alicja was a young, sweet child, Halina would let her.

Despite the paucity of her home life, manifested in the shabbiness of her school uniform and scuffed shoes, Alicja was a popular child with her peers and teachers. Her prettiness helped and while some children are taunted and bullied *because* of their generosity and openness, Alicja wasn't. She excelled at Games, particularly hockey. She didn't mind being out in inclement weather or attending inter-school matches after school. 'Home' was somewhere she often wanted to avoid going back to. When, on occasion, she was invited to friends' homes for tea, she was struck by the comfort of their living rooms and the warmth of the welcome extended to her.

Rarely, when she arrived home after school, would her mother be alone. Usually, there'd be a man – or men – sitting around in the kitchen, smoking and drinking coffee. They'd appraise her with their eyes and make the odd comment, embarrassing her.

It was around the time of the diary that Alicja began to understand the nature of her mother's relationships with these men, shocked by her own naivety in not seeing it earlier. Whilst they didn't stay overnight, there were times when she returned from school to find a naked, or semi-clothed, man emerging from their bathroom. He would scuttle into Halina's bedroom and slam the door without acknowledging her. Soon afterwards, he'd leave the flat and Halina would go into the bathroom and stay for a long time. Alicja would hear the taps running while the bath was filled. When she knocked, wanting to use the toilet, her mother wouldn't answer her. Alicja would curl up on her bed and pray to God that her mother was not dead. It took her a long time before she stopped being fearful, putting her key in the lock after school, of finding Halina drowned in the bath or her mutilated body on the living room floor.

Alicja's life changed one Monday afternoon on a summer's day. She'd played netball after school and arrived home ravenous, hoping there might be some bread so that she could make toast. Otherwise, it would be a trip to the shops, assuming her mother had the money to give her.

Since the radio was playing, her mother and her male friend didn't hear her when she entered the flat. Halina's bedroom door was wide open, as were all the windows in their small lounge. It was a hot day; the flat could become unbearable without some form of ventilation. Initially, Alicja went into the kitchen to look for something to eat. There was bread, but nothing to put on it.

"Mum," she shouted out. "Is there any butter?"

When she didn't get an immediate response, she went towards her mother's room.

They were lying on their backs, looking at something and laughing. Alicja couldn't recall seeing the man before. He was bald, a great bear of a man with a scar running from one corner of his eye to his chin. Her mother looked small beside him. Neither of them showed discomfort at Alicja standing at the bedroom door, staring in at them.

"Oh hi, honey," said her mother. Whatever they had been looking at was placed under the covers by Halina.

"My bag is on the settee. Go and get something for our meal, would you? Chips, burgers. Oh, and milk and butter, too." She smiled sweetly as she said it. *Putting on an act*, thought Alicja. *She must like this one.*

"How many for?" asked Alicja. She was wearing tracksuit bottoms and a tee-shirt, her blonde hair pushed back from her face with an Alice band.

Her mother laughed and looked over at the bear.

"Staying for some food?" she asked him.

He fixed his gaze on Alicja, ignoring Halina.

"Pretty girl," was all he said.

"Just the two of us, then," snapped Halina. "Shut the door, would you?"

Alicja stayed out as long as possible, hoping the bear would have gone by the time she got back but she met him as she was climbing the stairs on her return to the flat. She hated the small smelly lift, preferring to walk the six flights.

"Ah," he said, towering over her. She stepped away from his garlic breath. "The pretty one." She ducked under his arm, catching an unpleasant smell as she did so, and sprinted up the stairs. His laughter followed her.

Arriving, breathless, back at the flat, she heard the familiar sound of the bath being filled. Her mother's bedroom door was open, the bed unmade. Lying on the top of the duvet, she caught sight of a book. She walked in, unable, at first, to believe it was her diary. She thought back to watching the two of them, lying together, entertained and amused by her private thoughts.

It was one of those times in a life never forgotten. Her mother reading it was treacherous, certainly, but to invite a stranger to share it with her cast that treachery in a different light. *I mean nothing to her*, she thought. She retrieved the diary from the jumble of bedclothes and went to her room. That night she ripped out every page and tore it into as many strips as she could, thinking briefly of scattering the shredded paper over her mother's bed but her courage was lacking.

It was a topic never raised between them. Her mother knew she had found the diary because later she tried to be nice to her, saying she would cook their meal and asking Alicja why she hadn't bought herself some coke.

"That would have been ok," Halina said to her from where she stood at the cooker. Her long hair stretched down her back, still damp, and she was wearing a silky, pink robe which Alicja had not seen before. A gift from the bear, perhaps?

Alicja did not respond. Without asking, she took her burger and chips into her bedroom on a rusting metal tray they'd had for as long as she could remember. It was an old Polish one, showing a snowy scene somewhere in the mountains. There was a church nestling in the folds of the hills, lit up on the inside. Alicja had always liked the tray; it reminded her of Christmas. She stayed there for the rest of the evening, even though she had no television to watch and her radio was in her mother's room.

The following morning, she gathered up the tattered remnants of her diary and thrust them into her rucksack. They were decanted into the third-floor rubbish chute on her way down the stairs. And she wept all the way to school, grieving not just for the diary but for something else which she knew was irreplaceable.

~ ~ ~

Jane was pleasantly surprised when Richard messaged her after her first day in her new role – a Thursday – to ask how she'd got on. She hadn't expected him to remember, let alone bother to enquire. It was a thoughtfulness he appeared to be trying to cultivate.

She had enjoyed the day and told him so, her voice full of genuine enthusiasm. Even after just a few hours in the job, she left feeling that she'd made a good choice. Being surrounded by shapes, colours and textures, which changed according to the light from the large windows, was a stimulating environment to inhabit. Their customers tended to take pleasure in the experience, lingering over their choices rather than it being a feat of endurance as in crowded supermarkets. Often, it was the culmination of a project, the part they'd been looking forward to, choosing the wallpaper and matching paint. And then there were the new homeowners, almost ecstatic after years of renting and living with someone else's choices, unable to even put up a painting in the living room for fear of losing their deposit.

Perhaps it will fade, Jane thought, when the novelty has worn off. And did she have the patience for a customer's indecision without exhibiting some impatience? How many different shades of white were there actually? It must have required an impressive imagination for them all to be given different names: chalk, bright white, off-white, vanilla white. She'd been warned that, at times, the shop was very quiet and there would be little to do but go through the stock in one of the back rooms, re-organize the soft furnishings or stack the fabric rolls yet again. But there was relief in leaving at night and carrying no anxieties back with her, happy to exchange tedium for the stress which had been her constant companion with Max. Obviously, the corollary was that she wasn't paid much but it would supplement what she already had and keep her afloat as long as some restraint was exercised. Her life was acquiring some structure. It felt like another step on the path to adapting to living alone.

Yet, it was rare that she didn't think of Larry as she let herself into her empty, dark home after returning from work. Occasionally, she would see a shadow in the hallway and imagine what life might have been like had he been there to greet her. How wonderful it would be to walk from the front door into a warm kitchen, with music blaring and a pot of his usual pasta bubbling on the stove. There'd be two empty wine glasses sitting on the kitchen table, ready to be filled once they were together. *As with so much in our short lives,* she thought – *youth, health, companionship, freedom – only truly valued when lost.* Inevitably, such musings on her own circumstances would lead to reminiscences of Gladys. Contrition would invade her then, an unwanted rodent scrabbling and scratching at her conscience. *You were cruel, Jane, cruel.*

Lilly was delighted when Jane got the job in *Magnifique*. She'd only been in post a few days before she was on the phone eager to know Jane's first impressions.

"Look, I know we shouldn't invite ourselves, but I wondered whether we could visit you this weekend. I'd love to see the shop. You can introduce me to the manager if they're around or I can drop some of my cards off. Or are you otherwise engaged?"

Privately, Jane thought this was somewhat pushy of Lilly. She'd hardly got her feet under the table, not even being sure if she remembered the manager's name. There were buyers and traders and assistants. They all merged together on what she'd found, together with the hour and a half commute, amounted to quite long, busy days.

Only a few minutes beforehand, Jane had agreed with Richard that he'd come over for dinner that Saturday evening. They'd contemplated meeting up in Cheltenham after work, but Richard had reminded her that he'd have to bike over and then bike back. It didn't seem 'the best way of expending energy on a Saturday evening'. The implication of this latter comment had made Jane smile. She was thinking of that now as she wrestled with whether to admit to Lilly that she did indeed have a prior commitment. Lilly would be surprised as, Jane concluded, the question had been added out of politeness. No-one, with the possible exception of Debbie, believed she had yet forged any independent life from the ashes of her widowhood. Widows stayed widows for a long, long time, didn't they?

Thinking she could swap Richard to the Friday, she agreed, trying to sound grateful for the company.

"No, I'm free. And that sounds great. I'll look forward to seeing you both. Friday evening's no good as I'm not sure what time I'll be back from the shop. But there's a spare key in the rockery to the left of the front door so by all means arrive at the house at your leisure on the Saturday and, of course, stay over."

"Well, we'll probably drive straight to Cheltenham and then come back to the house late afternoon – or something."

"Yes, of course," Jane answered. "That sounds more sensible."

Richard was happy to change their date to the Friday although it wasn't ideal for Jane, as she had to leave the house by 8 30am the following morning. After many months of indolence, she was struggling to adjust to a new regime; early morning showers and blow drying her hair while eating toast and drinking coffee. Richard was scornful of her complaints. He was usually out on his bike by 7am.

Their evening together was enjoyable. As trust entered what was now becoming a relationship, their insecurities diminished. He still lectured her. She still teased him. But there was now affection alongside the sex. They'd lingered in the bedroom and then lingered again over dinner. Jane drank too much, partly out of relief at having survived her first few days in a new job and also because she liked looking at him over the dinner table. He didn't ask to stay the night. It was just assumed.

When she left on the Saturday morning, in a great hurry, Richard – for all his sermonising over the joys of rising early – had still to shower. He'd forgotten what it was like to share this part of his morning with someone. There was much less reason to leap from your pit when there was a warm, soft body beside you. He'd waited for Jane to dress, watching her from the bed, admiring the confidence she showed as she walked around the room, naked.

"See you later," she'd called out as she left the house, wishing it were true.

He'd pulled on a tee shirt, wandering over to the window where he watched her reverse her car and drive smartly away, leaving tyre tracks in the gravelled drive. Larry's cars were still there. He wondered briefly what it was that attracted other members of his sex to such gas-guzzling machines, before deciding that he too should make a start on his day.

So Richard was in the shower when Lilly and Michael let themselves in to *The Old Byre*. Whilst he knew that 'relatives' were visiting that day, he distinctly recalled Jane saying that she was meeting them in Cheltenham first. She'd said nothing, by way of warning, that they might turn up in the house. And, anyway, it was only just gone 9. What were they doing driving up from London so early on a Saturday morning? He never found out. Neither did Jane, for that matter.

Richard wasn't sure who was the more surprised, he or Michael, when they met, one fully clothed, the other definitely not, in the en-suite to the master bedroom that Saturday morning. Having noted the absence of her car, he and Lilly assumed Jane had left for the day. They were confused when, as they entered the house, they heard the drumming beat of a power shower. Lilly had remained in the hall, texting Jane in fact, while Michael, suspecting a leak of some sort, had wandered into a few rooms before finding the source of the noise.

"Who the hell are you?" asked Michael, unsuspecting for the moment. Perhaps he was a tradesman, taking advantage of the owner being absent for the day.

Richard exited the shower without rinsing the shampoo from his thick dark hair. As Michael looked at the muscled body in front of him, the realisation of the man's identity suddenly struck him.

Richard said nothing in response, casting around for a fresh towel, unable even in such extreme circumstances to bring himself to pick up the one, now draped over the radiator, Jane had used that morning. Once he had covered his modesty, he might be able to formulate a reply. Desperate, he lunged forward, genitals swinging, to retrieve one from the towel rack adjacent to where Michael stood. Michael took a few steps backwards, bumping into Lilly who had come to find him.

Richard wrapped the towel around his waist and dragged his hands through his soapy hair.

"Don't worry, I'm a friend of Jane's," he said, wondering whether it was appropriate to smile or not.

In unison, Lilly and Michael looked over at the unmade bed, seeing Richard's jeans and navy shirt. *A friend indeed*, thought Lilly, trying not to run her eyes over the lovely male body displayed in front of her.

"Come on, Lilly," muttered Michael. "We're going."

Within seconds Richard heard a car engine and, once again, the swerve of tyres over the gravel drive. He let his towel fall back onto the bathmat and restarted the shower so that he could rinse his hair properly.

CHAPTER 12

It just happened

Alex Snow was thinking back to his meeting with Veronica Stern, recalling the initial judgements he'd made about her on the basis of her looks. Now he was wondering if appearance wasn't a much less superficial guide to character than people thought. Oscar Wilde was probably right. He should have stuck with those first impressions.

Heather Sharpe had been on the phone to him. She'd squawked into his ear for almost fifteen minutes, barely pausing for breath or even to allow Alex the opportunity to comment. She'd begun by describing her client, Bradley Blake, as 'a serious young man' who had been 'terribly misrepresented' in the letter sent by Alex setting out his client's allegations of undue influence.

At the beginning of the conversation, Alex was content to let her prattle on whilst he scrolled though some of his more mundane emails. A few minutes in and he was pacing his office, unsettled by the extent of the differences between their respective clients' accounts of the last few weeks of Tim Blake's life.

"Veronica Stern cut Bradley out of his father's life," Heather maintained. "She did everything within her power to fracture the bond there was between father and son. It's actually quite tragic."

Heather said her client had broken down during their initial meeting. Bradley himself had been shocked at how much his father appeared to hate Veronica, the woman he'd lived with for fifteen years, the woman he'd left his wife and Bradley for. It was a relationship which had become sour and Tim had begged Bradley to help him change his will so that he could die knowing that his son would inherit all his worldly goods and not the 'harridan' he lived with.

Tim Blake had been ill for a long period of time. Had he been a well man, he would have left Veronica many years ago, Bradley told her. He and Tim had been meeting up secretly for some time, his father saying that had Veronica known, the fall out would not have been worth it. When he became bedridden, he'd had to pretend he hadn't seen Bradley in years.

"Bradley said his father was desperate to put matters right between them, saying he'd made a terrible mistake in leaving him and his mother. It was Tim who contacted the Wills company from his sick bed and they may be able to confirm this. Anyway, I've written to the firm and requested some details from them. Obviously, I'll furnish you with copies of those letters as soon as I can."

"But why did he leave her out of his will altogether? She's clearly got some come back, even if the facts as set out by your client *are* established. As a dependent, she's probably got a claim under the Inheritance Act. Frankly, it was bound to end up in a dispute the way he went about it. Why in Heaven's name didn't they take some proper legal advice on the matter? It's all so unnecessary."

"Tim was dying, Alex," Heather replied. "It was done quickly and without proper thought. But look, we should be able to get them to agree something between them. Bradley comes over as a very reasonable man."

"Not sure I feel the same way about my client!" said Alex. "It's likely to be an interesting meeting with Miss Stern. Anyway, drop me a line about all this, will you? I may send it out to her by way of preparation."

After putting the phone down, Alex couldn't help but feel some consternation. Whilst he'd await Heather's further correspondence before taking matters forward, Bradley Blake appeared to be able to cast sufficient doubt over Veronica's claims for the case to be one for negotiation and settlement, rather than litigation. In light of the assurances he'd given Veronica Stern, he wasn't looking forward to imparting any such advice.

Calling Jane Sedgefield would not present such a challenge. Probate on Larry's estate had been granted.

"Thank goodness for that," breathed Jane. "Those cars need disposing of quickly before they deteriorate further. Although I've grown used to seeing them in the drive. I'll miss them when they're gone."

"I'll send the Grant out to you. How many copies do you think you'll need? They'll need to be certified ones."

"No, I'll come and collect them."

"Are you sure? It's a long way for you to come when we can just post them." Alex wondered why he was being so amenable in this respect. If he posted them, he'd never see her again. His professionalism simply did not allow him to remind her of their proposed lunch date.

"No. it's fine. I've got friends I'd like to see so I'd be coming up anyway. And what about our lunch date? If you can spare the time, of course. What day is good for you?"

She told him about her new job and how it meant she was no longer available on three days of the week.

"I look forward to hearing about it," he said.

They arranged their lunch for a day the following week. After the call, Alex re-examined Veronica's file, still wondering at her ability to have spun him such a tale.

Jane had picked up her phone, determined to try Lilly again when Alex had called her. It was the Monday after the disastrous events of the Saturday morning. She and Lilly had exchanged some short texts – *we've just met your new boyfriend and decided to leave you to it!* – but had yet to speak. Much to her relief, Lilly answered immediately.

"Jane," was all she said by way of greeting.

"I just wanted to apologise. You know. You weren't supposed to meet. Obviously. I can see just how difficult it must have been for Michael. I'm truly sorry."

There was a pause.

"Personally, Jane, I think it's your business and no-one else's. I suppose Michael sees it differently. That it – you know, dishonours his brother. Or he thinks it does. And he wondered how long it had been going on."

It hadn't even occurred to Jane that Michael might have seen it as an affair pre-dating Larry's death.

"God, Lilly. No! I met him in February, actually. I hadn't planned to meet him. It just happened." She wondered how many times in the history of man and womankind that such a phrase had been employed to excuse shameful or, in her case, embarrassing behaviour. *It just happened.* It was pathetic. But she shouldn't have been musing on those three words. Considering she'd virtually invited Lilly to ask the next question, she should have been formulating her reply.

"As a matter of interest, where did you meet him? Is he a neighbour? You know, a gamekeeper with a snug little hut in the woods."

"No. I met him at the local hunt." She was tempted to carry on with the joke and describe the horse he rode and how they cantered over the fields together, the hounds by their side. Instead she swallowed hard, regretting the flippancy of her response. "Seriously, though, do you think I can put this right with Michael? I'd like to try. He was so good to me when Larry died. I really do feel awful about disappointing him so much."

"Look, I'll speak to him. But he remains extremely cut up about Larry and I guess he just can't understand how you could, you know, well – get over him so quickly. He sees it as your forgetting him."

"I haven't forgotten him, Lilly. But... why does having a lover amount to that? Why does being with someone else *occasionally* mean I've forgotten Larry?"

Jane surprised herself with her honesty. Perhaps, when you have only yourself to answer to in the world, there's more scope for being honest. She wondered too if there wasn't some basic sexism in Michael's response. Would he have felt the same had she been a man whose partner had died? Or would that be seen as 'just a fling' – 'his emotions are all over the place, poor guy'. But she didn't go this far. She thought she'd probably already said too much.

She was relieved when Lilly answered.

"No, I understand. This is a matter for you, Jane. I don't believe it is for anyone else to cast judgment. And, between you and me, and for Christ's sake, don't breathe a word of it to Mike, I told him as much. He doesn't own you, nor did Larry.

But… but, I think he is still in the depths of his grief and we don't always make the best judgements in that frame of mind."

There was a pause in their conversation. Jane battled against some tears and, hoping Lilly would not hear the wobble in her voice, muttered her thanks.

"Give him a few weeks, Jane. I'll suggest he calls you and we make another date to visit. I can see the shop then. How's it going? I've been dying to find out."

~ ~ ~

A foster placement had been found for Alicja. It was in Guildford and she wouldn't have to change schools. It wasn't the nearest school to where she was being placed but at least, Barbara Todd said, she had a choice in the matter.

"Which is a huge relief."

"Has she been introduced to the family yet?" asked Debbie, even though she was sure that, had she been, Alicja would have already told her.

"No," said Barbara. "It's why I was calling you. I wondered if you'd be able to visit the placement with her this coming weekend. I know you work on Saturdays, but the Sunday would be fine."

"What about her mother?"

"Alicja has made it clear that she wants nothing to do with her mother. And it's not a family she's going to, actually. It's a single woman whose children have left home. There'll be just her and Alicja in a two bedroomed flat. I think it's ideal for her."

Debbie was in the deli, replenishing the various containers of salads and vegetables, mobile clamped between her shoulder and ear. It was mid-afternoon and the shop was quiet, so she'd been able to return the social worker's call.

"I'm sure it will be good for Alicja to be out of the refuge," said Debbie. "And, yes. Sunday morning is fine. If you give me the details, I'll pick up Alicja in the car. Or are you coming anyway?"

"No. I'll leave it to you, if that's ok and I'll catch up with Alicja early next week and get her views on the placement."

When Debbie picked up Alicja from the refuge at 10.30 the following Sunday, she was delighted to note that her little spat with Halina had had some lasting impact. Alicja was wearing her woollen coat and looked smart. Her thick blonde hair was neatly tied back with a velvet black ribbon. She seemed pleased to see Debbie and chattered happily throughout their journey, telling her of a school project on climate change which was taking up a lot of her time. There was no hint of any nervousness in going to meet a stranger with whom she would be living for, possibly, the next few years. Either she's desperate to get away from her mother or she's just used to her life changing at a moment's notice, Debbie decided.

The flat was in a high-rise block just off the main road. There were two similar blocks nearby. Debbie parked the car, refraining from voicing her doubts as to whether it might still be there when they returned. Initially, they went to the wrong block, Alicja realising just as they approached the lift. A group of young teenagers gathered around the entrance helpfully pointed out where they needed to go. A tall black kid called after them "I'll take you there if you like!" Alicja turned around and smiled at him which provoked a cheer and some back slapping.

Joyce Kehoe's flat was on the fourth floor which, Alicja said, was 'great'. It meant that using the lift would not be necessary. The corridors and hallways were reasonably clean and, for a Sunday morning when most people would be at home, it appeared quiet.

Mrs Kehoe answered the door in her coat. Her face suggested she was in her early fifties, but her dress indicated an older woman. Still wearing her coat, she ushered them in.

"Come in, come in, my dears," she said, in a strong Irish accent. "I'm only just back from Mass so let's us all take off our coats and I'll make us some tea."

She beamed at them both and then added, "I'm Joyce. Very pleased to meet you. Alicja, is it?" She pronounced it 'Aleesha'. Saving Alicja the embarrassment of correcting her, Debbie intervened.

"I'm Debbie," she announced, sticking out her hand. "And, yes, this is *Alicja*."

Mrs Kehoe grasped Debbie's hand with one hand and Alicja's with her other. "You're very welcome. Both of you. I'll do my best with your name," she said, looking at Alicja. "Polish is a very difficult language, isn't it?" Alicja gave her a brave smile as she handed over her coat.

In the living room, there was a picture of The Sacred Heart over the mantelpiece and a large three-seater sofa, positioned perilously close to a gas fire. The worn carpet was partly covered by a bright red rug. Debbie and Alicja sat together awkwardly on the sofa, listening to Joyce clattering about the kitchen, clinking cups and humming. There was nothing to say. It being already painfully apparent to them both that this was no place for Alicja, Debbie was plotting their exit strategy. Joyce was clearly a warm-hearted, well-meaning soul but she doubted she and Alicja had much in common. She suspected that part of the 'matching' process – if anything so sophisticated had taken place, which seemed unlikely – was Alicja's Catholic heritage. Unable to find a Polish home, social services had plumped for a devout Irish foster mother who would provide the warm, nurturing environment needed to see Alicja through to adulthood. Had Barbara Todd actually visited Joyce Kehoe? Or had it been a paper exercise? Such questions occurred to Debbie as she imagined the nature of the conversation she would have with Barbara when they next spoke.

Over tea, which Alicja declined, accepting a glass of tap water, Debbie established that Joyce came from County Wicklow, having lived in the UK since she was a young woman. She spent a lot of time helping out in her local church and went to Mass each Sunday and, sometimes, twice. Having been a nurse in the past, she now lived on her foster earnings and her late husband's pension.

"You don't need much to lead a God fearing and good life," she declared. She nodded at Alicja. "You'll come to understand that, my dear. Now come along, let me show you your room."

There was a brief guided tour of the tiny flat. Alicja's room was a single bedroom, dominated by a large wardrobe in one corner. Over the bed hung another image of Christ although, refreshingly, he was alive and even smiling on this occasion. His hand was raised in a blessing, reminding the room's occupant that if they wanted to enjoy the sleep of the virtuous, they should not forget to get down on their knees and offer up a prayer to his Father. There was no desk. When Debbie inquired as to where Alicja would do her homework, Joyce said she was welcome to use the kitchen table.

"There'll be plenty of room there for you, my dear, once we've cleared up after our dinner."

Debbie glanced at Alicja, seeing the hollow look in her eyes as she scanned the cell-like room. She'd never had her own television, but doubted she'd want to spend her evenings with Joyce, each occupying a corner of the sofa, their knees being scalded by the gas fire.

After a discussion about school and which buses Alicja would need to catch to get there, Debbie said they would leave Joyce to 'enjoy the rest of your Sunday'. Joyce seemed disappointed, asking them to stay longer so that she could get to know 'this dear girl a bit more' before she moved in.

"I do hope it's what you want," she said. There was something imploring in the way she looked at Alicja who shifted nervously from foot to foot so obviously anxious to get away from the woman and her piety. Joyce tried to hug Alicja as Debbie, holding both their coats, hovered by the front door. Once out, they charged down the walkway, as if escaping a burning building, and descended the stairs quickly. Emerging into the light, expressions of relief spread across their faces.

"Which way is the car?" asked Debbie.

Once they'd found the car, they sat together for a while waiting for the other to speak first.

"It's not what you want, is it?" asked Debbie, turning to look at Alicja. Her blue eyes looked even bluer in her pale face.

"I would be better off living with my mother," she said simply.

"I'll speak to Barbara if you want," said Debbie. "I'll ask her to find somewhere more suitable. I don't suppose you care whether the family is Catholic, do you?"

Alicja shook her head.

"Why don't you come back to mine for the rest of the day and I'll drive you back to the Refuge later on. We can have lunch and then go to the nature reserve. It's a good time of the year to be there."

"Are you sure? That would be awesome."

"Of course I'm sure. And if you want to work on my laptop for the afternoon, you know, on your project, that's ok too."

The contrast between Joyce's light-starved flat in its claustrophobic setting and Debbie's bright, open plan one with its view of the nature reserve, could not have been starker. As Debbie brought out a plate of sandwiches and crisps for their lunch, Alicja was standing at the window gazing out at the bright sky. She turned and came towards Debbie, saying she should help. Her face had regained its rosiness and the smile she gave her convinced Debbie that the idea she had been harbouring in the last hour, was the right one.

"Why don't you come to live with me?" she said, handing the plate over to Alicja.

CHAPTER 13

Wordless, but effective, communication

Richard and Jane had yet to emerge, with any level of commitment, into the social world. There was still something clandestine about their meeting up, as if like vampires they might be stuck down in the daylight. Their lunch in Cheltenham had been their only public outing and, even then, they'd bought sandwiches and eaten them on a park bench in the spring sunshine. Jane remembered at the time that they probably looked like colleagues. They didn't hold hands or kiss or show any sign of affection outside the bedroom. If this was more to do with Richard's natural reserve than with anything else, Jane was content. While professing not to feel any guilt, she felt nevertheless more comfortable conducting their relationship along the lines of some casual affair.

Larry came and went. She saw him in her mind's eye when least expecting to, popping up when she was emptying the bins or turning on the car's ignition. *You'll need to secure that bin properly or the fox will turn up. Have you checked when your MOT is due?* It wasn't always practical advice which sparked her memories of him. *Yes, but you're my heartless cow.* Someone on your side. Faithful like no other ever was – or could be.

A tragedy had brought Larry and Jane together; a death. That most tormenting of deaths, suicide. If they never spoke about it in their married life, it was because it was Jane's experience, not Larry's. He just happened to be around when she was struggling with the aftermath. The body of a fellow student hurtling its way through the air to land at her feet in the grounds of their halls of residence was not a sight she was likely to be able to shrug off, particularly when the girl involved was a member of her own tutor group. Bridie was a quiet, studious girl whom Jane, popular and outgoing, had little time for. She hadn't been cruel to her; she'd just paid her little, if any, attention – which might amount to the same thing in the minds of the vulnerable.

She and Bridie were both studying Psychology and in the middle of their first year of university. Jane had been ambivalent about going in the first place but her parents, neither of whom had attended university, were so clearly overjoyed at the prospect of their daughter achieving what they hadn't, that Jane felt obliged to enter the choppy sea of her parents' unfulfilled ambitions. She dropped out just before sitting her first-year examinations denying that she'd been affected by Bridie's death, or more precisely, the nature of that death. She said she was hungry to work in the real world, as opposed to wasting yet another year cooped up with self-obsessed people of her own age. Above all else, she wanted independence and saw paid work as the fastest route to that goal.

When Bridie had been scraped up from the ground, it seemed to Jane that everyone around her, particularly her tutors, were keen to forget her. There was no announcement in the faculty nor even when the tutor group re-convened, one person missing. Bridie was expunged from memory; an inconvenient statistic. Sometimes, Jane would think of Bridie's parents and how they survived such a loss as they grew old. What did they do on Bridie's birthday each year? What did they say to each other? *She'd be 40 this year, we might have been grandparents.*

It was a few days after Bridie's death. Jane was at a bar on Fleet street with some fellow students. She had decided against fleeing back home to the security of her parents' home, unwilling to provide an explanation for her return in case they worried she might be similarly inclined to harm herself. But she knew she wasn't coping. Later, looking back, she decided she must have been suffering from some post-traumatic stress as the images of Bridie's broken body would come, unbidden, into her mind at all different times of the day or night. That night she'd decided that company and booze might blur, if not blot out, Bridie's face. The face that would blush with nerves whenever asked to speak in their tutor sessions.

Larry came across Jane in the corridor leading to the toilets. She was standing with her back against the wall by the door of the Ladies, as if waiting for someone. Larry glanced at her as he passed on his way to the Gents. A woman used to being stared at, he thought, as she turned her face away from him sharply as he passed. But it wasn't as he supposed. Jane was crying and didn't want him, or anyone else, to notice. She was hoping that her alcohol-induced tears would soon abate so that she could slip away from her friends without fuss. When Larry emerged from the toilet, she was still there and he spoke to her then.

"Are you ok?" he asked, in a low, gentle tone. He leant against the wall next to her, his head knocking a picture, almost displacing it from its hook. Before she could answer, he turned to straighten it.

"Wouldn't be that much of a loss, would it?" he said, smiling. The painting was a still life: a fruit bowl, undistinguishable from thousands of similar depictions save for the outstretched, dead carcass of a hare lying on the table by its side.

Larry was slim, of medium height and with a head of thick dark brown hair, curling at the back of his neck. There was a confidence in his movements and his gaze which Jane, in her sorry state, found instantly comforting. She wiped away her tears with a sodden tissue and nodded.

"I'm fine, thank you."

Larry smiled again.

"Good."

He didn't hang around but later, back in the bar, after she'd rejoined her friends and he his, they sought each other out, their eyes meeting in wordless, but effective, communication.

When she saw him make his way to the bar, she made an excuse to her fellow students and joined him as he waited to be served. He ordered her a glass of wine and, after taking a round of drinks back to his table of mates, they stood at the bar, squeezed close together and talked. She spoke intimately as, occasionally, one can do with a stranger, revealing to him her terror at how little control she had over her mind. He listened, his eyes never wandering from hers, bewitched by her intensity.

He admitted to having no experience of what she'd described but said he was sure that acknowledging her feelings, no matter how devastating, was healthier than denying them. He suggested that *activity* would help her. Did she play any sport? Did she jog? It seemed to Jane such wise, old-fashioned advice to spring from the lips of a young man and yet she followed it. She discovered the university's Olympic sized swimming pool and even joined a synchronised swimming group for a few weeks before reverting to lane swimming on alternate days.

It wasn't a smooth, or particularly conventional, run-up to a marriage. Jane was a little younger, less keen than he on a long-term relationship. But Larry was always there: faithful, steadfast, forgiving. He made her laugh, like no other man quite achieved, with his off-beat humour. When they did decide to get married, it was she who asked him – certain, naturally, that he would say yes, while he could never have been so sure. He was always surprised when she returned to him after one of her brief intense affairs and although, rarely, he might accuse her of 'using' him, it was because he felt obliged to exhibit a modicum of self-respect. He might try to affect indifference when she arrived at his flat, after the pubs had closed, looking a bit wild and desperate for the comfort of his arms, but he was a transparent individual with no interest in being other than honest. It marked him out. Within ten minutes, she would be in a bubble bath, a cup of coffee in her hands while Larry, ordered to keep her company, perched on the toilet seat. At such times he was tempted to declare that one day, he might just surprise her by not being alone when she called.

Now he was gone, dead, Jane assured herself that she wasn't looking to replace him. To seek out companionship and take a lover didn't mean, as Michael appeared to think, that Larry was easy to forget or that she relished her freedom from the shackles of a long marriage, grown stale and predictable. It meant only that the transition from being with someone who loved and understood you, to navigating the world alone was a hard one. If she sought help along the way, defying the traditional view of how the recently bereaved should conduct themselves, she reassured herself that it was society's hang-up, not hers.

~ ~ ~

As soon as Debbie had given voice to her – impulsively devised – idea that Alicja needed a home, that she had a spare room and that she had grown increasingly fond of her young friend, she wondered if she shouldn't have spoken to Barbara Todd first. Supposing she wasn't deemed fit or Halina had some fundamental objection? She would need to be assessed before becoming Alicja's foster carer although, from what she understood, Alicja was not the subject of any formal Order and was probably of an age to have a view as to where she should live. In any event, she thought, as she stood, still clutching her own plate of sandwiches and watching the tears roll down Alicja's young face, she should have kept quiet until she'd considered the possibility in more detail.

Debbie went over and took the plate back from Alicja. Crisps were floating down onto the carpet as Alicja's hand wobbled with her sobs.

"Dear, oh, dear," said Debbie, laughing, while also wondering where these maternal murmurings sprang from. "Is it such a bad idea?" she joked.

"Do you mean it?" Alicja asked, wiping her face with both hands and trying to smile.

Debbie nodded. "Of course, although I should probably have spoken to Barbara before blurting it out like that."

"But that would be the best thing that ever happened to me," said Alicja, looking like she might begin crying again. "Living here, in this beautiful place with you, near the trees and the birds. It would be," she paused, searching for the right word "it would be paradise!"

She rushed over and flung her arms around Debbie, almost knocking her over. "Thank you, Debbie. Thank you so much."

"Let's eat, for goodness' sake," said Debbie.

Over their lunch, Debbie explained that there would be procedures she needed to go through before Alicja would be allowed to move from the Refuge. Alicja looked surprised.

"But I am nearly 15, I can make up my own mind where I live, surely? And how could anywhere not be better than living with my mother?" adding, after some hesitation, "and her men."

"I suppose, as a minor, social services owes you a duty of care. They would be failing in that duty if you were just allowed to go off and live with whoever you wanted to. For instance, someone who might harm you. I suspect I'll have to go through a thorough assessment process. But that might be necessary anyway as I might need some financial help."

Debbie hadn't meant to raise the issue of money. But there was little point in pretending she had enough to support the two of them. She didn't.

"I can get a Saturday job!" Alicja announced. "In one of the clothes' shops on the high street."

"At 15?"

Alicja shrugged.

"Maybe. I look 16."

Debbie laughed.

"Don't start worrying about that. That's my concern, not yours. Let me speak to Barbara. But don't say anything to your mother yet, will you?"

Alicja shook her head.

Debbie looked at her, studying her. She'd seen so many expressions pass across her face that day already; the entire gamut. The poor girl must be exhausted. But she wasn't going to comment.

"What's the matter?" asked Alicja.

"I was just thinking. You've told me quite a bit about yourself, but you don't know much about me, do you?"

"I know I like you," said Alicja. "I know you're the kindest person I've ever met. Do I need to know more?"

Debbie laughed.

"I haven't got any skeletons in the cupboard, if that's what you mean!"

"Skeletons?"

"Secrets. Bad ones."

As she said this, she wondered about Marie. Was she a skeleton? Much of our past is made up of skeletons, she decided, although perhaps this wasn't the time to embark on such a discussion with Alicja.

On their walk that afternoon, blessed with some sun, the paths were busy with young families. Debbie now knew the places to go within the reserve which were much less visited, made up of mud flats and reed beds. Her delight was to stop by the lake and stand quietly until a rustling might indicate that a wader of some sort was about to reveal itself. Like all who love birds, she had fantasies of what she might see. She was sure, last time, a wild afternoon when the wind whipped across the water, she heard the whistle-like cry of a red knot. But when she'd looked at the black board on her way out of the reserve, where other birders chalked up what they'd seen that day, there was no mention of this black-billed bird. Instead there were all the regulars – the grebes, herons and kingfishers, occasionally the egret and shelduck. This time, she made sure they looked at the board before they started their walk so that she, particularly, didn't suffer any disappointment. Alicja was fascinated with the precision of the recordings: 3 Redshank, 20 Lapwing, 8 chiffchaff, 1 Sedge Warbler.

They saw plenty of Lapwing that Sunday afternoon and spent time watching the antics of a Great Crested Grebe as it dived and then resurfaced some distance away. Debbie described to Alicja the mating ceremony of the Grebe and how she still hoped one day to catch it.

"I wonder why we humans love birds as much as we do," she said. "Do you think it's because they fly in the sky and we can't do that, except with the aid of machines which is not quite the same thing. What do you think?"

"I think they weave a magic on us. Wiser than us, I'm sure. They don't go to war with one another."

"Oh yes they do," said Debbie, sad to insert such a grim fact into their perfect afternoon. "All creatures show aggression. They have to, to survive. Magpies and crows murder small birds and attack each other and, as for the sweet little Robin, he is one of the most territorial birds in the garden. Don't be fooled by them."

Alicja laughed, her hair blowing around her face as a sudden breeze blew in over the water of the lake.

"Let's see if we can catch the café before it closes, shall we?" said Debbie, feeling in need of some sugar.

Over their drinks and chocolate bars, Alicja took out her mobile. It had always surprised Debbie that she didn't seem as wedded to the device as most of her peers. Sometimes, she wondered if it was simply politeness on her part. It was Jane who had pointed out, on their weekend away, that Alicja's phone was old and out of date, clearly a cast off of her mother's. She was ashamed to bring it out and it didn't seem to pick up much of a signal either. Debbie doubted that Alicja had access to the internet at home, let alone on her mobile.

Debbie could almost see the happiness leaking from Alicja's face as she absorbed whatever message it was flashing up at her.

"What's the matter?" Debbie asked.

Alicja looked at her.

"It's a message from my mum. My father has been contacted by social services and he's just called her to say that he's coming to the UK as soon as he can. He wants to take me back to Poland with him."

"Oh, I see," murmured Debbie. Anger towards Halina swelled within her. Intent on spoiling their day, she must have known the effect such a message would have on Alicja. It was cruel.

"He can't do that! He just can't!" Alicja slammed her mobile back down on the table.

"Calm down, Alicja." She reached out to hold her hand.

"You know, it just might be that your father cares for you. Let's wait and see what happens. I doubt very much that anyone could force you to go to Poland against your wishes. I really do. Let's cross that bridge when we come to it, hey?"

"I've heard nothing from my father for years. Why would he suddenly care for me now?"

"If he comes, you'll find out."

"I'll refuse to meet him," Alicja declared, her cheeks blazing. "I'll get his number off Mum and then tell him not to bother coming as I don't want anything to do with him."

Debbie kept silent. She wanted to say, 'give him a chance – people change'. But it didn't seem the time to foist her advice on Alicja.

"I want to live with you," Alicja said, tears welling up in eyes.

"I know," said Debbie, scrabbling in her bag for a tissue to give her.

Alicja looked at Debbie imploringly, repeating her earlier question.

"You did mean it, didn't you?"

Debbie nodded.

"I did," she said, thinking how complicated matters had become in the course of just a few hours – not least because of her own impulsive behaviour.

CHAPTER 14

What panache the man has

Alex had not really planned to see Victoria Stern and Jane Sedgefield on the same day although while reading back through his notes of the call with Heather Sharpe, he now thought it was fortuitous. Lunch with the second 'grieving widow' might compensate for the difficult hour he was about to endure with the first.

Victoria looked pleased to see him. She was much more smartly dressed this time. Gone were the flat shoes and the thick stockings: sheer tights and smart black court shoes had replaced them. Her hair looked newly washed.

"You're looking well," Alex commented before regretting the compliment when he saw a faint blush travel up from her neckline to her face.

Alex linked his hands in front of him and tightened his lips.

"I've heard from Bradley's solicitor." Before he could continue, Veronica let out a snort.

"Oh yes," she snapped. "That must have been interesting." She wound her legs around each other as she spoke, her back rigid.

"He takes issue with your version of events. He...."

Again, she cut him off rudely.

"Well, he would! I didn't expect anything different. He's a scheming young man. I thought I'd made that clear to you." Veronica expanded on her view of Bradley's character until Alex stopped her.

"Miss Stern," he said, as patiently as he could manage. "Please listen to me."

She shifted a little on her chair, as if embarrassed that she'd been told off. Alex was beginning to see how she might have worn Tim Blake down over the years. With the aid of his notes, he went through the details of his conversation with Heather Sharpe. By the end, Veronica was pale with anger.

"I asked her to respond formally to us, although I've yet to receive anything," he concluded.

"How dare he!" she said, loudly. "How dare he distort the truth in such a calculated manner and expect to get away with it. I trust you made it clear that I'd be contesting his lies?"

"There are, indeed, significant differences of fact between you. A court would be faced with a difficult task – who to believe. I'm not sure litigation is the answer."

"I don't understand. In our first meeting you assured me that I had a cast iron case. Now, it appears, you've changed your mind because of Bradley's lies."

She shook her head at him.

"I'm not sure I used that terminology."

"You most certainly did! It was on the basis of that advice that I paid you a considerable sum on account of costs. Now you're saying something entirely different."

"If you'd allow me to continue, I'd be grateful," said Alex.

He waited to see if she was about to embark on another rant. She shook the stiffness from her shoulders and fixed him with an antagonistic glare.

"You'll recall my advice on the last occasion we met that you had more than one method of legal redress. I can go into that in more detail later but, in short, I think you'll be able to establish an interest in the house in any event. I don't know the details of what other assets Tim had but I'm sure there's scope for negotiation. When we spoke, Bradley's solicitor intimated that she wouldn't be against entering into such discussions. That would avoid a bruising, expensive and risky court case."

"Let me make myself entirely clear, Mr Snow. I have no intention whatsoever of negotiating with that despicable man."

"Very well. But I'd be grateful if you'd take some time to consider my advice over the next few days. I understand that they're seeking some additional evidence from the firm who attended Tim to re-write his will. I'd like to see that before we proceed further."

"What for?"

"Because it might support Bradley's case. We need to know what we're up against. Obviously, if you decide to go down the litigation route, I'll need to go into matters in much more detail including the nature of yours and Tim's financial affairs such as who paid for what. The discussions you had between you concerning the house will also be relevant but, for the time being, I'll let Bradley's solicitor know your initial view."

"You mentioned entering a caveat on the last occasion. I assume you're going to take that step immediately in order to safeguard my position?"

"I'm going to set out my advice to you in writing, Miss Stern, and then await your instructions."

"You already have my instructions, Mr Snow. I don't need your advice in writing. It will just cost me more money."

"That's not the way I operate, I'm afraid," said Alex.

Veronica gave a little smirk.

"I thought I was the client."

"I have a professional duty towards you. I can't fulfil it if you do not allow me to give you the benefit of my advice."

Veronica shrugged.

"I'd like you to enter a caveat without further delay. Those *are* my instructions. Please adhere to them."

She got up and started buttoning her coat with shaking fingers.

"I'm sorry you're so upset," said Alex, moving towards the door to open it for her. She brushed past him without replying. Beyond her, in the waiting area, he could see Jane flicking through a magazine. She was over half an hour early. Looking up when she heard his door open, she smiled and gave a little wave with her fingers. It suggested intimacy; the sort of wave you give a friend or lover. Whilst cheered at both the sight of her and the prospect of her company, Alex, for reasons not entirely logical, would have preferred to have seen Victoria Stern off the premises before engaging with Jane.

"Hi Alex, sorry I'm a bit early. The traffic was so much less than I'd expected," she said getting to her feet and then standing back as Victoria, casting an unfriendly glance in her direction, marched past her.

Alex beckoned Jane into his office.

113

"Lord, she had a look of fury about her!"

"Best if I don't comment," Alex replied. "Anyway, your documents are ready. Please, take a seat." He pulled out a chair for her and went over to one of his filing cabinets where he extracted a large brown envelope.

"The original Grant plus five certified copies. That should be enough for your purposes."

Alex looked at her as she tucked the envelope into the side of her black leather tote bag. She was wearing a belted green trench coat with a high collar. Her jeans were tucked into knee high black boots as if she was on her way to ride a horse.

"That's great. Thanks so much, Alex. I can dispose of the cars now and complete the formalities with Larry's life policy company."

"Yep. Should all be straightforward. But any problems, just call me."

She smiled warmly at him.

"I hope you've time for a quick lunch."

"Yes, of course. I'm ravenous! There's a place around the corner which does a couple of lunchtime specials each day. *Toni's* – shall we go there?

"I'll be an hour or so," he said to the receptionist as they passed her on their way out. Inevitably, she looked over at one of the secretaries, raising an eyebrow.

At *Toni's*, Jane and Alex sat at a table in the window. Had they chosen differently their experience might have matched their expectations.

Alex removed his suit jacket, hanging it carefully on the back of his chair. He loosened his tie and then removed it entirely. Jane looked at the collar of his gleaming white shirt; it was in pristine condition. Clearly, Alex Snow took much pride in his appearance. Politely, he checked that Jane was comfortable and then asked her about her new job. There wasn't much to tell him, she said, confessing that the novelty was unlikely to last long without some progression to visiting clients in their own homes. She laughed when Alex asked her whether she had 'a background in interior design', telling him about Lilly and her Japanese screens. They chatted about

Cheltenham, Jane saying there were some lovely properties in the city and that she suspected that she may well end up there.

"Sometime in the future," she said, as the waitress placed her 'chilli con veg' in front of her. They had both ordered the vegetarian dish, Alex saying he had converted to vegetarianism some two years ago but doubted he'd graduate to veganism.

They were deep into a conversation about the pros and cons of living in the countryside when Victoria Stern appeared outside their window. Alex noticed her, as he looked up from his plate to pour them both some water. Much to his relief, she was only there a few seconds before disappearing into the lunch time crowds. He relaxed back into his chair, grateful that Jane had not seen her. But his relief was short-lived. Suddenly, Victoria was standing by their table. The anger generated from her meeting with Alex had not abated. And seeing him there, with that attractive woman, chatting and smiling, enjoying the day as she was now unable to do, she felt incensed.

"Ah, Mr Snow," she said. Alex could not quite believe that she felt it appropriate to interrupt his lunch. It had never happened to him before, relations with his clients being almost invariably good and always civil. And how often did he lunch out? Rarely. He nipped out for sandwiches and some exercise. He'd been so hopeful of this meeting with Jane, so *very* hopeful it would be the beginning of something. *No chance now*, he thought, bitterly. *I'll never hear from her again after this debacle.*

He stood up quickly before Victoria could get more than a few words out, flipping his jacket off his chair.

"Excuse me," he said to Jane.

He placed his hand underneath Victoria's elbow and steered her toward the exit of the restaurant.

What panache the man has, Jane thought, recalling Max and how completely inept he had been at dealing with irate clients.

Outside, he struggled into his jacket as if unable to engage with anyone in a professional manner without being suitably attired.

"Had you wished to speak to me, Miss Stern, it might have been more appropriate to have telephoned me." He fought to keep his tone even, reminding himself that his one objective was to avoid a scene. "Would you like to make another appointment to see me? If so, I can call you this afternoon when I have access to my diary. I can understand your feelings. But let's talk later, shall we?"

It had been Victoria's intention to inform him that she would be seeking to instruct another solicitor. She wanted to hurt him and sacking him in front of his lady friend would be a fitting act of vengeance for his unwelcome advice. But now, discombobulated by his lack of hostility towards her, despite her behaviour, and struck by his kindness, she was flooded by feelings of embarrassment and regret.

"I'm sorry," she stuttered. "That was wrong of me. Of course, I'll call you later."

Before Alex could say anything further, she'd scurried off and he was able to return to Jane.

Jane smiled at him when he sat down at their table.

"That was quick," she said. "Is she stalking you?"

"No. She's just upset after our meeting this morning. I apologise for that… that interruption. Hideously embarrassing!"

He looked down at his half-finished meal.

"I think I've lost my appetite. Coffee?"

Jane nodded and Alex motioned to the waitress when she next passed them.

Seeing Alex's troubled expression, Jane leant across the table.

"It's fine, Alex. Actually, I'm impressed with the way you handled it. I'm just sorry it's spoiled your lunch."

"These things happen. I probably bear some responsibility for her reaction. I should have been more – more, what's the word – *circumspect* when I first advised her."

Over coffee, they chatted about Alex's love of walking and how he'd completed the *Monroe challenge* some years ago. He described a difficult night on one of the mountains when a mist had fallen without warning on his descent, saying he spent eight hours in a flimsy tent contemplating his end. Jane asked if he always climbed alone and he admitted that he did. He said it was the perfect antidote to his working life during which he was inundated with demands on his time, whether in the form of telephone calls or meetings or court hearings. In turn, he asked Jane what she did 'for recreation'.

She struggled to answer.

"Well, nothing really. I had designs on taking up pottery or keeping some animals but I've yet to fulfil any of those fantasies." Her words had a familiar ring to them. "And they are fantasies. I've learned that about myself – recently," she added.

"Come on" said Alex, gently, surprising her with the way in which he picked up on the note of sadness in her words. "There's nothing wrong with having the odd fantasy."

Before they could talk further, Alex said he had to get back to the office. There was a tussle over the bill which Jane won.

"God, Alex, it's twenty quid. Allow me to pay it! This was my idea."

She walked back to his office with him, explaining how she was staying with her good friends, Stella and Bob, for the night before heading back to home the following day.

"Back to rural seclusion – and then work, of course. I look back to this time last year and cannot quite believe how different my life is now. I could never have predicted it."

"Well, have a good evening. And if you're ever back in town, perhaps we can meet up again? And if there is a next time, I'll make sure I have no disaffected clients hanging around to ambush us!"

Jane laughed and pecked him on the cheek, where the scent of whatever cologne he used lingered. Standing back from each other at the door of Alex's office building, their eyes locked briefly.

"You're less of an enigma to me now, Alex Snow," she said, flirtatiously, as she turned away. *But no less attractive*, she decided, before wondering why she considered it acceptable to engage in such predatory behaviour. In the past, friends had said to her that they believed it was the very essence of being human to want to share your life with someone, to be in a long-term relationship or marriage. To be alone was unnatural, harmful even. Most people, if they were honest, wanted the security of a mate; preferably an exclusive one. Jane had scoffed at this. These are society's expectations, she declared, arising from religious beliefs, marriage being as much about the control of women as anything else. *We've moved on, surely, from the straitjacket of monogamous love, the tyranny of possession!* Had she spoken out of ignorance? It appeared that *she* was hell bent on securing a partner as though the prospect of being alone for the rest of her life terrified her.

Back in his office, Alex thought wearily of the promise he'd made to Victoria and perused his on-line diary in case she really did want a further meeting. Perhaps now, wishing to make amends after her extraordinary behaviour, she would agree to a consideration of his written advice before demanding that they plunge headlong into an unnecessary court battle. He thought too, less wearily, of Jane Sedgefield and how soon he could see her again, despite all formal business between them now having been concluded.

~ ~ ~

Now back in *The Old Byre*, Jane was standing in the cloakroom with a police officer. During her thirty-six-hour absence, she'd been burgled. The burglars had forced their way in by smashing a small window. There were smears of blood over the windowsill and spots of it on the tiled floor. She'd noticed the break-in as soon as she drew up in the drive and being concerned they might still be in the house, had called the local police who sent someone over immediately. It was one of the same officers who'd run her home the night of Larry's accident and insisted on staying until she'd contacted someone. An older man in his late fifties, he remembered her.

"The last thing you needed," he said, squatting on his haunches, inspecting the blood. "I'll get someone to come over and take some samples. You never know."

"I can't leave the window as it is. It needs securing," said Jane. They'd yet to examine the extent of the damage throughout the rest of the house, although she expected the worst. They would have known they were unlikely to be disturbed.

"Sure. I'll see if anyone is available this afternoon. Seen anything suspicious lately?"

Jane told him about the damage to Larry's car at the end of the previous year and the two hooded figures she thought she'd seen on the morning after Larry's death.

"But they hadn't come back. Not so far as I know, anyway."

"You need some proper security," he said, stating the obvious. "A panic button, security lights, an alarm linked up to us." It was evident he was surprised she hadn't installed anything. "Particularly now you're on your own."

"I've been meaning to. I'm worried now they *will* come back."

"Only natural," he said. "But if they weren't disturbed, they've probably taken all they wanted. So it's unlikely." She wondered whether this theory was based on his actual experience or whether he was just trying to reassure her. It seemed the opposite to her. She was an easy target. If they thought there might be cash on the premises, why wouldn't they come back again?

They patrolled the interior of the property together. The intruders had trampled mud over some of the carpets and engaged in the usual practices of the burglar; drawers pulled out, cupboard doors opened, mattresses askew. All the wine had been taken along with the small television. For some reason, the large screen one had been left. Jane's gold watch, inherited from her grandmother, was missing.

"Could have been worse," said Jane, as she saw the officer to the door. He promised to get someone over by late afternoon.

"I can give you the name of someone who can secure the window for you, but I can't guarantee they'll come out tonight."

Jane thought of Richard.

"No, it's ok. I know someone who might help. Thank you anyway. And thanks for coming out so quickly."

Jane glanced over his shoulder as she spoke. Larry's *Alfa Romeo*, in its damaged state, remained in position. His *Morgan* was gone.

"Oh my God," she breathed.

The officer turned around with a jerk.

"What?" he asked, seeing nothing but tranquillity in the scene before him. A flock of sheep grazed happily in a field in the distance. The only noticeable noise was the sound of bird song. A rustling sound beside them came from a bright-eyed robin, hopping about near the camellia bushes looking for grubs.

"My husband's car. His pride and joy. They've stolen it. How could I not have noticed that before now?"

"I'd better take down the details."

Jane's eyes brimmed with tears. The burglary had generated anger towards the interlopers and frustration at her own neglect in failing to secure the property when she had received so many warnings. What more had she needed – a letter of intent? She didn't feel *violated*, as she heard some people describe the experience of their home being broken into. But Larry's car being stolen *did* feel personal. Yes, she was going to sell it in due course but that was different, somehow.

Later, as she nipped around with the vacuum cleaner, she tried to not think about how sad Larry would have been at the loss of his beloved *Morgan*. She imagined his expression. It came back to her with such force that she had to sit down on the cold floor of the utility room to recover. The dam she'd built to keep the flood waters of grief at bay was breached that day. They rolled over her, filling her lungs with a regret so intense that she struggled to breathe.

She did not call Richard. After the forensic guy had been, she found some pieces of wood in the garage and, using a hammer and a variety of mis-matched nails, she managed to board up the window. She couldn't lock the cloakroom door from the outside, so she barricaded it with a large cupboard, dragged on a rug all the way from one of the smaller bedrooms. Then she stuffed the cupboard with as many heavy objects as she could find. If the bastards returned, they'd make a hell of a noise trying to get in, she decided.

It was a therapeutic exercise. She felt much stronger by the time she went to her bedroom that evening, clutching a large whisky and locking the door behind her. She rarely drank whisky, but there was no wine and it was the single malt one which Larry had loved. The smell of the spirit brought him even closer although, this time, it comforted her.

"I haven't forgotten you," she whispered, wondering whether to keep her bedside light on all night.

CHAPTER 15

She said home

Relations between Halina and Alicja had reached breaking point. Debbie hadn't observed this for herself. She'd been told by the staff at the Refuge and, in a 'phone call received that day, by Barbara Todd. Some of the other residents reported hearing a loud row between mother and daughter in the early hours of that morning and were fearful for Alicja's emotional welfare. The louder voice was Halina's, they maintained. *Get Alicja out of there before there's an incident.*

"There's no suitable emergency placement for her at the moment," Barbara told Debbie. "Now she's rejected Joyce Kehoe. And there's no spare bedroom in the Refuge either."

"She can come to me," said Debbie, boldly. *Might as well get the ball rolling immediately,* she thought. "I've got room."

There was a brief silence at the other end of the phone as Barbara absorbed Debbie's offer.

"Have you discussed this with Alicja?"

"Well, yes, actually. I have. In fact, I'd like to offer her a permanent home with me."

"I wish you hadn't done that without speaking to me," said Barbara, an 'official' tone entering her voice. "We can't just place her with you without a proper assessment."

"But this is an emergency," Debbie persisted. "I'm happy to be thoroughly assessed as soon as your resources allow. In the meantime, surely, she can stay with me. She's not a child! She's capable of saying should anything untoward happens or she changes her mind."

"It's not the way it works, I'm afraid."

Debbie was tempted to push Barbara further – so what would they actually do if Alicja came to stay with her and refused to go back to the refuge? Drag her away kicking and screaming? It was a ludicrous position to adopt.

"So, you're happy for Alicja to remain in an abusive environment rather than allow her to make an *informed* choice and come to live with me?"

"I think that's overstating it, Debbie, but listen, I'll speak to my manager."

"That's good," said Debbie. "I'm relieved to hear it."

"Before you go," said Barbara. "Did you know Alicja's father is due to arrive in the country this week? The day after tomorrow, I think."

"Yes. She told me. She's not happy that contact was made with him without her knowledge."

"Would you speak to her about it again? Perhaps reassure her that she's not going to be whisked off to Poland overnight," asked Barbara, hesitantly. It appeared they trusted Debbie enough to ask this of her but not enough to allow Alicja to move in with her.

"I will if she asks me," said Debbie.

Alicja called Debbie some few minutes later. She sniffed and swallowed throughout the conversation as she fought to keep her emotions under control.

"Everyone is on my back," she complained. "I'm sick of it. Now my father has started texting me. I can't stay with my mum any longer. Can I come to you – now?"

There was another swallow and then a hiccough. *"Please."*

Debbie repeated her conversation with Barbara.

"She's speaking to her manager," she finished off.

"And how long will that take?" Alicja said. "I've heard that before."

"Look, Alicja. I don't want to get on the wrong side of social services although, God knows, they complicate things which are, essentially, simple and vice versa." She knew this generalisation wasn't helpful. She knew she should be encouraging Alicja to trust Barbara. *Yes, in an ideal world. But we're not in one.*

"Let's give them a couple of days to get things sorted, shall we? I just feel we have to try to be fair to them."

"And what if they say, no? That I can't come now because of this *fucking* assessment."

It was the first time Alicja had sworn in front of her.

"We'll cross that bridge when we come to it. I can promise you Alicja that I will do all in my power to get you here as soon as possible. Trust me."

"I do, Debbie."

She did trust Debbie, but she didn't say she agreed with her. Halina was out when she returned to the Refuge from school. Taking advantage of her mother's absence, Alicja stuffed her sports bag with as many clothes as she could fit in. She used her rucksack for her schoolbooks and the various toiletries she'd acquired over the last few months, courtesy of Debbie and her unending generosity: a hairbrush, body lotion, shampoo, moisturiser. The two staff on duty were chatting in the kitchen but, just in case, she left by the fire exit which, surprisingly, given it was supposed to be a secure place, was not alarmed.

In town, Alicja went to a café where she ordered a diet coke and a muffin, leaving her penniless. She knew Debbie didn't leave the deli until after six so she had an hour to kill. When a boy, Matthew, she knew from her school year group sidled over and asked if she fancied company, her first impulse was to tell him to go away. But she was charmed by his big grin and changed her mind. When she was younger and said goodbye to her friends at the school gate or the bus stop at the end of the day, she'd felt the occasional pang of envy, imagining them all going back to their nice, normal homes where dogs, or siblings or grandparents or – even – parents might greet them: making toast, chatting at the kitchen table, watching television together. But wiser now, she noticed there were kids like herself who wandered around after school because they either feared going home or hated the idea of being alone for the rest of the day. Matthew said his mum did shift work – the four to midnight shift four days a week. On those days, he usually hung about town for a couple of hours for something to do. He bought Alicja another coke and then, looking at her luggage, asked where she was off on holiday.

"Anywhere nice?" he joked. "Or are you just on the run?"

"Staying with a friend for the night," she replied, and then added "maybe longer."

Her friends knew about the Refuge. It had been pointless keeping it from them, especially since her closest friend lived in the same block of flats which she and Halina had lived in. So she took a deep breath and regaled Matthew with her recent troubles, stopping short at disclosing her mother's occupation. He listened intently as if she were telling him a bedtime story or relating the plot to a film she'd just seen.

"Shit," he said, after she came to a stop and went back to drinking her coke. "I'd never of known. You always look so together."

Alicja didn't pull him up on his grammar, although she was tempted.

"But your Dad coming over," he said, after a moment's pause. "That might be ok. Why would he come unless he wanted to see you?"

"He's left it a long time. It's too late now. I don't need him."

Matthew shrugged.

"I'd hear what he's got to say first."

Alicja glanced at the clock on the wall.

"I've got to go," she said. "Thanks for the coke."

"Do you want me to help carry your bag?" Matthew asked. He was a tall, lanky boy with straggly dark hair which needed cutting. But he has nice eyes, she thought, and he seems kind.

"No thanks, I can manage."

She could tell that her refusal disappointed him.

"Can we meet up again – you know, when you're settled, like? Maybe after school one day?"

Alicja nodded.

"Yeah. Sure."

Outside, he asked her which way she was going, and they walked to the deli together. At one point, he took her sports bag from her hand and hauled it up over his shoulder. She glanced sideways at him, shyly, taken aback by how comforting it felt to have someone by her side at that moment – like having a brother.

At the deli, they exchanged numbers, her cheeks burning as she took out her old mobile. But Matthew didn't comment. He adopted a serious face, masking his happiness, as if he were always exchanging numbers with pretty girls. Before turning to see if Debbie was behind the counter or in the back, she watched him as loped off down the street. He'd listened so patiently to her and she hadn't asked him a thing about his own life.

Emerging from the interior of the shop, Debbie started as she saw Alicja's face pressed against the window, *like the little match girl*, she thought. Except Alicja wasn't little and it wasn't snowing and, although she couldn't see her feet, she was almost certain she would be wearing shoes. A beam spread across Alicja's face at the sight of her. Debbie had her coat on and was clutching a set of keys.

"Alicja?" she said as stepped out and began locking up.

"Please don't send me away," pleaded Alicja.

Debbie looked at her plaintive expression. The beam was gone, replaced by an almost palpable anxiety reflected in her large blue eyes.

"Come on, then," said Debbie, picking up Alicja's bag. "Let's go home."

Home, thought Alicja, *she said home*, as they made their way to the bus stop. *I'm going home.*

~ ~ ~

Back at the flat, they made up Alicja's bed together in the spare room and Debbie suggested she unpacked her clothes into the set of drawers which doubled as a bed side table.

"I'll take one of the lamps from the living room for you tonight and pick up another one tomorrow when I'm in town."

She patted the side of the bed and Alicja sat down next to her, looking nervous.

"It's ok," said Debbie, putting her arm around her. "Don't look so worried. I just wanted to say something. I want to ask something of you."

Alicja nodded.

"I want you to promise me that you'll meet up with your father when he comes. Give him a chance. Don't reject him."

Alicja thought back to Matthew's words about hearing what he'd got to say.

"I don't want to go back to Poland," she said.

"I understand that. And, as I said before, no one can force you to. You'll be 16 next year, able to make up your own mind." As she said this, Debbie wondered about Alicja's immigration status and whether she was being too emphatic about Alicja's rights. "But your heritage is important. Perhaps not now, but it may become so as you get older. Most of us need to know where we come from – and *who* we come from. Give your Dad a chance."

"What about staying here?"

"I'll call Barbara again tomorrow. No doubt the Refuge is panicking. So I'll call them now to tell them you're here with me and that you're safe."

Alicja leant over and kissed Debbie on the cheek.

They had dinner together at the small dining table by the window and watched the darkness roll in over the green expanse of the nature reserve. Every now and again, they'd hear the loud two-syllable honk of a Canada goose, calling for its mate now that the nesting season was underway.

"They can make a hell of a noise in the mornings," said Debbie. "You won't need an alarm clock."

"I will love that," said Alicja. She felt almost lost in her happiness; an unchartered land. To lie awake in her own space, listening to the geese, imagining the waterways and reed banks they flew over just outside her window, fulfilled every childhood wish. She thought about her mother, wondering whether she'd been concerned about her absence during the evening. If she had been, there had been no calls or texts from her.

After they'd said goodnight and agreed what time they'd leave together in the morning, Debbie to work and Alicja to school, Alicja saw she had two new WhatsApp messages on her phone. One was from Matthew saying he hoped everything was ok with her and to let him know when they could meet again. The other was from her father. Halina must have passed on Alicja's number to him. She scrutinised the little photo attached to his contact details. Of course, she thought, looking at his short crop of blonde hair and clear skin, he's still quite young. Halina was twenty-two when she had her. That would mean he would now be in his late thirties, much younger than Debbie.

Hi Alicja, it's your dad, Arik. I'm flying into Gatwick from Gdansk tomorrow, landing about 11. I know you will be at school. Perhaps we can meet afterwards? Let me know what is best for you.

There were some Polish words at the end of the message which she didn't understand. She didn't think long about him before falling asleep, but she did decide that Debbie and Matthew were right. And anyway, seeing his photo and his message, she was suddenly intrigued. He would have a story to tell and she wanted to hear it. Whatever might happen between them the next day, she now had somewhere safe to come back to. It was *that* knowledge which made all the difference to her.

CHAPTER 16

Who are you going with?

Richard saw the boarded-up window as he cycled up Jane's driveway in the pouring rain. Jane was always amazed at how the elements never interfered with Richard's plans. If he said he was coming over, only some meteorological catastrophe would prevent him from turning up when he said he would. *All the roads are flooded and I don't possess a canoe.* He noticed the *Morgan* had gone too.

"Have you sold it then?" he asked, as Jane came to the front door to greet him.

"What? Oh, the car. No. It's been stolen. I was broken into whilst I was away seeing Bob and Stella."

"Hence the window?"

Jane ushered him into the house.

"Yes. Please don't comment on it. It's a botched job, I know. I had no choice."

"I wasn't going to comment. You need to install some proper security."

"Yes, I've got that message, believe it or not."

"I'm sorry," he said, pecking her on the cheek which he had never done before. "You could have called me. I would have come over."

"I can't call you immediately anything goes wrong," she said. It wasn't an invitation for Richard to say, 'why not?' – which was as well, because he didn't. It was a statement of fact. Their relationship had yet to enter the zone where doing things for each other was part of the contract. They were still at the 'no obligation' stage.

Over coffee she entertained him with an account of her discovery of the break-in and the subsequent police visit.

"I've cleaned up the blood now. No-one attended from forensics."

"Burglaries no longer have any priority, I suppose. The police numbers have been cut over the last decade."

"I've got a security firm coming out this afternoon. But you know, I wonder."

"What?" asked Richard, draining his cup.

"I wonder what I'm doing here. In this house. Now. Its purpose – in so far as it ever had one – has gone."

Richard rattled off his advice in short, clipped sentences. "I thought you liked it here. Wanted to make a go of it. Summer is coming. The best time of the year. The burglary has rattled you. Don't make a decision in its aftermath."

Jane laughed.

"You're probably right. Anyway, enough of my gloom. How are things with you?"

"Fine," he said. And then, in typical, straightforward fashion, he came out with the reason for his visit.

"I've been asked to speak at a conference in Florence next month. I wasn't their first choice. He died. But I said I'd do it. Expenses paid and a small fee for the two lectures I'll give. Would you like to come with me?"

Jane blinked at him. "How long for? I've got work, remember?"

"Five or six days – if you can manage it?"

As light flooded the room, Jane looked out of the window. The rain had stopped and a golden sun glimmered behind a thin layer of cloud, as if to encourage her to say *yes* to the adventure she was being offered. Instead, she wanted to know a bit more about the man, so casually referred to, whom Richard was replacing.

"This guy. How did he die?"

"I don't know. I didn't ask." Richard looked non-plussed. *It's an irrelevance to him*, she thought. "Look, it's just a suggestion. It's fine if you don't fancy it."

"It sounds exciting," she said. "But I'll need to square it with work. Give me the dates and I'll speak to them on Friday – or is that too late?"

"No. I can wait until then to book my air ticket and accommodation. I've accepted the invite anyway." He got out his mobile and relayed the dates of the trip to her.

"Are you staying over?" asked Jane.

"No, sorry. I need to get back. Now I'm going away, I'm under some pressure on another project. How about Sunday? We can look at hotels or apartments together if you decide to come."

Within minutes, he'd gone. Whizzed off on his bike, after delivering a short lecture as he strapped on his helmet about the level of security she needed. No ceremony. No fuss. No kiss.

In a way, she was glad. She wanted time on her own to think about going away. *Why did it have to be Florence?* she asked herself, petulantly. It could have been anywhere else in the world *but* Florence. She and Larry had gone there on their honeymoon, more for the romance of being in such an old city rather than to devour its cultural wealth. They'd been put off by the queues and the intense summer heat. And those narrow pavements. A trip to Venice had been the highlight of their trip; the breeze which blew over the lagoon bringing respite from the searing temperatures. Knowing it would be an act of masochism, she went to one of the cupboards in her bedroom and rummaged around looking for an old photo album. Their honeymoon had been one of the few holidays she had documented properly. In the large plastic box underneath that album the rest of their photos lay, jumbled together, some of them creased and stuck to others. Those muddled contents represented her memory of their lives together much more accurately than any neatly organised album could do.

The cover was decorated with pink flowers: peonies and roses. *June 1990 – Honeymoon – Florence and Venice.* On the first page there was one photo only. She and Larry in a gondola, their arms around each other. Their gondolier was one of the singing ones although she couldn't now remember what he'd sung. Of Florence, she remembered the Boboli gardens above the Pitti Palace. It had seemed that day to be a place of relative quiet after walking across the city, over the Ponte Vecchio, jostling their way through the thronging crowds. Florence had been a bit of an ordeal, they had confessed to one another, when they returned home, tilting their faces into the soft, sweet English rain and vowing never again to complain about the weather.

She flipped through the pages of the album quickly. Would she want to return, even with a scholar of the Renaissance? *I am not the same person*, she told herself. This time, the idea of soaking up the riches of museums and churches and paintings was an appealing one. And, anyway, nothing was to be *gained* from passing up Richard's offer whereas, whatever introspection she might indulge in – whilst navigating those cramped pavements – there would be consolations along the way. And there was Richard, of course. It would be interesting to 'engage' with him in a different environment, although not without some risk. It was one thing to meet up intermittently. Quite another to spend a whole six days in his company.

Resolutely, Jane put the album back in the cupboard and then picked up her mobile and called work. It was short notice, they declared. Leave was not usually permitted in the first three months of employment. However, if she was prepared to work the entire week on her return, they would accommodate her. She agreed, expressing her gratitude.

Just as she was about to text Richard with the good news, her mobile vibrated and Michael's number flashed up.

"Michael!" she said, brightly.

They talked over each other for a few seconds, both eager to make amends.

"I was calling to say Lilly and I could visit in May – if you'll have us. Make up for lost time."

Even before he gave her the date, she guessed what weekend he would propose.

"Oh. That's unfortunate," she said. "I'm away then. How about the one afterwards?"

But she couldn't avoid his questions. He was being polite, she supposed – and genuine. It would be stupid and unnecessary to lie. He probably didn't even remember where she and his brother had gone on honeymoon twenty plus years ago. After all, she couldn't say where he and Lilly had honeymooned.

"Oh, that sounds wonderful," he commented. "Great time to go, too. Won't be too hot."

"Have you ever been?" asked Jane, quickly, hoping to stop him asking the next obvious question – *who are you going with?*

"Only for a weekend. A long time ago now, before we had children. When we were footloose and fancy free."

They didn't dwell further on the destination of Jane's trip. They arranged a different weekend and chatted about his work and Lilly's latest creative idea.

As Jane rang off, she sighed with relief and then texted Richard.

That evening, Michael gave the new date to Lilly and asked her if it was ok.

"Oh, why can't she make the weekend of the first?" asked Lily.

"She's off to Florence," he replied. "She must be going with her fancy man as she was keen to move off the subject."

"Isn't that where she and Larry went on honeymoon?" Lilly asked.

"Yep," said Michael. "Precisely. Beggars belief."

"You didn't say anything, did you?"

Michael shook his head. "No, Lilly. I didn't. I kept my mouth shut."

~ ~ ~

Alicja had struggled with her concentration throughout the day. It hadn't helped that they had a double maths period in the morning and she hated the subject, with a vengeance. She had almost been disappointed when she was placed in the top set, surrounded by some true nerds. Being at the top of the lower set might have been preferable to being at the bottom of the top.

Matthew had tracked her down during the morning break, loping towards her along the corridor wearing his happy grin. A few of her friends looked surprised when she smiled as he approached. Interpreting her smile as acquiescence, he stopped and offered her some gum. They shuffled away from the group, looking for a quiet corner where they could chat.

"I'm meeting him after school," she said. "He's flying into Gatwick. Probably there now."

"Where are you meeting him? Outside school?"

She nodded. She wondered all night if it hadn't been a mistake to tell him the school's address and agree to him waiting for her at the gate, like an ageing boyfriend. When she'd told Debbie of the arrangement, Debbie had expressed concern that their initial meeting would be unsupervised. Alicja had simply shrugged when she asked if Barbara Todd knew of the arrangement. Debbie discovered later that Arik had only informed Alicja of his impending arrival.

"Stay in a public place and have your phone charged and on, please," she said over their breakfast that morning, acknowledging to herself that living with a teenager might have more challenges than she'd considered initially.

Alicja had laughed, unable to understand why everyone appeared so much more suspicious of her father rather than her mother. It didn't make sense to her. She related Debbie's little homily to Matthew.

"Would you like me to wait with you?" he asked.

Alicja was touched by his offer. She shook her head.

"No, that's ok. We'll probably go into town so if you're hanging out there, I'll message you if there's a problem."

He grinned at her.

"Yep. I'll be around. I usually hang out at the café we were in last week."

When the bell went, before they went their separate ways, he shuffled around on his feet.

"I'm going for a haircut," he said, waggling his head at her. "You may not recognize me when you next see me."

"I'm sure I will," said Alicja. Glimpsing his eyes behind all that straggly dark brown hair, she'd been struck by his long, black straight lashes. She'd be interested to see his face properly. When she re-joined her group of friends on their way back to the classroom, she'd expected a bit of teasing. But it didn't come. Katia, from the estate where she used to live, asked her a few questions about Matthew but there were no jibes.

The night before, she had borrowed Debbie's computer to research the city of Gdansk. She knew nothing about it, nor about the region her mother's family came from. Alicja realised how ignorant she was about her heritage and wondered why she hadn't been more curious about her father. Her mother, she concluded, with some bitterness, had done a thorough job of convincing her of his indifference. Now she wondered if she wasn't about to learn a very different version of their story.

Arik was on the opposite side of the street when she emerged from the school gates. He was wearing a black bomber jacket, his hands thrust inside its pockets, and tight black jeans. He'd sent her a selfie that morning and asked for one back. She'd got Katia to take it and send it to him from her phone at lunchtime, as her camera didn't work. She was embarrassed to ask her, knowing she was going to have to provide an explanation. Katia had been pleased to help out, giggling and making some comment about Alicja's *'secret life'*. So, as Alicja suspected, there was a little gaggle of her schoolfriends watching her as she crossed the street to meet the father she could not recall. Katia had turned round, making a face to the others, signalling her admiration – "Jesus. That's her Dad."

They did talk about the past that afternoon, but Arik didn't dwell on it, as if he'd made a conscious decision to focus on Alicja's life, current and future. So he said very little about Halina although the look of relief which suffused his face when Alicja told him she had recently moved in with Debbie, told its own story of his concern for her. When she did tentatively ask him about what he remembered about her as a child, he was damning of his own behaviour.

"I was a stupid boy," he said, adding some words in Polish to replace the English ones which escaped him as he emphasised his contempt for his own immaturity. "I could not cope. I ran away. But now. Now I am a man, not a boy." Even to Alicja, the explanation sounded rehearsed.

He picked up his phone and showed her a picture of a sturdy little toddler with blonde hair.

"My other daughter. Your half-sister. Rosa."

Alicja took the phone from him and gazed at the cheerful face of the little girl.

"As soon as I held her in my arms, I knew I had to find you. It was just – how do you say it?" He used a Polish word again. "That the social people contacted me."

"A coincidence?"

He nodded.

"Yes. A coincidence. Your mother blocked me on her phone many years ago."

He was a manager at the Gdansk Shakespeare Theatre and said he'd harboured a wish to be an actor when young. But things hadn't worked out and he'd fallen into an admin role within the theatre and then worked his way up higher. He asked her if she liked Shakespeare.

"There's a festival every summer at the theatre. Perhaps, if you like, you could come and visit us then in the holidays. Meet Rosa and my girlfriend, Alia. We have only a small apartment, but you can sleep in Rosa's room – if you don't mind."

"I would like that," Alicja said, her face flushing with pleasure at the prospect of a trip abroad but, more so, of being part of a family.

"I can baby-sit for you and Alia," she said.

Arik laughed, throwing his head back, as much from relief at how easy their meeting was turning out to be as because, as he commented, the visit was for her benefit, not theirs.

"But I can't imagine anything I'd like better," she said. "Looking after my little sister."

Arik leant over and did what he had told himself he would never do on their first meeting. He kissed her on the cheek.

"Thank you," he murmured. And then he was off in Polish again, blowing his nose and hoping she wouldn't notice how emotional he'd become.

"I know very little of our language," said Alicja, cupping her chin with her hands, her elbows on the table. "But I promise I'll try to learn a bit before I come."

When it reached 6.30, Arik said she should be getting home. He would take her back if she liked as he'd rented a car. He was only staying two nights, but they could meet up again the following day.

Inevitably, Debbie invited Arik in and cooked dinner for the three of them. She had never heard Alicja talk so much, eager to tell her father about the nature reserve and her school life. She asked Debbie if she could take the day off school to spend it with Arik and Debbie had nodded in Arik's direction.

"He's your Dad! Ask him, not me."

"Dad?"

Debbie watched as daughter and father smiled at one another. Arik nodded.

"You bet," he said in a mock American drawl.

It's too soon to know if this will end happily, Debbie decided, before getting up to make them all some coffee. *But it's a hopeful beginning.*

CHAPTER 17

Bonfire of the Vanities

Girolamo Savonarola: born in 1452. Executed in 1498 – first hanged and then burnt at the stake.

"Burnt so that not one relic of him remained for his followers to sanctify. In fact, it is maintained that the burning went on for so long because his ashes were periodically mixed with brushwood to, I suppose, contaminate them."

"How gruesome," murmured Jane.

It was Sunday and, despite the hour, she and Richard were still in bed. They had been surfing the net, trying to decide whether an apartment or hotel would suit them better for their six-night stay in Florence. In fact, it was Jane who was doing the searching. Richard seemed less than interested; hence the lecture he was delivering regarding Friar Savonarola and his battle with Pope Alexander VI.

He'd called the night before, shortly after Jane had returned from Cheltenham, saying they needed to firm up the arrangements for their trip as soon as possible. He'd bike over unless she preferred to wait for the morning. Having arrived, all it seemed to Jane he really wanted was to rehearse the lecture he was going to give in Florence on its infamous inhabitant.

"I'm giving the lecture on May 23rd," he declared over their dinner of shop-bought lasagne. "Now why do you think that is?"

"I could guess but I have the impression you're going to tell me. So I won't bother." Richard had ignored her frivolous response.

"Because that is the very date on which his execution took place in the Piazza della Signoria. It's a pity I can't arrange an actual pilgrimage to the Piazza. But there's too many attendees for that."

Jane had been certain they had exhausted the subject over dinner the night before. But she was wrong. Before she could bring his attention to an apartment she'd discovered in central Florence – with a view of the Duomo from the bathroom window – he continued with yet more facts about the execution.

"And," he said, "why did they choose that Piazza for the site of the execution?"

"Plenty of space for the crowds to gather?"

Richard shook his head. He paused as if for dramatic effect and then reached over to the bedside table for his mobile and glasses. Jane assumed he wanted his glasses so that he could see what she was looking at on her laptop.

"No," he said emphatically. "It was chosen because that's where Savonarola lit his famous Bonfire of the Vanities. Have you heard of it?"

"I thought it was a novel by someone or other."

"It is." He barked out the author's name. *You would know that too*, thought Jane. *The man's not only an obsessive. He's a know-all.*

"The Bonfire of the Vanities was where Savonarola burned a number of items which he believed were corrupting the true word of God."

"Do you believe in God?" Jane said.

Richard looked irritated with the non-sequitur.

"No, of course not," he snapped.

"Ok, so what sort of things went on this bonfire, then?" in a voice suggesting she was now resigned to her fate.

"What would you think went on it?" Richard asked, suddenly forgiving her for her recent lack of focus. After all, she was the only audience he had on which to practice.

Jane sighed. Why was it necessary for him to treat her as one of his students? He appeared incapable of conversing along normal lines.

"Oh, just tell me, darling." The temptation to add the next few words simply overpowered her. "I can't wait any longer."

Richard, she observed, had an amazing ability to ignore her sarcasm. Perhaps he'd become accustomed to it when he was married. She imagined his daughters didn't exhibit the deference he expected from his students.

"Well, cosmetics, non-biblical art works, erotic writings –"

"Oooh. I'm surprised they had anything like that back then. Can you give me an example?"

For once, Richard did not give an immediate reply. Jane cheered, internally.

"I'm not sure I can – but it's a good question."

He handed his phone over to her.

"Look," he commanded. "This is a painting attributed to Francesco di Lorenzo Rosselli of Savonarola's execution. What's particularly interesting is the way in which the streets leading out of the square are depicted. Can you see? Those streets are actually parallel to each other, but the artist doesn't show them as such."

Jane peered at the three figures hanging from a cross at the top of the pyre. Hooded men – the Pope's henchmen – appeared to be bringing yet more poor souls to face imminent death.

"No," explained Richard, when Jane expressed this thought. "There's a time lapse to the painting. Rosselli is showing the trial – far right – and then the leading of the men to the end of the platform and then the hanging of them. It's fascinating, isn't it?"

Jane was beginning to believe that by the time they got round to looking at the apartment, someone else would have snapped it up.

"Richard," she said. "Let's decide on the apartment, shall we? We're booking really late so I think our choice will be limited."

He looked over her shoulder at the pictures of the three roomed, fourth floor flat.

"Location is what matters. It seems central enough so if you're happy, just book it. My credit card is in my wallet in my jeans. Pay for it on that. I can claim it back."

Richard got out of bed, located his card and chucked it over to her.

"I'll go for my shower," he said.

Their flights to Bologna were booked over breakfast and, by the time Richard left in early afternoon, all the arrangements were in place. Jane was committed. It seemed a significant step in their relationship. And, by virtue of this commitment, there was less hesitation in their interaction with one another. But she couldn't help but question whether she would be able to tolerate a trip of such duration with him. Just when she'd thought they had finally exhausted the history of Savonarola, Richard enlightened her as to the second lecture he'd been asked to give: the works of the Florentine artist, *Masaccio*. Apparently, Richard was less confident about this subject, saying although he recalled an earlier visit to the *Brancacci Chapel* in Florence which contained some of Masaccio's most significant frescoes, he felt largely ignorant of the man's work. He intimated that it was a shocking omission in his compendium of knowledge concerning the Renaissance. Whereas other individuals might express regret at the emotional mistakes they'd made – their failed marriage, the conflicted relationship they had with their father, the lack of support to a sibling – Richard defined himself, and felt judged, by what he *knew*. Or so it appeared to Jane.

"And one can't – shouldn't – make reference to Masaccio without also speaking about his fellow artist, Masolino," he went on. "Scholars of that era have concluded that the two artists were working from a single project in the Chapel. I've my work cut out in that respect."

Jane nodded, adopting an expression of sympathy at the grave task ahead of him.

~ ~ ~

After meeting up with her father, Alicja had been on a high all week. She was now keen to meet up with Matthew after school and tell him how positive the visit had been. She would be going to Poland in the summer. Arik would send her the air fare. In the meantime, she was hoping to learn some Polish so that she could talk to her half-sister. When she mentioned the Shakespeare festival, Matthew had said that he presumed the plays would be performed in Polish and wouldn't that be a bit of problem, even if she had picked up the rudiments of the language? She'd had to admit that she hadn't even considered this.

"I'm looking to earn some money before then and I don't have long. Any ideas?"

She and Matthew were sitting in their usual café on a Friday afternoon, both happy that the school week was over and that the weekend stretched out before them, particularly now it was the end of April and the nights were longer and lighter. Matthew looked different with his new haircut, his cheekbones more prominent, his green eyes now visible with their fringe of straight black lashes. He was wearing a new jacket too, courtesy of his mum, he said. Alicja had noticed that he was very loyal to his mother. While she was constantly lambasting her own, he stayed very quiet. Occasionally, he'd look at his phone and if his mother had messaged him, he always answered. He never put it down, making a joke about his mother 'fretting again', like it was fashionable for their peers to do. It wasn't cool to respect your parents – not publicly, anyhow.

"Not really but I'll ask my Mum. Maybe you should just trawl round the shops asking if they have any vacancies."

"Debbie says I'll have to have my mum's permission. That may be a problem seeing I don't speak to her."

"Well, you've got a dad now. Maybe he can give his permission?"

Alicja nodded. "I can't believe just how great he was. You know, after everything I'd believed about him. None of it was true. All that shit about taking me back to Poland made up by my idiot mother."

She filled him in on another few details she learned about her father over their two days together. As she talked, she saw Matthew looking more thoughtful.

"What is it?" she asked him, wondering if he was jealous of her admiration for her long-lost father or just tired of the subject.

"I was just sort of wondering, like, why he left. You know, went back to Poland. Did you ask him?"

Alicja shrugged. "He said he was young and immature, that's all. It's like Debbie said – people change."

"But he didn't stay in touch, did he?"

"He said mum blocked him."

"But weren't there other relatives who knew where she was – where *you* were? Don't your mum's parents live in Poland?"

Ripples of annoyance stirred within Alicja. She tried to suppress them.

"Look," she said. "I don't know. Why's it important? He's got in touch with me now. That's what matters."

"I just think it's easy, that's all. Coming back into your life, you know, when you're grown up." Matthew flushed as he said this.

In a sudden flash, Alicja realised that he was probably talking about his own Dad.

"Where's your Dad?"

"He comes and goes. Lives about thirty miles away with his girlfriend. We go out for a meal every now and again. On my birthday, Christmas. You know, the usual stuff."

"Don't you like him?"

"He's ok. But my mum struggled. Like, he left her with debts. She's still broke now." He fingered the cloth on his jacket, as if testing its quality. "Like this, she spends anything extra she has on me. Not herself. Dad gets to do the good stuff. Mum's had it hard." His face was burning now. He'd not meant to give away quite so much about himself. And talking about his mum? *Seriously* uncool.

"You think that applies to my dad too? Is that what you mean?"

Matthew was keen to reassure her.

"Fuck, no. I'm just saying, that's all."

But he'd made his point. Her dad had given her his version of events and she'd chosen to believe him. He could have found her before now and he didn't. And she hadn't questioned him about that because she hadn't really wanted to spoil the picture book look – and feel – of their reconciliation. She and her mother *had* been close when she was young. Perhaps there were good reasons why Halina felt bitterness towards Arik.

"Are you seeing your mum at all?" he added.

"No. We're not in contact. She doesn't want to know me. So there's no point."

"What about this man who hit her. What happened to him? Are the police involved?"

Alicja's expression suggested that he'd overstepped the mark.

"Sorry," he mumbled. "I just, like, wondered."

But, as was becoming apparent to her, Matthew's questions were not idle ones.

"Why? Do you think I should feel sorry for her?" It was Alicja's turn to flush, albeit with annoyance rather than embarrassment.

Matthew shook his head and tried to change the subject by saying he was 'fucking starving' and was going to order a burger. He took some change out of this pocket and looked through it. Alicja watched his lips moving as he counted the coins. And when she looked back – which wasn't often – she would remember that moment; in the café, the dust particles dancing in the light of an April afternoon, Matthew's sleeve touching hers. Staring at his profile, she wondered if she trusted him enough to tell him the truth about her mother. Would it be all around the school the following day? And anyway, why would she bother unburdening herself to him?

"I've enough for two," he declared. "Want one?"

"No, you're alright," she said. "You go ahead. Debbie will expect me to eat with her."

Matthew got up and then hesitated before going to the counter.

"You will be here when I get back, won't you?"

Alicja smiled at him, enjoying the look of relief which flooded his face as she did so. She nodded.

Taking her completely by surprise, Matthew bent down and kissed her lightly on the lips. Then he was off, walking jauntily and confidently, to order his burger. The interval allowed them to change the tone of their conversation without embarrassment. They swopped some school gossip. One of Matthew's mates – 'actually, we've never really hung out together' – was risking permanent exclusion for being caught with a knife on school premises. He was mixed up in something 'stupid', Matthew explained, although precisely what he did not reveal. Despite Alicja's background – the Refuge, the estrangement from her mother – he saw her as quite an innocent girl. He didn't want to scare her away by references to drugs and gangs and 'county lines'. She seemed happiest when talking about nature and her commitment to the climate change movement. He'd also noticed that she took her schoolwork seriously which suited him. He did too. He was determined to make his mother proud of him but would not have admitted that to anyone. Even her.

"Would you like to come to the nature reserve with me this weekend?" Alicja asked. "Or are you busy?" she added quickly.

Matthew tried to keep a straight face. He too had been intending to suggest that they meet up but donning a pair of wellingtons and tramping across muddy fields, bird spotting, was not what he'd had in mind. There was a *Captain Marvel* film on at the cinema he wanted to see. His mum would no doubt give him the ticket money for both of them.

"Yeah, sure," he said, glad at that moment that his burger had been plonked in front of him and he could pretend to focus on looking for the tomato sauce.

"You could meet Debbie," Alicja said. "I've told her about you."

"Really?" said Matthew, taking a gigantic bite out of his bun. "By the way, I don't have any wellingtons." He started to laugh, his eyes screwing up and then leaking tears with the effort of trying not to choke. Alicja looked on, perplexed.

"What is it?" she said. "What have I said that's so funny?"

Matthew tried to calm himself by gulping down the remains of his coke, but it was impossible. Every time he achieved some composure, he'd imagine them wading through streams and checking for pond life and it would set him off again.

Luckily, Alicja did not take offence. His laugh was so infectious that it set her going too and while she still had no clear idea what they were laughing at, it felt so good to be with him, free from adults and their unerring ability to complicate the world, she really didn't care.

CHAPTER 18

As clear as the full-throated song of the blackbird

Jane was on the phone to Alex. The *Morgan* – the *'flat rad'* *Morgan* – which had been stolen was not, according to the loss adjustor, Mr Moore, covered by her home contents policy. Since it was worth in excess of forty thousand pounds, it should have been specifically referred to. Mr Moore had not been unkind just firm. She'd called Alex to obtain his view.

"I don't expect there's anything I can do about it, is there? I just wondered what your opinion might be."

Alex said he couldn't say without sight of the policy but what Mr Moore had said was 'standard in the industry'. It was likely that the application form made the position on expensive items very clear. He rattled off a little more legal advice and then said, if she wanted to be doubly sure, given the size of the loss, he would be happy to cast his eye over the policy. Could she scan it and email it to him?

"Why don't you come here for lunch on Sunday?" Jane asked, impulsively. "You can see the house. See the size of what I'm living in! Tell me how mad I am and how I should be looking for a nice little flat in Cheltenham."

Alex did not hesitate to accept the invitation.

"If you're sure.....thank you. I would like that very much."

As ever, he'd tried to sound casual, but his words had come out stiffly, awkwardly. So he added some more in an effort to sound light-hearted.

"But I'll stick to providing advice on the policy rather than delivering lectures as to where and how you should live."

Jane laughed, thinking it would be nigh-on impossible to meet anyone so intent on 'delivering lectures' as Richard Marks. It would be a refreshing change to exchange some normal conversation with Alex without being periodically quizzed throughout it.

Dead on midday that Sunday, Alex's black BMW rolled into Jane's drive. He felt almost embarrassed at his punctuality. It suggested a man not inclined to spontaneity, a rigid thinker and planner. Someone, he imagined, whom Jane would find too safe and boring to be involved with – on any level, save a professional one where such characteristics were to be welcomed, not scorned.

Jane had been honest with Richard. No, they could not meet up, she'd said. Her solicitor was 'popping in for lunch' so that he could peruse a document for her.

"I owe him, you see," she explained, wondering why she felt it necessary to justify the visit. "He did the probate for Larry – *gratis*." She didn't refer to their recent lunch. Richard appeared indifferent to the news, adding that 'the girls' were likely to visit him that weekend anyway. She decided that he was probably unable to believe that she would find anyone more attractive than him. In Richard's eyes, surely, she had the perfect package: wonderful sex, followed by a discourse on some aspect of the Renaissance. There was no gossip or small talk. There wasn't much romance either.

Now, here was Alex, on a glorious morning in May. Having, seemingly, shed his professional persona, he was wearing denim jeans and an open necked shirt. As Jane emerged from the house to greet him, he pushed his sunglasses back from his face and smiled. He was holding a small bunch of spring blooms: yellow and pink freesias, white hyacinths. Their strong scent wafted over to her as he approached.

"What a lovely property," he said, casting his eye over the house's façade. He was perfectly groomed, his moustache trimmed and neat, his wavy greying hair a sensible length. There was a moment's awkwardness as they both pondered whether their relationship was one which now demanded that they peck each other's cheeks. Recalling that Jane had already signalled her consent on the last occasion when they'd parted, Alex bent down and pressed his cheek to hers whilst, simultaneously, proffering the flowers. Jane murmured her thanks.

She would acknowledge later, after the day's events, that no sentient being would believe that the invite she'd issued to 'my solicitor' was an innocent one. Had she had the power to roll back time as she welcomed him into *The Old Byre*, she would have done. A lone woman does not invite a single man into her home for the purpose of 'just lunch'. A single man does not drive 80 miles to peruse a document he could read online. This was a signal, as clear as the full-throated song of the blackbird which heralded from a Robina tree at the boundary of the garden.

They sat under the white wisteria, its first bloom already gone but now in full leaf and drank coffee and debated whether to go for a walk before or after lunch. Jane said she was now familiar with a few walks in the local area and suggested a round trip of about three miles. She didn't reveal the source of her local knowledge: Richard. In the event, she didn't need to. Alex would be introduced to him soon enough.

"That takes us to the local pub," she said. "We could eat there if you'd like although I know you can't drink. They do a good nut roast." Regretting that she'd sent out such a strong message, it occurred to her that a pub lunch was probably the better option. They could walk back then, have tea in the garden before he left and that would be that. She'd given him a lightning tour of the house, not lingering in any room and barely entering the bedrooms. As she announced – "and this is my boudoir" at the door of her own, she was reminded forcefully of the dénouement of Richard's first visit. She'd retreated quickly, and obviously, thus emphasising the implication of her needless remark rather than the opposite.

Before they left for the walk, Alex mentioned the insurance policy and then it was humiliatingly apparent that Jane did not know where it was. She'd obtained the insurance company's telephone number from a card she'd found in Larry's wallet, placed in the drawer of the console table in the hours following his death. The sight and feel of the leather wallet, one he'd had for as long as she had known him, had delivered another wave of remorse that day. Perhaps, on reflection, her invite to Alex had been a response to that anguish; a swallowing down of the pain which surfaced. The pretence of a normal life.

By the time Jane and Alex arrived at *The Lamb*, lunchtime was in full swing and there was barely an empty corner, let alone a table to sit at. At the bar, queuing had been abandoned as people jostled for position, waving notes at the harassed bar staff or calling their names if they were locals. But there was a queue for a table in the dining room and, after a brief discussion, they joined it, Alex noting that quite a few diners appeared to be sipping coffee and had finished their meals. As Jane cast her own glance around the room, she noticed a young woman, attractive with long dark hair, who looked vaguely familiar. She was chatting animatedly to a man with his back to Jane. As she watched them, their identities slowly dawning on her, another young woman, tall and slim, joined them at the table. It was Richard and his daughters, Cressie and Phoebe. She hadn't even considered that their paths might cross. However things were engineered, it would be impossible to avoid them. They were almost bound to pass each other.

Jane's first thought, regarding the forthcoming encounter, was how she would introduce Alex. *My friend, Alex* – or *my solicitor Alex*? *And for whose benefit was this distinction?* she wondered, irritated by her own indecision.

Within minutes, Richard and his daughters began to leave their table, pushing in the chairs, picking up mobiles. Richard turned to leave the room, catching sight of Jane almost immediately. Their eyes met and Jane gave a nervous smile. Still in the queue, Richard's little party blocked the aisle to the toilets as he stopped to exchange pleasantries with Jane. She thought he looked particularly suave that afternoon, as if he'd put some thought into his appearance with his grey gilet and black chinos.

"This is Jane Sedgefield," he said to Phoebe and Cressie, hovering by his side.

"Oh, wow," exclaimed Cressie, breathing wine fumes over them. "Dad was just talking about you! You're going to Florence together in a couple of weeks. That's amazing!" She stuck out her hand. "Hi, I'm Cressie."

"Yes, I've heard a lot about you," mumbled Jane, a blush developing over her face as she proffered her own limp hand.

Before she could introduce Alex, Phoebe started chatting to her, laughing, a head of glossy hair swinging around her lovely face, saying what a relief it was that "Dad has someone to bore on his travels, besides us – you brave lady! Just don't forget to pack your ear plugs."

Richard said nothing. A smile played on his lips as he contemplated Jane's embarrassment.

"This is Alex," Jane said, interrupting Phoebe. "My solicitor," she added. There was more handshaking and then Richard said they were in the way and should move. He put a hand on the shoulder of each daughter and steered them away, looking backwards towards Jane as he did so.

"Enjoy your lunch!"

Left alone, the awkwardness which descended over Alex and Jane was so intense, it was almost funny. But by the time a table had become available, Alex had recovered his equilibrium and was determined to display some dignity, however confused he felt at Jane's flirtation with him.

"So, you're going to Florence shortly. It's a wonderful city. Have you been there before?"

They were placed at a table for two, right in the centre of the room. It was noisy and hot.

"Yes, many years ago," Jane answered, looking at the menu intently, as if she might be called upon to memorise it before it was whisked away. Suddenly, she was back thinking of Larry, recalling the last time they'd sat together and shared a meal; this very place, on New Year's Day. She looked over at the large round table in one corner of the room. It had been a bit of a squash for nine people. Their elbows kept clipping one another's. She remembered some talk about how round tables were so much better for communal dining than rectangular ones. She remembered too how Larry had winced with pain whenever he moved. The outing had been an ordeal for him. She bit her bottom lip in an effort not to cry while, at the same time, attempting a brave smile for Alex. Seeing the redness in her eyes, a look of concern came over his face.

"Are you alright?" he said gently.

A tear dribbled down Jane's face. It was wiped away with undue force.

"Not really," she said, shaking her head. The relief she felt as she said those words was like removing a mask as the dawn arrived and the carnival finally ended.

"Do you want to go? It's a bit hot in here, isn't it?"

She indicated her agreement by standing up, fishing a tissue from her bag to stem the tears, now in full flow. Alex took hold of her elbow protectively, steering her around the tables while people looked up from their roast dinners, anxiously, wondering what could have possibly happened on such a bright, hope-heavy day. He smiled ruefully to himself as he remembered executing a similar exit with the rancorous Miss Stern. Was this now to be his fate? To escort middle-aged, emotional ladies from crowded eateries and then to comfort them with well-chosen words, softly spoken.

Outside, the sun beat down on them. The river opposite the pub flowed powerfully by, threatening to break its banks under the weight of water. Alex searched for a suitable secluded spot where Jane could recover from whatever had afflicted her. He could only guess at its origin – Larry – although that theory seemed to hang oddly with her forthcoming trip to Florence with the lover he'd just met. He could see a fisherman in the distance, standing still as a heron. The sport, as he understood it was now so defined, had never attracted him. But that day, he envied the man his simple, silent devotion.

"There's nowhere to sit," he said eventually.

"It's ok," said Jane. "Let's just go. I'm sorry to have ruined the day. I hope you'll forgive me."

On the way back to *The Old Byre*, she talked, and Alex, having little choice in the matter, listened. Although, when she embarked on her unburdening, he'd assured her that she didn't owe him any explanation, her view was the opposite.

Jane didn't mention how she had come to meet Richard, just said that 'yes, I'm involved with him but it wasn't an affair which pre-dated Larry'.

Alex was too polite to ask why she thought he might be interested in the details of her sexual frolics. But he was certain of one thing as they trudged homewards; once back he would get in his car and consign Jane Sedgefield to an experience best forgotten.

"I'm a bit of a mess, aren't I?" she'd said. "All over the place." If she was inviting him to disagree with this description, it didn't work. By the time *The Old Byre* came into view, his empathy button was firmly in the 'off' position.

"I'll fix us something to eat, shall I?" she asked, as they arrived back though the gate at the bottom of the garden. "We can sit outside." She turned to look at him, smiling and shaking the hair back from her face, summoning his gaze.

"I've certainly worked up an appetite," she added.

"No, it's fine," Alex said, taking his car keys from one of the front pockets of his jeans. "I'm going to get off."

He could have made some excuse about avoiding the Sunday traffic or having work to do for the following day, but he made no further concessions towards Jane's feelings. He felt enough had been expected of him already that day. Turning away from her, he headed towards the side gate which led into the front drive. Shocked and embarrassed, Jane followed him.

She stood, her face pale despite the day's warmth, and watched as from the wheel of his car, he lifted his hand to signal goodbye. She lifted hers in response and then started to move towards him, suddenly anxious to make amends and say, yet again, that she was sorry. But, although he saw, he didn't stop. He kept his eyes firmly ahead, reversing swiftly before driving off at some speed.

~ ~ ~

Alicja and Matthew did not spend Saturday as either of them had planned in their imaginations. Alicja needed some more clothes and, when she mentioned this briefly to Matthew, he suggested he accompany her to the Refuge. She had intended to ask Debbie to run her over there in the car, but Debbie was at work all day and it would be good to get the visit over with. She had been dreading seeing her mother again. Turning up with Mathew might curtail Halina's customary flow of wounding comments towards her. When she mentioned to Debbie that she and Matthew were meeting up, Debbie asked her if she wanted to invite Matthew over for a meal that evening.

"So you can check him out?" asked Alicja.

"Of course!" said Debbie, laughing. "Or is spending the evening with me not what either of you had in mind?"

"I'll ask him and text you – but thanks, anyway."

She broached the subject with him when they were on the bus on their way to the refuge that Saturday lunchtime.

"Yeah, sure," he said.

"You don't mind?"

"Why would I mind?" he said, throwing his arm around her shoulders, squeezing her. "Chill. It's no big deal. She sounds ok, your Debbie."

Halina was in their bedroom when they arrived. Alicja had hoped fervently that she might be out, but she was lying on her bed. She looked startled when they came in, without knocking, as if she'd been asleep. Sitting up, pushing her long hair back from her face, she blinked at them. Seeing her mother's puffy eyes, Alicja apologised.

"I'm sorry," she said, quickly. "I should have let you know I was coming."

Matthew hovered in the doorway behind her.

"I'll wait outside," he muttered.

"Who are you with?" Halina demanded, stretching her arms up to the ceiling and yawning. "And how is my baby girl?"

The question surprised Alicja.

"I'm fine. And I'm with a mate from school, Matthew."

"Matthew!" Halina called out. "Matthew, come in and say hello."

Matthew appeared again at the door.

"Hi," he said, blushing a little and glancing at Alicja for guidance.

Halina wandered over to him, tying her hair in a ponytail as she did so.

"How do you do, Matthew," she said, in formal tones, holding out her hand and inclining her head in a mock bow. "I am very pleased to meet you. Would you like some tea or coffee?"

Alicja sighed, wondering why her mother had suddenly decided to speak as if in an English language lesson. She was trying to be funny, she supposed. To Alicja, she just sounded weird.

Matthew looked over at Alicja.

"We weren't going to stay," said Alicja, indicating her sports-bag which she'd placed on her old bed. "I only came to collect some more of my things. I've run out of clothes."

"Actually," said Matthew. "Tea would be great. I'm parched." He grinned at Halina.

"Wonderful!" She turned to Alicja. "You collect your things, darling, and I'll make us some tea." She went over to the mirror on the wardrobe and scrutinised her face.

"I look like a witch. If I'd known you were coming, I would have made myself more presentable." She winked as she walked past Matthew on her way out of the door to the kitchen.

"She wants to be friends with you," Matthew declared when he saw Alicja's expression.

"She puts on an act," said Alicja.

"Does she have many friends?"

Alicja shrugged. "How should I know?"

"She's probably a bit lonely in here," said Matthew, looking around him. There was little colour or comfort in the room. Even the duvet covers were an indeterminate shade of beige. The single beds looked narrow and uncomfortable, like you might find in a prison cell. The walls were bare, just a scrap of tape where the picture of Greta Thunberg used to be. Alicja didn't look at him, rifling through drawers and stuffing garments into her bag, determinedly. "Hey," he said, "it's just a cup of tea."

Alicja zipped up her bag and waved to him to leave the room. He came over and took the bag from her. "Allow me, madam," he said.

"Don't you start," said Alicja. And then she began to laugh at her own pettiness. She linked arms with him and they jostled each other as they tried to fit through the door.

When they emerged, Halina was staring at them from where she stood in the kitchen, her back to the cooker, three mugs of steaming tea on the table in front of her. Two things had struck her about her daughter. She was happy, for one. And two, she saw the outline of the young woman she would become: beautiful and smart. There was a third thought as well, but that was too painful to dwell upon.

They stood around and chatted for a few minutes. *Like ordinary people do*, thought Alicja. Matthew's initial hesitation had disappeared. He was quite the conversationalist when he got going, Alicja decided as she watched him, mug in hand, answering Halina's questions. He chatted about where he lived and his mother's job as a Healthcare support worker. Alicja was perplexed by Halina's volley of enquiries concerning his mother's role in the hospital, wondering if she was merely being polite or whether it suggested she might be considering a change of occupation. Matthew's pride in his mother was reflected in his eagerness to chat about the challenges she faced in working the night shift in the accident and emergency department. *The stories she comes back with – you'd hardly believe*. Halina clearly liked him and bringing someone – not Debbie – had worked. There was none of her usual carping and criticism. She appeared to want to make a good impression. Before they left, she told them to 'wait a moment' and ran back to her room, returning with something in her hand.

"Buy yourself something with this," she said to Alicja, pressing a ten-pound note into her palm. "And let me know," she said, swallowing back what seemed like tears, "that you're ok, from time to time."

Alicja had rarely seen her mother cry. Halina's default mode was anger; the fuel of fury kept her moving, fighting some enemy, invisible to Alicja.

"Thank you, Mum," she said. She hesitated and then kissed her quickly, and lightly, on the cheek. "I will."

Matthew looked on, quietly confident that some bridge had been built that afternoon – or, if not an *actual* bridge, at least the footings of one.

Later, back on her bed, Halina wasn't thinking of bridges. She felt shame as she acknowledged what had occurred to her as she watched Alicja, smiling at Matthew's description of how he and Alicja had met.

It was quite likely that her daughter was better off without her.

CHAPTER 19

A desperate urge to see him

"So, how was lunch with your dashing solicitor?" Richard asked. "We found the food pretty average, actually."

It was a Friday evening. He had suggested he make dinner for them and Jane had driven over to his house, direct from Cheltenham. Work had been more interesting than usual. She'd accompanied a colleague to a client's spectacular Regency home and helped with the choice of curtains in the beautifully proportioned reception room. The two windows were to be dressed in swags and bows and frills with a final bill estimated at ten thousand pounds – although the lady owner had not appeared troubled at spending a similar amount needed to buy a small car on thirty yards of various fabrics. After spending a few miserable days hanging around the house, not seeing anyone, Jane had welcomed the experience. She had called Alex at least twice since their catastrophic meeting, leaving messages. Her calls had not been returned. Alex Snow wanted nothing more to do with her, she concluded. And who would blame him?

"Oh, fine," she said.

"What did you have to eat?"

"He had the nut roast and I had – oh, I forget – something traditional. The beef I think."

"Oh. That's odd. Cressie wanted the nut roast and they said it was all finished."

Jane shrugged.

"How are the girls? Was it good to spend time with them?"

"They're both doing well. We had the usual generational debates. Sunday's exchange of views was about cancel culture and whether it's in conflict with the principle of free speech."

"Are they interested in politics?"

Richard raised an eyebrow.

"They have strong views on most of society's current obsessions – some of which are political, I suppose. And Phoebe writes for some online discussion forum."

They were sitting in Richard's living room, a bottle of wine on the table in front of them. Jane was thinking how crucial light was in a home. Richard's terraced cottage lacked light; wherever they sat, it seemed gloomy without some artificial lighting. Outside, the dusk gathered. She had switched the side lamps on in the room when Richard went back into the kitchen for a corkscrew. Although she'd been looking forward to an evening in someone's company, now she was here, an ambivalence had crept over her. She'd resisted his attempts to lead her upstairs when she arrived and an awkwardness had settled over them from then onwards. She'd brought a small bag with her as it had been assumed she'd stay. Putting it down in the cramped hallway as she came in, Richard had suggested its contents were decanted and left there.

"The girls know about you now – so a few feminine things lying about the house won't matter."

The remark had been further confirmation that they were now in a relationship.

Richard poured Jane a glass of the Shiraz and handed it to her.

"Why did you tell them?" she asked, swirling the liquid around before tasting it. She grimaced.

"What's wrong? Would you have preferred a white?"

"It's a better aperitif, I think." She put her glass down.

Richard jumped up. Knowing him enough now to read him, she could sense the irritation in his movements.

"Richard!" she called out as he exited the room. "It doesn't matter."

He came back in with a bottle of white in a cool bucket and a fresh glass.

"It either matters or it doesn't," he said, placing them down on the now over-crowded little coffee table. It wasn't a snap exactly. His words just conveyed perfectly his ill-temper. He unscrewed the cap and poured her a half glass. If it was not at the required temperature, Jane did not dare comment. Taking a sip, her face remained impassive. After knocking back his half glass of the offending wine, Richard carried on as if there had been no interruption.

"Would you have preferred I'd not done so? Told them, that is. Kept it a secret."

"How did you say we met?"

"I didn't. And they didn't ask. I wouldn't have told them the truth. Not without asking you first."

"I'm surprised they didn't ask. It's usually the first question asked of a couple – if that's what we now are."

Richard made no observation on the latter part of Jane's reply.

"I wouldn't know what's usually asked of couples," he said, waggling his fingers to indicate imaginary quotation marks around the word 'couples'.

Pouring himself another glass of wine, he added "I doubt I've had as much experience as you in that department."

They hadn't spoken to one another about their past relationships. If Richard felt any curiosity at all, he believed it to be forbidden ground given the strange circumstances in which they had met. He had had dalliances with colleagues on occasion in the decade he'd been separated but Jane was his first one of any significance. He assumed she'd picked this up. It didn't need to be spelled out.

"Thanks!" Jane said. "You make me out to be some sort of whore. Larry and I were married for over 20 years."

"Don't be so sensitive," Richard said. "I meant nothing of the kind. I'm a bit of a hermit, that's all."

"What did the girls say when you told them? Women, I should say – they're young women."

"They were pleased for me. And when they met you –," Richard hesitated for a moment. "They were very complimentary – if a little sarcastic. They are practised in the art of sarcasm. Can't think why."

"Go on tell me. What did they say?"

"Why does it matter? It's trivial nonsense."

"Oh, I see, that's what we are, is it? I'm enlightened now."

Richard turned to look at Jane from where they sat – at either end of a three-seater sofa.

"Jane, if you don't want to be here, it's fine. Just say so."

Jane looked away from him.

"You mean, go?"

"I don't like these types of games. They're played by the bored and the stupid."

"Aaah. So I'm bored and stupid as well as a whore, am I? Good to know where I stand in your eyes, Richard."

"Jesus," breathed Richard.

Jane got up. At the front door, clutching her overnight bag, she heard the beginning of Mahler's fifth symphony. She left without saying goodbye and nor did Richard acknowledge her leave-taking.

In the car, she wondered at the speed with which her brave new world appeared to be disintegrating. Since Larry's death she had built sandcastles quickly and adeptly, her spade shovelling aside sand, patting and moulding. Now, even more speedily, more skilfully, she was kicking them down, not waiting for the more natural force of the waves to destroy them – as they surely would have done, given time. It went against the words she'd held close since reading them below the tiger and the man.

Living in the mountains, just let the year advance entirely as it likes.

Back home, she gave in to her mood, scrabbling in the wardrobe until she found the box of photographs. At the kitchen table, emptying them out carelessly, some of them slipped from the table to the floor. In the morning her heel would catch on one, bringing her crashing down onto the cold tiles. But that evening, she was seized with a desperate urge to see him. There was one photograph which had haunted her all day. In it, he was young, not yet thirty. He'd bought his first classic car – the *flat rad Morgan* – and was draped over its long bonnet as you might expect a young woman to be in the bygone age of car advertisements. The joy radiated from his youthful face.

She got a duvet from one of the spare bedrooms and went outside, arranging herself, in a little cocoon, under the wisteria tree. It was a warm, still night and there were pinpoints of light coming from the sky as the stars appeared. She pressed the photograph to her chest and closed her eyes.

In the morning, as she sat on the kitchen floor, she picked up the offending photograph. It showed the usual group in their old dining room, gathered around the table. Larry stood at the head with a cake in front of him, ablaze with candles. His fortieth, she recalled. And it struck her then – although why it had not done so the day before she could not explain. Perhaps, on some subliminal level, she *had* known. It explained the agitation, not just the unwillingness to spend time in Richard's company but the overwhelming urge to be alone.

Yesterday had been Larry's birthday.

~ ~ ~

"My mother liked you," said Alicja, poking Matthew in the ribs playfully, as they stood at the bus stop on their way back to Debbie's.

"I thought she was ok," he said.

"You don't know her," said Alicja. "She was on her best behaviour."

"I felt sorry for her – stuck in that place, alone."

"I know you did. She's a good actress."

Even though Matthew wanted to establish why Alicja felt such little pity for her mother, he didn't pursue the subject. As he understood matters, Halina had ended up in that sorry place because she'd been battered by some toe-rag of a man, so why was *she* the object of Alicja's anger rather than him? It didn't seem to fit with the fair-minded Alicja he spent time with. But then family relationships were often hard to work out. If anyone asked him why his parents split up, he wasn't able to tell them. From what he recalled his father had formed his new relationship following their separation. He had a strong memory of his father moving back in with his parents, Matthew's grandparents, when he left. He was there for some time too. Matthew had been disappointed when he eventually moved out to live with the girlfriend, Frieda, and he'd never felt comfortable going over to the new place – hers. It had felt more natural to spend time with his grandparents and his father when he went to visit, and he could pretend that very little had changed.

It was getting on for seven before Debbie arrived back in the flat, bringing a carrier bag of leftovers from the deli which she piled into the fridge as she chatted to them about their visit to the refuge.

"Was your mother there?" she asked, glancing over at Alicja as if her response would be better gauged by seeing Alicja's expression than hearing her words.

"Yes. She was ok. We had a cup of tea with her."

Debbie stood back with her hands on her hips.

"Well, that's just great. I'm pleased."

Alicja shot a look at Matthew who grinned at her.

"Why is it so important to you both that I get on with my mother?" she asked, looking at them both in turn, trying to inject some lightness of tone into the question. It fooled none of them.

Debbie turned back to the fridge, answering her at the same time.

"Because life will be easier for you – in the long run. And because it leaves a door open for a future relationship with the person who gave birth to you."

A silence descended. She hadn't meant to be so heavy about the issue.

"Anyway," she added. "Go into the living room – put on some music or something. I'll get dinner on."

"Why not let us do it," said Alicja. "You've been at work all day."

Matthew nodded vigorously, despite hoping the offer would be turned down. He could use the microwave and, occasionally, put something in the oven at the correct temperature. Beyond that would be an ambitious step.

"Lord, it's fine. It's only a spag bol. I took it out of the freezer last night so it's just a matter of heating it up and putting the spaghetti on. But thanks, anyway."

She smiled at them both, ushering them out of the room.

"Matthew will never come back if I put him to work in the kitchen!"

They sat eating dinner at the table by the window, watching the layers of clouds building up along the horizon. Occasionally, the geese would row with one another, emitting

159

angry squawks and honks. Alicja said she was growing used to the sound of them and could never consider them a nuisance. She told Matthew about the daily tally of birds which were listed on the board by the bird hide, her enthusiasm evident in the shine in her eyes. He listened politely, trying to think up questions which might demonstrate his interest. Debbie looked at them both and wondered at her good fortune having such lovely young dinner companions. Before Alicja came to stay, she spent most of her Saturday evenings alone – having dinner on a tray on her lap while she watched a film.

Matthew left at around 9 30, refusing both a lift from Debbie and Alicja's offer to walk him to the bus stop. He said he'd text immediately he got home, not scoffing when they asked him to. Their request had made him happy; people who cared about you always wanted to know that you were safe. His mum asked the same of him. Debbie pressed him to take some of the deli leftovers with him, saying she and Alicja would not get through them by the weekend and, eventually, when Debbie maintained that the fresh food would just be wasted, he agreed.

Lying in bed that night, after insisting to Debbie that she cleared up the kitchen and that Debbie sit down with a well-earned glass of wine, Alicja's thoughts drifted towards her mother. While they were chatting happily around the dinner table, what was she doing on her own at the refuge? She had surprised Alicja by seeming pleased to see her; welcoming Matthew, giving her the ten-pound note, asking her to keep in touch. Perhaps the separation had been good for them, allowing for a perspective simply not available when living on top of one another in such a charged environment.

She picked up her phone and messaged Halina. *Goodnight mum x*

A few minutes later a response from Halina appeared.

It was good to see you today, my darling. See you again soon, I hope.

She lay for a minute, feeling sleepy, but unable to properly relax until she'd heard from Matthew. It was after eleven – he must have arrived home by now.

Matthew *had* arrived home. But no sooner had he stored the food he'd been given in the fridge when the doorbell rang.

Suspicious at such a late hour, he kept the chain on the front door as he peered through the crack to see who it was. His father was on the doorstep, looking pale and nervous. A surge of adrenalin shot through him.

"What is it?" asked Matthew, standing back as he opened the door.

"Your mother," his Dad said, his voice breaking. "She's been hurt. In A and E. There was a fight and she tried to break it up. She didn't wait for security."

"Is she alive?"

His father nodded.

"Yes. But we need to go to the hospital now. They said to go."

Matthew wobbled on his feet and his father moved to catch him, steering him through to the kitchen where he could sit down and recover from the shock of the news.

"I've been drinking," his dad confessed as he pulled out his phone to call for an Uber.

They were in the cab within ten minutes. His father kept repeating the same phrase – "she didn't wait for security", shaking his head, making Matthew angry.

"Shut up, Dad."

"That's what they said. She didn't wait for security."

Matthew yelled at him then.

"Fucking shut up."

The Uber driver eyed them in his rear mirror.

"Sorry," his father said. "Sorry."

The rest of the ride to the hospital was undertaken in silence.

At the reception desk, when they asked where Maureen Jones was, a big burly security officer came over to them when he heard her name. "She's fine", he said, surprising them – "probably just concussed, follow me." As they walked the corridors with him, he filled them in on the number of assaults there were on NHS staff in any given year. He was a Union man. "The stats are shocking," he continued, relaying figures to them which, given the circumstances, were immediately forgotten.

But Maureen *was* fine. She had been knocked over, she explained, temporarily losing consciousness. They were monitoring her for concussion. When she came to, she'd asked them to contact Matthew's Dad so that he could tell Matthew. She knew Matthew would want to come and see her, but she was horrified to learn the confused and confusing message which had been relayed – the sort of message which suggests the loved one is about to die or, worse, already dead.

"It was an accident," she said, smiling at them both from her hospital bed. "That's all. I slipped on someone's beanie! I didn't see it. Imagine that. How stupid! They were a pair of pratts, having a scrap but they didn't attack me or anything."

Matthew asked if she'd be out by the next day.

"God, I hope so," she exclaimed. "Twenty four hours, they said."

"I've got lots of food for us, you see," he said, telling her of his visit to Debbie's with Alicja. "There's loads of different salads and a whole quiche thing and some chicken pasta. We can't waste it. We should get lunch and dinner out of it. You won't need to cook. You can rest." His mother put a hand to his cheek.

"It's ok, sweetheart. Shhh. I'll be home, I'm sure."

And then he put his head down on his mother's blanket-covered lap and wept with relief.

CHAPTER 20

Mad with grief

Matthew had messaged Alicja around midnight, apologising for the delay and saying he'd speak to her in the morning to explain. But Alicja couldn't bear to wait until then, feeling something terrible had befallen him on his journey home. So she called him, despite the lateness of the hour. It went to voicemail but half an hour later, he rang back. He was in a cab with his father on their way to his flat, having refused his father's offer to stay at his place for the night.

"I'm ok, Dad. I'm used to being on my own."

"Not for a whole night," his father said.

Matthew didn't say anything. There *were* nights when he was on his own. Usually, his mother worked the late shift, getting home around 11pm but, just occasionally, she'd work the night shift. They'd had a conversation about his going to his grandparents on those nights, but Matthew had persuaded her that at 15 he was quite capable of 'putting myself to bed, Mum'. His grandparents lived over fifteen miles away and, whilst they'd said they'd drive him to school, he knew it would be a hassle for them. In the end, his mother had given in, once she'd had a word with a friend of hers, four doors down, who was happy to be on stand-by should Matthew need her.

He was now whispering to Alicja, his phone cupped to his ear, providing a brief account of the night's events and suggesting they meet after school on Monday.

"Who are you talking to at this time of night?" his father asked.

"A friend."

"Well, they must be very special."

"She is," said Matthew.

His father laughed. "I see," he said. He tapped Matthew on the knee. "Thought you were looking a bit smarter these days. The hair. The new jacket."

When they parted company a few minutes later, his father fumbled in his wallet, eventually bringing out a crumpled twenty pound note and pushing it into Matthew's jacket pocket without saying anything. Matthew was shocked when, later, he saw the colour of the note. He thought back to Alicja and her mother. What had prompted these acts of generosity? The sudden realisation that their children were children no longer but on the threshold of adulthood? Perhaps they recalled these times themselves – the heady excitement of that first love – and hoped fervently that things might work out better for their offspring than they had done for them?

The walls were thin in Debbie's flat. She'd been reading when she heard Alicja's voice from the adjoining bedroom as she talked to Matthew. It was 12.20am but, despite the lateness of the hour, she decided not to interfere. Alicja would tell her in the morning if there was a problem. She was luxuriating in the knowledge that the following day was Sunday – no work. She'd turned down an invitation to a litter-picking session over at some beauty spot on the edge of Guildford, feeling a bit guilty, citing some prior commitment. The commitment was Alicja and their usual Sunday ramble around the reserve even though Alicja would have been just as keen to be take part in such a worthy environmental project.

To date, Debbie hadn't involved Alicja in any of the discussions going on with social services regarding Alicja's placement with her. If she were to obtain a fostering allowance for her, an assessment was necessary with all its attendant intrusions, such as references, background checks and interviews. Having been supplied with a number of forms, she was due to meet with a social worker in the fostering team in the next few days. It had been her intention to speak with Alicja on their walk that Sunday, warning her that the process was about to start and its ramifications. She assumed that Halina would be informed too and so, if Alicja and Halina were really on the brink of healing their relationship, transparency was vital.

Debbie hadn't told Alicja she was gay. It hadn't cropped up in any of their conversations and, anyway, it seemed of limited relevance. But now that she was seeking to be Alicja's foster parent, perhaps she should disclose the fact to her. Whilst Debbie had no current desire to form another relationship, should one materialise in the next couple of years, then it might appear disrespectful to Alicja to have withheld the information from her. She assumed too that during the forthcoming assessment, the subject of her sexuality might be referred to. Thus, she concluded, it needed to be part of their forthcoming conversation.

Over breakfast on the Sunday morning, Debbie and Alicja watched happily as the sun broke through the clouds into a patchy blue sky, agreeing that it was the perfect morning for a ramble. Alicja was regaling Debbie with Matthew's tale from the night before and she was suitably shocked.

"Poor lad," she said. "But at least his mum is ok. I suppose it could have been worse."

"Poor *mum!*" said Alicja.

"Have you met her?"

"Not yet – but I think I will soon. I know she wants to meet me."

Alicja blushed as she said this, thinking it might sound rather boastful.

"She'll be delighted, Alicja. You seem well suited. He's a very nice boy."

Alicja nodded.

"Are you happy?" Debbie asked. "Living here."

Alicja looked startled at the question.

"Of course," she said. "Why?"

"I just wanted to check, that's all."

Debbie didn't expand. She started clearing away their breakfast bowls, saying they should make a move while the sun was out. Within the hour, they were in the bird hide with the bird book which Debbie produced from her rucksack.

"For once," she said, picking up a large heavy pair of binoculars which, surprisingly, were left there for the use of birders and had not been stolen, "I've remembered to bring it."

Alicja now had her own pair: lightweight with their own little case: 20 x magnification. On the second day of her father's visit, he'd suggested he buy her something for her birthday and she'd asked for binoculars. Arik had expressed some surprise, had even thought she might be joking – wanting to know who she was spying on. *'Your mother?'* It had been the only awkward moment between them. Alicja had talked a lot about ecology, the nature reserve and her love of birds. Had he not been listening? She could have asked for things that would be expected of a fifteen-year-old girl: a pair of trainers or some jewellery or to have her ears pierced. But none of those even came close to the extraordinary sense of elation she felt when she put them around her neck before they left for their walk. She felt it was her first real possession of choice. *This is who I am.*

After they'd left the hide, walking back along the rough paths towards home, Debbie suggested they sit for a while. She led Alicja to a spot by the stream, where they could lounge in the warmth. Sitting side by side on a fallen log, they watched the sun's sparkle on the water. Alicja looked around with her binoculars, hoping, she explained, to see the flash of a kingfisher. Debbie opened her bird book and related a few facts about the bird while telling Alicja that she'd never been lucky enough to see one in the area.

"Anyway, I thought we should talk a little about the fostering application I've made. They'll want to interview you in due course, so be prepared for that."

Alicja put her binoculars down and turned towards her.

"I'm ok with that. They already know what I think. You know, about my mum. Will they speak to her?"

"I guess so."

"Do you think it will be ok – they'll let me stay?"

"I don't see why not. But I just wanted you to know a bit more about me, before the process gets going."

"Like what?"

"Well, I'm gay, for a start. I'm not sure whether it – my sexuality – will be relevant but I thought you should know. Rather than be told by a social worker."

"Wouldn't that be discrimination? Making out that it matters?" Alicja asked.

Debbie laughed. *Hers is a different generation*, she thought. *It's me who's hung up on it.*

"It might crop up, that's all."

Alicja nodded.

"Well thank you for telling me," she said. "You treat me like an adult, Debbie, not a child. It's the difference between you and Mum." As she said this, she picked up her binoculars to indicate they didn't need to say anything else. Debbie squeezed her arm, deciding that by the time Alicja reached eighteen, she would probably know far more about how the world worked than she herself had done at forty.

~ ~ ~

Until Stella rang to invite her over for a girls' night out, Jane hadn't anticipated she might have to disclose to her close friends that she was going on holiday with Richard. The evening proposed was the night before Jane was due to travel, so it was impossible for her to accept the offer to stay overnight at Stella's. She could lie, she supposed, and pretend she was holidaying with another of her girlfriends. But such lies often came home to roost in these days of social media, so she determined on the path of truth.

She and Richard had patched up their quarrel 'over nothing' – as Richard referred to it, waving their words aside, seeming gracious. She had called him the following evening, apologising. He said post-mortems were very rarely helpful so they should move on and look forward to Florence. She didn't tell him that it had been Larry's birthday that Friday. However liberal their relationship, it did not feel comfortable confiding in one lover how much she missed another. And for a man who imbued such passion in lumps of bronze or stone, his disinterest in the emotions which sprang from an actual human heart were puzzling. So, apart from her brief apology, Jane kept her counsel.

"I can't make that night, I'm afraid," she said to Stella.

"Oh, that's such a shame. We decided on that night as I know you work Thursday through to Saturday. A bit presumptuous of me. Sorry."

Jane was keen to reassure her.

"No, that was really thoughtful of you all. I appreciate it."

Since it was a re-run of her conversation with Michael, she felt she should be well practised by now in telling people she had another life besides the one which most had allotted to her.

"I'm going away the following morning, so it won't be practical."

"I see. A work thing?" asked Stella, before Jane could move the conversation on swiftly to setting another date.

"No, it's not, actually. I'm, er, going on a short trip. To Italy. Florence."

"Oh, that's nice. Such a lovely time of the year to be going there. Who are you going with?"

Stella's antennae were twitching: the hesitancy, the lack of detail. It pointed in one direction only. Stella waited for the big reveal. *Who?*

"I'm going with a friend, a male friend. He's a lecturer. A renaissance scholar, to be precise. Which is what he'd want me to be. Being a precise sort of individual." Even to herself, Jane sounded mildly deranged.

"That sounds interesting," Stella said. The nervousness was very un-Jane like, she decided. It was obvious to Stella – as it would be to all those who knew her well – that Jane was spending a few romantic days away with a new lover. "Is it a working break for, sorry, what's his name?"

"Richard. Richard Marks. Yes, he's giving a couple of lectures. One on Savonarola and another on – I forget – some Florentine artist, famous in the Renaissance."

A bell sounded in Stella's exceptional memory. Aah, yes, *the note*. Perhaps Jane had forgotten that, back in February, she had read out the contents of Richard's note to her over the telephone, asking her opinion about whether she should respond. Stella could not have stated the cyclist's surname, but she did remember that he was called Richard. It was the same name as her elder brother.

"How did you meet him – or should I mind my own business?" asked Stella, laughing.

"I'll tell you sometime," said Jane.

"Well, I hope you have a wonderful time in that amazing city. Have you been before?" As soon as the question was uttered, Stella realised that it was an insensitive one. If Jane had been, her most likely companion would have been Larry.

"Yes. Way back. Look, perhaps we can all meet up another time? Should we set a provisional date now?"

"Let me liaise with the others first. You know what Jill's diary is like. Call me when you get back from Florence. I'll look forward to hearing all about it. And take care, Jane."

"I will, Stella. You too. Thanks for calling."

In the minutes which followed their conversation, Stella attempted to project herself into Jane's shoes. Alone, grieving, without her beloved Bob snoring contentedly beside her, his absence reflected in the big dip in the memory foam mattress: his numerous suits hanging in the wardrobe, his wig and gown. Would glimpsing his expressions in the boys from time to time bring comfort or torture. Or both? She could not imagine being able to control her grief sufficiently to find solace in the arms of a stranger. Grief, so far as she had experienced, didn't operate like a tap to be switched on and off at will. It wasn't like the tide either, subject to a timetable. *Hold on, I'll just check when it's likely to strike again.* You were never sure when it might capture you in its suffocating embrace, inflict its blows with such ferocity that you wondered how anyone survived it without being permanently disfigured. You feared for your sanity. Like Hamlet. *Mad with grief.*

Thus, if grief were a type of madness, was that the context in which she should place Jane's new relationship? Had Jane and Richard become lovers on meeting, she calculated, then Larry had been dead for only a few weeks. How was Jane able to engage in such intimacy without being reminded, as forcibly as must be possible, of the person she had lost?

Stella's thoughts spilled out that evening. She unloaded them onto Bob as they were finishing dinner, their offspring having made their excuses and scarpered. The boys had wolfed down their chicken and mountains of chips in eight minutes flat, grabbing apples as they departed, more to pacify their mother than because they intended to eat them. Stella would find the fruit days later – after seeking out the provenance of a smell of something rotting – chucked into a wastepaper basket.

"I don't want to be judgmental," she said, having recounted her conversation with Jane.

"But you're going to be," interjected Bob. He hadn't known about the note from the cyclist. Jane had sworn Stella to secrecy over it. But now, since she was – in her mind, anyway – only speculating over the identity of Jane's lover, she felt able to mention it to Bob, finishing off her account by commenting that while Jane had sought her advice, quite clearly she hadn't taken it.

"I'm just sort of shocked I suppose. She's in bed with another man in a matter of weeks following dear Larry's death. Who does that?"

"She's looking for comfort, probably. I'm sure honouring the dead still has some application in today's times. But he's not a fallen soldier who gave up his life for the sake of the nation. His death was a tragic accident. I don't think it means she loved him any the less because she's able to have sex with a stranger."

"Could you do it?"

They looked at one another and laughed.

"It would depend on the circumstances," chortled Bob.

"A lawyer's answer!"

"Would you have felt the same sense of shock if it had been widower Larry rather than widow Jane?"

"I don't know," Stella replied, getting up to clear the table. "But, somehow, I don't think Larry would have wanted anyone else after Jane – well, not for a long time, anyway."

"Wanting sex and wanting a relationship are not the same thing, are they?"

"No, granted. But Jane's going on holiday with this man. That's a relationship, surely? I can understand the odd fling for the purposes of sex. But forming an actual relationship so quickly?" Stella shook her head. "No, I'm not sure I can understand it at all, if I'm honest."

"Grief does strange things to people."

Stella patted Bob on the head as she went past him, carrying a tray of plates and glasses into the kitchen.

"Yes, that can be the only explanation."

"Why on earth don't you make the boys take their plates out and put them in the dishwasher?" he called after her, taking advantage of her brief absence from the room to top up his wine glass.

CHAPTER 21

Where the hell was he?

Terminal 3 was heaving.

The run to Heathrow had taken them much less time than they'd anticipated and depositing Jane's car in the long-term carpark had also been a surprisingly smooth process. Having breezed through security without having to endure the body scanner, there was now over two hours to kill before their plane to Bologna departed at 2.05pm.

"Let's have an early lunch," said Jane, anxious to sit down. Her shoulder was already aching. Richard had insisted that they carry hand luggage only so that there would no hanging around at the other end, waiting by the bag collection conveyer belt. He was not a traveller, Jane decided. True travellers relished the journey as much as the destination and planned their trips accordingly. Assuming they survived the next six nights together, it was unlikely that he'd be drawn to a few days on the Trans-Siberian express or take the long route to Spain on a car ferry. She'd always been attracted to going to New York by cruise liner, approaching that iconic skyline from the sea. If she ever did embark on such a voyage, it was quite clear to her that it would be with someone other than Richard Marks – or alone.

Throughout their lunch at a Starbucks outlet, Richard sat studying his laptop, barely speaking. Occasionally, he would look up to glance at the departures board.

"Are you rehearsing your lecture for tomorrow?" she asked.

He nodded.

"Then I'll leave you to it and wander around the shops."

"What are you after?" he asked.

Jane raised an eyebrow at him.

"Maybe a lipstick. I just want to stretch my legs, really. Can you watch my bag?"

"Of course. Keep an eye on the time."

Their flight was delayed. She heard an announcement from British Airways as she was leafing through an interior design magazine in WH Smith. She scurried back to find an elderly couple now sitting at their table, sipping tea and buttering scones.

There was a message on her phone – *I've moved over to the general seating area – to the left of Starbucks as you face it.*

She espied him in the middle of a row, their two bags at his feet. He looked exactly what he was: an academic. His black framed glasses were a clue to his internal workings – intense and focused on what to him was important, struggling to understand those for whom the generalities of living were sufficiently challenging. He wasn't warm or outgoing, perhaps the opposite of Larry. It made the relationship possible for her. For now, anyway. She didn't expect others to understand the effect of the distinction she made, having been sure that Stella had bitten her tongue when learning of the gender of her travelling companion. It was only later that Jane remembered she had told Stella of Richard's note. She recalled Stella's response too.

"I'd be wary of meeting up with him, Jane. He sounds a bit weird to me."

Stella was usually inclined to give people the benefit of the doubt so, at the time, Jane had decided she would heed her friend's advice. That was less than four months ago. Now they were sitting side by side in an airport; a couple.

Richard looked up as she approached. He didn't need to say anything; his irritation at the news of a delay radiated from him.

"Fucking typical!" he expostulated. "And, naturally, no information as to how long the delay might be. I'm going to the BA desk to see what I can find out." He got up as she sat down. "Watch the bags," he ordered as he strode off, making a beeline for some official looking person with a clipboard. After a brief exchange with the individual, he disappeared into the crowds which seemed to Jane to have swelled by another few hundred in just the short time they had been there. To shut out the sight of the sprawling human mass surrounding her, Jane closed her eyes. But its effect was simply to intensify the level of noise:

voices, laughter, crying children, announcements, the incessant clatter of suitcases being wheeled around the concourse.

The board had already been updated by the time Richard returned. The delay was around an hour – "Something to do with a fault on one of their aircraft," he explained.

"Shall we go for a drink?" suggested Jane. She'd noticed a champagne bar on her travels. It had looked very inviting.

"Not for me," said Richard. "But I can have something soft if you're desperate."

"I'm not desperate! I just thought it would be a nice thing to do while we wait. We are supposed to be on holiday, after all."

She squeezed his knee as an afterthought, hoping to adopt a playful pose.

"I'm not," Richard said, opening up his laptop.

Jane got up.

"Ok," she sighed. "I'll see you later."

At the champagne bar, she perched on a stool and ordered a glass from the chirpy bartender, who whizzed around with his bottle, topping up glasses as soon as they were emptied. He'd pause and watch as the glass was drained and put down and then await the punter's nod before going further. After a few minutes, the stool next to her was occupied by a middle-aged man, smartly dressed in an Armani suit and an open necked light pink silk shirt. Placing his designer man-bag on the bar in front of him, he turned briefly to acknowledge Jane. She knew before he spoke that he was European, probably Italian. She could tell from his exquisite two-toned leather shoes. British men were, largely, a scruffy lot. Their choice of shoe often proclaimed their nationality.

As he sighed, audibly and happily, on taking his first sip of champagne, Jane smiled at him.

"Just what you needed?" she enquired.

"As they say, just what the doctor ordered!" he said, in a deep accented voice. She was suddenly reminded of Alex. She'd found his voice mellifluous. Would she ever hear it again, she wondered, nodding at the barman as he flashed by with his bottle expertly held in a white linen napkin?

They chatted about their respective trips. The Italian was returning to his home in Rome. He managed a chain of classy restaurants in the major cities in Italy and had been investigating the prospect of expanding into London. '*Mayfair or Chelsea*'. Jane was given his card and recommended a restaurant in Florence. "Mention me," he said. "You will get a better table overlooking the rooftops, by the fountains. You will not eat in a more beautiful place, trust me."

Jane was too cultured to enquire about the prices, but, since the man reeked of wealth – with a chunky gold bracelet on one wrist and a Rolex on the other – she doubted she and Richard would follow up his suggestion.

Halfway down her second glass, she felt someone's hands on her shoulders. Richard was standing behind her, their bags at his feet.

"We're being called," he said, with a nod to the departure board. He glanced at the handsome stranger sitting next to her, his hands remaining firmly in their proprietorial position on Jane. She rose, picking up her bar bill, her eyes searching for the barman.

The Italian took the bill from her, their hands brushing against one another as he did so.

"Allow me," he said. "It has been my great pleasure to meet you."

"Are you sure? That's so kind of you. Thank you," she said. Richard gave the man a cursory nod.

On their way to the gate, she was handed her bag.

"What a creep," he said, plucking his passport and boarding card from his jacket pocket.

"A charming one, though," said Jane. "And very rich, too."

Richard speeded up, almost tripping as he stepped onto the travellator.

"Be careful," said Jane, laughing. "You wouldn't think it was me who'd been at the booze!"

Richard ignored the remark, pointing out a poster for some exhibition currently on at the *Bargello* Gallery in Florence.

On the plane, when Richard nodded off, looking uncharacteristically vulnerable with his mouth a little open and his glasses askew, Jane retrieved the Italian's card from the pocket of her jacket. *Alonzo Sterlini*. There was an email and a mobile number for him together with a little painting of a building in Rome which she imagined was one of his restaurants. She placed the card in a pocket of her purse. She knew it would probably remain there for many years, tucked discreetly away between her debit and credit cards. But there had been something faintly glamorous about her encounter with the suave Mr Sterlini which, on bleak grey days back home, she might just wish to recall.

~ ~ ~

Somewhat later than had been originally agreed, the owner was outside the building, patiently awaiting their arrival. A woman of indeterminate age due to the amount of foundation caked over her face and neck, her large, hooped earrings glittered and shook as she spoke rapidly about where to leave the keys when they left and which night to put out their rubbish. She took screenshots of their passports, extracted the city tax from them and then, saying she had other guests to greet and was now late, left them abruptly.

Lots of holiday rentals, Jane commented to Richard, do not match the description promoted by their websites. If the gallery is peppered with photographs of vases of flowers, toiletries or bales of white fluffy towels, it usually means the owner is trying to compensate for something; the tatty kitchen, the four flights of exceptionally narrow stairs up which the tourist has to lug their luggage – there being no lift. But the apartment just off the *Piazza della Santissima Annunziata* charmed Jane on first sight. The walls were colour washed in varying shades of terracotta and there was an old and interesting wooden ceiling in the living room. On the small balcony there were pots of lavender and baskets of herbs. The black and white marble shower room looked recently installed.

"Wow, it's beautiful!" exclaimed Jane, dashing from room to room, before opening the French doors onto the balcony. The scent of mint from one of the herb baskets wafted over her as she stood admiring the view of red-tiled rooftops.

"Pity it doesn't get the sun at this time of the evening," said Richard from behind her. "And what are they growing in those pots? Cannabis?"

"I suppose we should unpack and look for somewhere for dinner," she said.

Richard took out his mobile.

"Look, I've just got a message from Antonio, the guy running the course, and he wants to meet me – us – for a drink in about half an hour to discuss tomorrow's lecture. We can go on to dinner after that."

"Right," said Jane, the prospect of the romantic evening she had envisaged in one of the nearby piazzas nearby rapidly disappearing. "It's half seven now. So it'll be a late meal. How long will you be? Any idea?"

"No, not really. Why?"

"Well, I'll wander around on my own and you can text me when you're free."

"You're not coming, then?"

"No. You don't want me hanging around. It's fine. Don't worry."

Richard, she noted, did not protest.

"Ok, I'll just have a quick shower and I'll be off. Don't get lost, will you?"

"No, daddy."

Richard looked at her, scratching his chin. She could tell he had already departed in his mind, no doubt thinking of some aspect of Savonarola he'd forgotten to cover.

Twenty minutes later, she was alone, sitting on the balcony looking out over the buildings, trying to identify a church she could see in the distance. There were some guidebooks in the apartment together with a large tome entitled 'The Art of Florence' and a couple of maps of the city. Spreading one of them out over a little tiled table, she proceeded to orientate herself. Richard said he always relied on Google maps for directions and, thus, there was no necessity to cart round the printed variety. Your mobile was all you needed. Jane wasn't sure she entirely agreed. The map in front of her provided a splendid overall view of the centre of Florence. She could see the main buildings and attractions in relation to each other and to their apartment.

Although Jane had planned to walk down the *Via dei Servi* to the *Duomo*, she didn't reach that destination – not on that day anyway. Stopping in the nearby Piazza to admire the statue of *Duke Fernando 1*, a party of tourists exited the *Chiesa di Santa Maria Della Scala* chattering excitedly. On a whim she decided to take a look inside. It would be something to impress Richard with when they chatted over dinner. And she wasn't to be disappointed. Like an over rich cake dripping with icing and decorated excessively, it was a place stuffed with treasures: frescoes, paintings and sculptures. Jane's neck ached after gazing up at the ornate golden ceiling for so long and, within minutes, she had decided that if the church was all she saw during her visit to the city, it would be enough. And Richard would be bound to already know the *Pieta* sculpture – Joseph and the dead or dying Jesus – by *Baccio Bandinelli*. She later discovered that Bandinelli portrayed himself in the figure of Joseph of Arimathea. Apparently, he had a penchant for inserting his 'likeness' into his artistic works. It was one way, she supposed, of securing his legacy.

After an hour in the church and a few minutes walking in the cloisters of the nearby 'hospital of innocents', she was sure that Richard's meeting would have ended and he would be ready to meet up. But there was no message on her phone and her text to him remained unanswered. Since it was now past nine o'clock, and dark, Jane made her way back to the apartment in case he'd returned and was waiting for her there, his irritation growing as the minutes clicked by and his hunger intensified.

The heavy wooden door clanged behind her as she entered the vestibule to the apartment block. Momentarily it was pitch black and she spent a panicky few seconds trying to locate the light switch. Walking past the other flats, there were no strips of light coming from underneath the doors and no voices. The place seemed eerily absent of life. The landing lights throughout the building snapped off just as she reached the door to their apartment. By then, she was certain that Richard was not inside.

Where the hell was he?

CHAPTER 22

Flotsam and jetsam

One can chart a life from a particular event; seeing it as belonging to *before* or *after*.

Jane knew this following Larry's death the previous year. And so it was that Richard's 'disappearance' that May in Florence turned out to be yet one more such 'particular' event in Jane's life. It seemed deplorable ill-fortune for it to happen so speedily following her last tragedy, confirming for certain not only the unpredictability of life – save for it being predictably unpredictable – but how little control we have over our own happiness. Like flotsam and jetsam, we are tossed around in the choppy cruel sea of existence, so much more dependent on the elements than we are on our ability to swim or build sea-worthy vessels – even though we are intent on telling ourselves otherwise.

Of course, on that first night, Jane had no idea that she was on the cusp of one more particular life event. By midnight, she'd decided Richard had had an accident and must be in a hospital somewhere.

Unable to sleep, she got up at 3am to look for any coffee or tea which might have been left by the previous tenants. There was none. All she found was a bottle of white wine in the fridge. She hadn't eaten properly since the airport but at least had stowed away the two packets of nuts offered to them on the plane. Intending to have a glass of wine with them, in an effort to relax, she couldn't find a corkscrew. The nuts were horribly salted and mixed with the adrenalin accumulating in her system – which she seemed powerless to control – she became nauseous. Richard's small wheelie remained where he'd left it in the bedroom. He hadn't unpacked it but the leather shoulder bag, in which he carried all his work and work-related documents, he'd taken with him. His iPad wasn't in the apartment either; no doubt he'd needed it in his meeting with whomever he'd gone out to see. Had he arrived there? How could she find out?

She hadn't listened properly to him. She wasn't even sure if she could remember the name of the academic institution he was speaking at, let alone recall the name of the person he'd taken the call from the previous evening. But she knew it should be relatively easy to find out and, after she'd gulped down a couple of tumblers of water, she managed to calm herself and think logically of what she should do if, come the dawn, he had still not materialised.

She went back to bed, curling up in a ball and pulling the bedclothes over her head, telling herself that he'd be back. That he'd got drunk and passed out on someone's sofa on the other side of Florence, intoxicated not just with the wine but by being with people who held the same passions as he did and were equally knowledgeable. People who were happy to listen to his interpretation of '*Savonarola's doctrine on salvation*'.

But that wasn't the Richard she'd known during their short time together. Even if he was selfish and prone to allowing his obsessions to dictate his actions, he wouldn't have left her alone on their first night in Florence. Or would he?

Perhaps she didn't know very much at all about Richard Marks and was about to find out. But despite this train of thought, and the lack of consolation it brought, eventually an exhausted Jane fell asleep.

~ ~ ~

At 8am, awakened by bells summoning the faithful and the not-so-faithful, Jane was on the phone to the lady who'd greeted them at the apartment. Although Signora Greco's English was good, she still had to ask Jane to 'please speak slowly, Signora'. Jane started again on her account of the last twelve hours and Richard's extraordinary disappearance. There was silence from the other end of the phone when she eventually came to a stop, such that Jane wondered if they'd been cut off. Evidently, this scenario was a new one for the landlady. She was more accustomed to lost keys and passports, food poisoning and mosquito bites, missed planes and water shortages. But missing people? Never before.

"Hello?" enquired Jane, a tone of irritation in her question.

"I will come to see you," Signora Greco replied crisply. "I arrive in one hour. At the apartment. If Signor Marks turns up before then, you will let me know, yes?"

"Of course," breathed Jane, relief flooding over her. "Thank you so much. That's very kind."

Jane had already explained that she didn't have the details of where Richard had gone to the previous evening and nor, to her embarrassment, did she know where he was supposed to be delivering his lecture that afternoon. She knew there were two possible topics – Savonarola or Masaccio. She'd conducted a brief search on google – *lecture on Savonarola in Florence by Richard Marks* – just before she made the call that morning but it had revealed nothing. She presumed it needed to be done in Italian and, so, she decided to wait for Signora Greco's visit before trying again. In the little time she had in the meantime, she'd go out for coffee and something to eat.

It was a perfect morning; the coloured stones of the ancient city highlighted in the spring sunshine. In the *Piazza Filippo Brunelleschi* she picked up a black coffee together with a cheese and prosciutto panini, devouring the panini with a hunger she'd rarely experienced. Enviously, she looked around at the other tourists, strolling the cobbled streets, clutching their cameras and phones. And then, in one corner of the square, at the entrance to a building – which turned out to be the Humanities department of the city's university – was a billboard advertising that afternoon's lecture. *Savonarola: Ascetic, puritan and heretic.*

Knowing she was likely to be late for her meeting with the Signora, she ventured inside the building. There were lots of students milling around, the noise from their laughter and chatter almost overwhelming. Without the language, she had no idea where to start with her enquiries. But seeing a sign to an office – *Ufficio* – she headed in that direction. There was a long queue and there appeared to be only one official behind the desk. While waiting, she sent a text to the Signora letting her know that she'd established some information regarding where

Richard might have gone to for his meeting and she was likely to be half an hour late. Her message was answered immediately; Signora Greco would not set off until she heard further from Jane.

The bespectacled young lady behind the desk spoke reasonable English. Her brow furrowed with concern as she absorbed Jane's account of Richard's disappearance.

"One moment please, Signora," she said, before scurrying off into the back office where she had an animated conversation with someone in her native tongue. Then a side door opened and Jane was ushered into their inner sanctum. A man in his fifties pulled out a chair for her and then sat down himself, his pen poised over a notepad.

"I am so sorry to hear about this," he said, before asking for her details and then Richard's. He scribbled it all down on the back of a prospectus and then, apologising again, said he'd make some enquiries and return as soon as he could. In his absence Jane tried to relax. Her relief was short-lived.

"Signora Hedgefield," he said, opening up a further button on his crisp white shirt.

Jane did not correct him. "Signor Marks did indeed make his meeting with Signor Antonio Fiore. I have spoken with him – Signor Fiore, that is," he added swiftly. "But your friend left around 21 hours and there has been no contact since. His phone, according to Signor Fiore, is – *e morta*."

This needed no translation. She swallowed down a little surge of panic induced by the word *morta*. Was this the fate not only of Richard's phone but of Richard also? Was he now wedged in the sludge at the bottom of the Arno, his limp body having been dragged to the river following a brutal mugging on his way back to the apartment?

"Are there many such disappearances in your city?" she asked.

The man blinked at her, not sure of her meaning. *And who could blame him*, she thought. Whether the answer was in the affirmative or otherwise, it was unlikely to be consoling – let alone helpful.

"I think we need the police to be contacted," he said, attempting to put some authority into his tone. "He must be reported as a person missing."

She rearranged the syntax. "A missing person?" He nodded and then leapt up. He disappeared again for a few moments, returning with a glass of water which he handed to her, accompanied by a brief but warm smile.

"And I cancel his lecture," he added, nodding as she gulped down the water.

"Will *you* call the police for me?" she asked. Something had occurred to her. Hadn't the previous incumbent in Richard's position died suddenly? She recalled asking Richard the cause of his death. No reply had been forthcoming. Coincidence – or was there some disaffected psychopathic student on the loose? Despite her wish to remain calm in front of this stranger, in this even stranger place, her voice wavered and tears filled her eyes. *Please dear God*, she said internally, *please let this fucking nightmare be over*. Before she could give voice to this uncomfortable train of thought, the man, whose name she had still yet to establish, patted her hand.

"Please Mrs Hedgefield, do not upset yourself. Yet."

In the space between them, the word 'yet' hovered like a wasp about to sting.

CHAPTER 23

How do I say this?

The visit Alicja had made to the refuge with Matthew could have represented a turning point for mother and daughter. They started to message each other, guardedly at first, their uncertainty reflected in the formality of their exchanges. Halina seemed more respectful of her daughter, realising perhaps that unless she changed, she could easily lose her. Having both Matthew and Debbie, Alicja was no longer dependent on her. She now saw that it was she, Halina, who would suffer more the loss of their relationship – lose that bright, happy girl, on the cusp of blossoming into someone special. Might they even become friends, she wondered?

She recalled the pride Matthew had shown when speaking about his mother's job in the hospital. It contrasted wildly with the path she herself had chosen and it was difficult not to feel some shame. Had Alicja told him? She'd had her reasons at the start – although she could not imagine divulging them. The exposure would risk breaching the barriers she'd spent so much of her adult life constructing.

After Matthew and Alicja had left that day, watching them walking down the driveway, hand in hand, she'd returned to her room and wept. Their obvious pleasure in each other's company had underlined her own isolation. Trust remaining an issue, Halina didn't go so far as to reach out for help but there was a shift within her. A shift but, it transpired, not a gear change as when Alicja messaged her one morning to ask if she wanted to meet up for coffee, instead of accepting the invitation gracefully, she enquired as to her daughter's motivation.

For any particular reason? Did that lady you live with suggest this?

Alicja was with Matthew when the text came in. They were sitting in her bedroom, side by side on her bed, trying to decide what to do with their Saturday afternoon. A sky heavy with dark clouds suggested rain was on its way. Their combined cash amounted to £6.52p. Options were limited.

"The lady I live with!" Alicja expostulated, her face flushing with fury. "I bet she knows her name. She's just being her usual awkward self. I don't know why I bother."

"Oh, cut her some slack," said Matthew who, while not being privy to the conversation, just knew from Alicja's response that she was referring to her mother.

"Why? Why should I? I'm the one who's suffered in all this. Losing my home because of her stupid, selfish actions!"

"She's insecure. Proud too, probably. After all, she's the mother and you're the one acting with some maturity."

It was a clever remark, diffusing some of Alicja's anger while complimenting her at the same time. Initially it worked. Alicja stared at her phone, her lips drawn tightly as she pondered her response. Matthew suddenly pushed her down on the bed and kissed her passionately on the lips.

"This doesn't cost anything," he said, grinning. "Put your bloody phone away for an hour. Let her stew."

Alicja struggled back up.

"I can't concentrate," she said, "until I've answered her."

"You don't need to concentrate," said Matthew, his hands now clasped behind his head, knowing he had to exercise some patience. He let out a heartfelt sigh of disappointment.

Alicja glanced at him and smiled.

"Just one minute."

She stared back down at her phone and then started to type quickly with her thumbs.

"What have you said?" asked Matthew, more to affect interest rather than because he had a burning desire to know.

"This - her name is Debbie. And she didn't suggest anything. It was my idea but no big deal if you're too busy. Have a nice day."

"Right," said Matthew, pulling at Alicja's arm and trying to get her mobile out of her hand.

"No wait. I just want to say something else to her."

She started typing again, smiling as she did so.

"Go on then. Tell me."

Alicja placed her phone on the bedside table carefully and lay down next to him.

"I just told her that Debbie is gay, that's all. And how much I like her. *Really, really* like her! Should freak her out a bit."

Matthew laughed.

"She'll think we're in a threesome and be on the phone to social services if you're not careful. Hope you haven't shot yourself in the foot."

"I'm willing to risk it," said Alicja, jumping up again and going over to the window to look out over the reserve.

"Shall we go for a walk later?"

"Later, sure," said Matthew who could not fathom why anyone would go for a walk just for the sake of it rather than for a specific purpose. "So long as it's not pissing it down."

"You can stay for dinner too. Debbie is always happy to see you. She told me."

"Come here," said Matthew.

The first drops of rain sounded as if someone was throwing handfuls of tiny pebbles at the window. Alicja remained where she was, suddenly transfixed by the sight of the wind rolling over the wetlands, moving through the reeds and grasses like an invisible army. She longed to be out in it.

"Looks like we're stuck in here for the rest of the day," said Matthew. "What a pity! I was looking forward to a ramble."

Sheet lightning illuminated Alicja's silhouette against the darkening sky, followed immediately by a crack of thunder which made them both jump.

"It's overhead, Al. Move away from the window, for fuck's sake," ordered Matthew.

"No I won't. The view is spectacular, Matt. Come and look."

Matthew rolled off the bed and came to stand next to her. Their arms around each other, they stood in companiable silence and watched as the storm gathered force outside.

"It's better than a movie," said Alicja, as she took his hand and led him back to the bed.

~ ~ ~

Jane spent most of the day in the office at the University with Benito, who had eventually got round to introducing himself. He made several calls to the police, intermittently putting his hand over the receiver to ask her further questions about Richard. Had she a recent photograph? What was the address of their apartment? Who was the agency they'd booked with? Did she have a copy of his passport?

At around lunchtime, Benito went to the café and brought back a selection of sandwiches together with small cups of coffee so strong that Jane's few sips induced immediate heart palpitations. Seeing her pale face, Benito suggested she take a walk 'in the air, to clear your head and no worry, Mrs Hedgefield, I will still be here when you return.'

Outside, back in the Piazza, Jane struggled to calm her breathing. With their chatter and laughter, the lunchtime crowds milling around her served only to intensify her feeling of isolation. Her palms damp with perspiration, she dialled Stella's number. She'd thought about calling her parents before she remembered she'd not actually told them about her trip – or about Richard, for that matter. The explanations would take up time; time which would be unnecessarily spent. Stella at least knew where she was and was bound to offer some practical advice.

"You need to go to the British Consulate," said Stella. Tears filled Jane's eyes as she listened to the comforting sound of Stella's voice. "You can't navigate the whole Italian system on your own. That's what they're there for. This Benito chap sounds great but the Consulate will have dealt with these situations before. And they'll have the contacts which Benito might not. I'll look it up and call you back. Ok?"

"That would be great, Stella, thanks."

"Hang on in there, darling. I'll be right back to you."

She'd expected Stella to be back to her after a few minutes but when ten minutes had passed, Jane decided to go back in and find Benito. He was on the phone and looking even more harassed than he had done throughout their brief time together. Tiny beads of sweat had appeared at his hairline. He gestured that she should take a seat while he finished his call. The Italian so rapid, she could follow nothing of his conversation with whoever he was talking to. At one point, he grabbed a pen and scribbled down an address, nodding vigorously.

While he talked, Jane looked around the room. Along the walls, there were various prints of buildings in Florence. She hadn't felt particularly excited about the prospect of the trip, accepting Richard's invitation because she thought a change of scene with him might offer something lacking in their relationship to date: *fun*. But now, the thought of not being able to explore the city's cultural treasures acquired a loss of significant proportions. And forever, the city would be tainted for her; the Duomo, Michelangelo's *David*, the Ponte Vecchio bridge would always be associated with this shocking time – not knowing if he was dead or alive.

Her phone buzzed and Stella's name flashed up. Before she could answer, Benito placed the receiver down and sat back in his chair, running his hands through his hair, gathering his thoughts. *How do I say this?*

"Signora. I have just spoken to someone at the ... It appears -"

Gripping the side of the desk, Jane was certain he was about to deliver the news that Richard's body had been found. Benito glanced from the pulsating vein in Jane's neck to her large eyes, reddened from lack of sleep.

"Signor Marks has been kidnapped."

A look of incredulity spread over Jane's face.

"Kidnapped," she repeated. "*Richard*? Why for God's sake? Where is he? Do they know if he's...."

Benito held up his hand to stop the inevitable questions which Jane was now firing at him.

"I know very little. They – the carabiniere want to speak to you – they're sending a car here. They suggested you went there in a taxi but I said this was, well, not appropriate. You are in shock. So – any moment they will be here."

"Where am I going?"

"Let's wait outside."

Jane stood up, putting her phone in her bag even though it continued to vibrate. Benito ushered her to the door and she followed him down a corridor and then turned left instead of right as she had done so previously to exit the building.

"We're going out the back way," he said, by way of explanation. For a brief moment, she wondered if she too were about to be kidnapped. But seeing the back of his head and the manner in which he nodded at colleagues as he passed them, she banished the idea. She heard the police car before they emerged onto a side street at the back of the university. Inside were two uniformed Carabinieri, alongside a plain clothes man who leapt out as soon as the vehicle came to a screeching stop.

After a brief exchange of words with Benito, the man, young, swarthy and, Jane sensed, exuding some excitement at the unusual challenge presented to him that morning ushered her into the back of the car. Jane gave Benito a brief wave, realising immediately that she hadn't even thanked him for the kindness he'd shown to her during the course of the last few painful hours, and then, tyres squealing, blue light flashing, siren wailing, they were off. She turned briefly as they waited a few seconds at the junction before emerging into the traffic but he was already gone.

The carabinieri sitting next to her completed a full, visual, examination of her before turning to stare out of the window for most of the journey. It was clear that the young man was in charge. He turned round from where he sat in the passenger seat to introduce himself. He was from the Special Operations Unit, he said, in heavily accented English. *Luca Pavesi*. Jane was finding it difficult to focus. The lurching of the car, as they weaved their way through lines of traffic in dramatic movie-style manner, was making her feel sick. He added a few more details which, given her nauseous condition, Jane did not absorb. She concentrated on staring straight ahead, keeping her eyes on the road in order to still the waves of nausea which rose to her throat from her churning insides.

When they came to a stop outside a building which looked nothing like a police station, Jane tried to open the door, desperate not to lose all dignity by splattering the occupants of the car with the foul-smelling vomit which, having pulsed its way through her system, now resided in her throat. But the door was locked. Clamping her hand over her mouth with one hand, she pulled at the handle with the other. A viscous liquid oozed through her fingers and then there was click and she was able to vomit the entire contents of her stomach into the gutter which, fortuitously, they had drawn alongside.

As sure as she could be that her body's revolt was now over, she stood up, wiping her mouth with a tissue handed to her by the silent officer with whom she'd shared the back seat. He had already left the vehicle and was standing beside her, a look of genuine concern on his face. He muttered some words of Italian and then retrieved her handbag from the car, offering it to her. He hadn't spoken to her because he doesn't speak English, she decided, not because he's an unfeeling man.

Jane smiled weakly at him.

"Let us go inside," said Pavesi. "Get you some water. We have a room where you can rest."

Inside the station, she was taken past the reception desk and introduced to a woman officer who, on receipt of instructions from Pavesi, took her to a suite of rooms where there was a shower and a couple of sofas. She was given a towel and a jug of water together with a glass and then, almost abruptly, left alone to recover.

She sat down heavily on the brown leather sofa and took her shoes off. Her phone vibrated again but she didn't answer it, sending Stella a quick text to say that she was with the police and would get back to her as soon as she could.

It was a long and lonely hour before the same woman officer returned to collect her. Jane had peered into the shower cubicle, wondering whether to strip off and enjoy the experience while she could but then, overtaken by a combination of exhaustion and apathy, she found herself back on the sofa – like a robot returning to its docking station.

At one minute past five, the female officer returned, unsmiling, straight-backed, behaving as if Jane were a suspect in a criminal matter rather than someone caught up in a nightmare scenario not of her own making. Trailing behind her warder, she wanted to hiss at her – *Excuse me, Signora, I happen to be the victim's partner.* Instead, she followed meekly, contemplating her description of her relationship with Richard. 'Partner' suggested something of length and durability; commitment. *Love.* And much as the thought of

Richard suffering and afraid was horrible, she knew she didn't love him.

Luca Pavesi was waiting for her in a small, dark room. Both uniformed officers remained with him, leaning against the walls, their weapons apparent on their belts. He did not stand himself when she was delivered into the room, merely beckoned to her to sit at the opposite end of a long table.

"You are not married to Mr Marks?"

"No. We haven't..." Jane stuttered over her words, shifting in her seat, embarrassed, as if she were facing Savonarola himself questioning her moral laxity. "We haven't known each other that long."

"How long?"

"Since, well, February of this year."

Pavesi nodded.

"How did you meet?"

"Look," said Jane. "I really don't mean to be awkward but what is happening? The man from the University said that Richard had been kidnapped. Please, *please*, let me know what is going on."

Pavesi held up his hand.

"I will explain. I promise. But first, just some background information."

"But why is it relevant?" Jane persisted.

She knew it wasn't wise to display such irritation but she distrusted this line of questioning. Wasn't time of the essence here? Pavesi replied swiftly.

"In this situation, I assure you it is."

There was a brief pause in their conversation while they eyed one another. Jane knew she was defeated.

"I'm sorry," she said. "I'm just anxious."

"I understand," he replied, flashing her a brief, if insincere, smile.

"We live near one another," she explained.

"A dating app?"

Jane shook her head. *For God's sake.*

"He was involved in a road accident with my late husband... so we met in, well, unfortunate circumstances."

If the man was after salacious detail, hopefully he would now be satisfied.

"I am sorry. When did this accident happen?"

Jane provided the date, sent back, suddenly, to the scene outside in the drive. The dense fog. As far away as possible from here, in sultry Florence, with its colour and light.

She studied Pavesi's expression on receipt of this information.

Yes, that's right, just weeks after my husband's death did this man became my lover.

He sat back, then picked up a lighter that was sitting on the cigarettes in front of him, switching it on and off a few times, shaking it when it didn't light immediately. Jane suppressed a smile. His actions were copied from a hundred films in which hard-nosed, stressed detectives contemplated their next move.

Jane provided the date. New Year's Day.

"This year?" asked Pavesi. His eyebrows raised a fraction when she nodded.

A rap on the door interrupted them. One of the uniformed officers answered it and, within seconds, Pavesi had left the room, swiping up his cigarettes and lighter as he did so.

"I will be back," he shouted as he slammed the door behind him.

Jane looked at the two men in turn, hoping for some enlightenment.

It was a vain hope.

CHAPTER 24

'He is worth nothing dead'

In the two weeks before Halina had an excuse to contact her daughter, there was something resembling a stand-off between the two. Alicja was hurt that Halina had reacted so defensively to her offer of meeting up over a coffee. In turn, Halina had not been taken in by Alicja's bait regarding Debbie's sexuality. She knew her daughter was trying to goad her and she retaliated by remaining silent and refusing to *be* goaded.

But then Halina received an offer of rehousing. Her original request for a two bedroomed apartment, much to her surprise, was honoured. The housing department did not appear to have liaised with Social Services so, as far as her housing officer was concerned, Alicja was still with her. Halina, no innocent when it came to the workings of the system, decided that she should accept the offer immediately and face any consequences once she was in occupation. On looking through the details of the flat – not in the best of areas, and not as large as her previous one – she declared she was happy to accept without seeing it. The money side of matters was much less straightforward. It involved a swallowing of pride, two meetings with a kind man from Citizen's Advice and several calls to the Department of Work and Pensions; several since one had been terminated as a result of Halina's inappropriate language and another because she'd hung up, irate at being asked to repeat various bits of personal information.

It wasn't the new flat, the escape from the Refuge, the beckoning of independence at last, which motivated Halina to contact Alicija. It was a job.

In the weeks since Alicja had deserted her, Halina, driven as much by boredom as by the need to have some money coming in, was now working shifts in a pub a few streets away from Debbie's deli. It was safer than her previous role in the sex industry, although, ironically, physically more demanding. On her feet, sometimes for what felt like most of the day, she would flop onto a seat on the bus on a Saturday evening and close her eyes. On more than one occasion she'd gone sailing past her stop and had to hobble back to the Refuge where, at almost midnight, the reception was an icy one.

When she complained to one of the residents about her aching arches, she was advised to 'ditch the heels, you silly sod.' This suggestion, kindly meant, resulted in a text to Alicja.

Hi darling I need some trainers. Where's cheapest? Xx

"I wonder what she's up to," Alicja commented to Matthew. "I doubt she'd taken up running."

Matthew said he didn't think it mattered. It was an 'olive branch'.

Alicja let out a cynical laugh.

"Oh yeah. She wants money, more like."

Intrigued, despite her cynicism, she texted her mother back and they arranged to meet up at a Costa in town that forthcoming Saturday morning. Separately, Matthew and Debbie hoped it was the beginning of some form of reconciliation, although each had the sense not to voice their optimism.

"I pay for these," said her mother as they approached the counter at the café. "I have a little bit of money now."

"Really?" Alicja responded, her heart rate increasing as she wrestled with the implications of the remark. Did this mean *The Bear* was back in her life? Halina laughed when she saw Alicja's expression.

"No need to worry darling. I've decided to become a respectable woman. Go and sit down. I have lots to tell you."

Over the next hour, Alicja learned of the new flat and the new job.

"It is very hard work," she told her daughter. "But it's regular. You and the boy can come and visit me there."

Alicja reminded her mother that neither of them had turned 16 and so were not legally allowed in a pub without being accompanied. But Halina waved her concerns away. "Who knows?" she said, with her familiar shrug of the shoulders.

"Mum!" exclaimed Alicja, but with a smile. "You'll lose your job with that attitude."

Halina turned, briefly cupping her daughter's face, before dropping her hands to her lap.

"You called me Mum," she said.

Alicja made a face at her.

"So? You are." It elicited the response she wanted. Halina laughed.

In the shop where, only a few months ago, Debbie had bought Alicja the black woollen coat, they found a pair of cheap trainers for Halina.

"I don't look stupid in these?" asked Halina, standing in front of Alicja awaiting her verdict on the blue and black trainers with their thick white soles.

"Are they comfortable?" asked Alicja. "That's the main thing."

Halina walked up and down a few times and then nodded.

"Like walking on air!" she said.

Before they parted for Halina to get to the pub to start her shift, they embraced and agreed to meet again the next weekend.

"I think we have some talking to do darling," Halina admitted.

"Yes, Mum," said Alicja. "It's about time we did."

~ ~ ~

Jane didn't have to wait long before Pavesi was back, startling the room's occupants as he burst through the door. He didn't sit down. He surveyed them all, theatrically. *He's a frustrated actor*, thought Jane, noting his splayed legs and folded arms.

In his rapid native tongue, he spoke to his comrades first. They looked shocked and one of them shook his head, assuming a grave expression. Then he turned to Jane.

"I have some new information. It is a case of – how do you say – of inaccurate identity. They have kidnapped Signor Marks instead of ….. well, a rich man, the head of a multinational organisation."

"So Richard *has* been kidnapped," said Jane. "And he's still alive?"

"He is worth nothing dead," replied Pavesi.

"Who is the man they wanted" asked Jane, ignoring the lack of sensitivity on the part of the detective.

"I cannot reveal his name at this moment. It is too sensitive." Pavesi accompanied this remark with a wave of his hand. "A ransom was requested late last night. Three million euros!" One of the officers whistled as the figure rang out. Jane glanced at him and he had the decency to look away. She wasn't sure why she'd chosen him on whom to vent her distaste at their collective excitement. Pavesi was setting the tone here.

"This man's family thought it was some joke as the initial contact came though just as he climbed into his bed. No-one answered at first but their landline rang and rang until his wife took the call. She didn't speak, she said. They were not interested in a discussion, just that they would ring again in the morning and then the usual threats about contacting the carabinieri."

Pavesi gave another rapid translation of this information to his colleagues.

"So what will you do? Surely they will let Richard go once they know they have the wrong man?"

Pavesi shrugged.

"I hope so, Signora. From you, I need a photograph of Signor Marks. So we can prove to the idiots they are mistaken!"

Jane scrabbled in her bag for her mobile. As she clutched it, aware of the three pairs of eyes observing her, a worrying thought occurred to her. She had no pictures on her phone of Richard. He wasn't a man who needed the camera to perpetually remind him of where or who he was – or who mattered to him. The only photograph of him in Italy – unless there was one at the University – was in the copy of his passport taken by their landlady. And that, probably, was small and grainy. And useless.

Jane explained the situation as best she could, summing up with the words that would haunt her.

"We haven't known each other that long, you see."

Pavesi's mouth twitched. He sighed.

"Then we have to contact his relatives in the UK and get them to send one urgently. He has relatives?"

Jane nodded.

Christ, the girls, she thought. *Phoebe and Cressie should be told as soon as possible.*

"He has children," she said, and then, hoping this might indicate that she was not the whore they now believed her to be, she added. "Two adult daughters. I've met them."

Yes, I met them when out with another man.

"Please contact them," said Pavesi. "Give them this email address. I should speak with them. Yes. It is important. There may be things they can tell me."

"Like what?" asked Jane, wondering how she could ever have found herself in such a ridiculous situation.

"They are *related* to him, Signora. Not …. friend…..like you."

"I don't have their numbers," said Jane, keen to get this admission over as soon as possible. "But I can get them. Just give me a few minutes."

Pavesi sighed.

"I leave you here to do this. I will be back in a while."

Issuing some instructions to his colleagues, Pavesi left the room, returning a few minutes later to pick up his cigarettes.

Jane's phone was low on battery and she indicated this to the officers, one of whom went off in search of a charger. In the meantime, Jane googled Phoebe's name and came across several sites, including Facebook. Although she used it little, Jane was at least familiar with its workings. She left a message on her wall as she did on Cressie's also. They're young, she thought. They're bound to keep an eye on such things. She left a message on another of Phoebe's pages before putting her phone down on the table. She visualised Richard, imagining him lying gagged and bound in a damp cellar. Images from a dozen films added details to this scenario.

It was only minutes before Jane's mobile rang. Plugged into the charger, she had to cross the room to answer it. Bending down awkwardly, an unknown number came up on her screen.

"Is that Jane? It's me, Phoebe Marks."

"Yes it's me, Phoebe. Thank you for coming back to me."

"What's wrong? What's happened to my Dad?" Her voice sounded strained.

Jane swallowed. She felt movement behind her. One of the officers had placed a chair near the socket so that she could sit and talk. She nodded her appreciation to him.

"There's no easy way to say this, Phoebe...."

She heard Phoebe give a sharp intake of breath. *Poor lamb*, she thought, *she thinks he's dead. And for all we know, he may be.*

"Your father has been kidnapped – that's what the police here think. I'm in the police station with well, God knows who, but I understand it's a case of mistaken identity. They've got the wrong man. The officer in charge – Signor Pavesi – wants a photo of him. And I don't have any and he wants to speak to you anyway. You're his next of kin."

"Oh my God!" shrieked Phoebe. Her voice, despite the fact the phone was not on speaker mode, was loud enough to be clearly audible in the room.

There was further conversation between them, Jane providing the answers to the questions being fired at her. Then they rang off, Phoebe begging her to get Pavesi to call her as soon as possible. But her phone rang again half a minute later.

"I'm coming out there," said Phoebe. "On the next available flight. And Cressie too, probably. I assume we can stay in the apartment you've rented."

She didn't wait for an answer.

CHAPTER 25

The over-heated plot of a depressingly bad drama

Once Jane had passed over Phoebe's number and details, Pavesi's interest in her diminished. She was told, instructed even, to return to her apartment and 'await developments.'

"There is nothing more you can do here," Pavesi informed her. "I will speak to Signor Marks' daughter. We will of course let you know if we .... discover anything…of significance."

"Do you know anything about how Richard is – anything at all?" Jane asked him, as she was ushered out of the room.

Pavesi shook his head but said nothing else, his lips drawn tightly together as if, having learned of the existence of Richard's blood relatives, he had little further obligation to Jane. He barked some orders to the two officers and then Jane was escorted out of the building to the police car she'd previously travelled in. Asking for her address, they drove her home, fortunately in a less frenetic manner than before, weaving though lines of taxis and bikes with the authority enjoyed by law enforcers throughout the world.

Despite her uneasiness at the manner in which she'd been dispatched by Pavesi, Jane's predominant emotion on letting herself into the apartment was one of relief. She could bathe, eat – once she'd bought some food – sleep and, above all else, be alone for a few hours. Solitude might help her absorb the awfulness of her situation.

An hour later, thirty minutes of which she sat on the balcony practising some relaxation techniques she recalled from her thirties, she was back out navigating the busy streets under a hot afternoon sun. She was searching for a supermarket where she could buy some provisions to see her, and possibly Phoebe and Cressie, through the next forty-eight hours. Finding one, she grabbed a basket and made her way swiftly through the various aisles, snatching wildly at products without formulating any particular plan for the meals to come. Three bottles of cheap white wine also saw their way into the basket which was so heavy by the time she came to the checkout, she struggled to lift it onto the counter. There were no bags and she was provided, somewhat grudgingly, with a square cardboard box in which to store her items. Staggering back to her apartment, knocking into the tourists who clogged the pavements and the office drinkers now assembling outside the various bars, she tried not to think of the image she undoubtedly conveyed; a batty English woman with a minor drink problem.

Jane's upper lip was slick with perspiration by the time she reached the door of her apartment. Dumping the box onto the step, she fumbled in her bag for a tissue. As she stood with her back against the peeling stucco wall of the building, dabbing at her face, the door miraculously opened and a middle-aged man emerged. Smartly dressed in beige slacks and an open necked, immaculately pressed, cotton, pale green shirt, he gave a short bow and held the door for her.

"Grazie," murmured Jane, bending down to collect her shopping.

"No, please, Signora!" he said, almost clashing heads with her as they vied with each other to pick up the box.

Jane had no strength to resist his gallantry. *What does it matter*, she decided, even as she suppressed a giggle seeing him struggle with the weight of the thing. *Bet he's thinking twice now.*

Once Jane had given him the flat number, they trudged silently – and slowly – up the stairs together.

In the apartment, Signor *Gallant* placed the box on the kitchen counter, looking around as he did so.

"You are here on your own, Signora?"

Jane looked at him, wondering how she could possibly answer the question. His brown eyes blinked back at her, seemingly confused as to why she appeared unable to answer.

"You're English?" he asked, eventually, having decided that perhaps he had guessed her nationality wrongly.

She nodded.

"Thank you for helping me," she gasped, suddenly overwhelmed with her predicament, the ill fortune which appeared to stalk her.

Signor Gallant looked shocked at the fat tear he observed rolling down the pink face of the lady he'd sought to assist.

"There is something terribly wrong," he said. It was spoken as a question.

Jane wiped the tear away hurriedly.

"I'm so sorry," she said. And then she forced a smile. "Your English is very good."

"I spent four years in London as a student."

"A student of what?"

"Art history. My final dissertation was on the Renaissance. I made many trips here and then, one year, I did not go back to Naples, my hometown. I stayed."

Jane struggled not to convey her thoughts in her expression. *Well, it would be, wouldn't it? It couldn't have been the works of D H Lawrence or economic theory. No, here stands before me Richard's ideal companion!*

"Look, I'm fine," she said. "I'm so grateful to you for carrying my groceries up all those stairs. I can eat now!"

He surveyed her. Not lasciviously. There was something honourable about this man, she decided.

"I'm Sylvano Bussotti," he said, holding out his hand. "Not the composer Bussotti, of course."

Jane took his hand hesitantly and introduced herself.

Sylvano gave a slight bow of his head.

"Well, Jane – why don't you join me for a drink in my apartment when you've unpacked all this," he said, gesturing towards the box. "I make an excellent cocktail. You can relax a little and, perhaps, tell me what is troubling you. Sometimes, Signora, it is easier to unburden yourself to a stranger."

Sylvano raised his eyebrows, seeking her response.

"I won't be good company and, anyway, I'm expecting an important call at any moment."

He nodded and smiled.

"Of course."

He walked smartly towards the door.

"Number 14. If you change your mind."

~ ~ ~

The 'important call' never came.

During the evening, Jane bathed and ate and rested, jumping whenever her phone pinged, usually with unsolicited email. Two messages came in from Stella, 'desperate to know how you are' and 'please let me know if you're ok'. Jane answered the second, briefly, ashamed that she could not bring herself to actually call her.

By nine thirty she'd consumed the best part of a bottle of wine. It emboldened her to message Phoebe and ask if she had any further news. She didn't have any contact number for Pavesi, had never thought to ask for one; just assumed he'd keep her informed.

There was no response from Phoebe either. As she climbed into bed, knocking her knee painfully against its wooden base, her thoughts returned to Richard. She imagined hearing his key in the lock, a light coming on, his silhouette appearing in the doorway. In that moment, she recalled his peccadillos – those long lectures, his impatience with trivia of any description, his self-absorption – with more affection than irritation.

An intermittent buzzing sound awoke her. The digital clock on the bedside table showed 7.58am. It took her a few seconds to realise that she had a visitor. Stumbling over to the entry phone, she spoke into it, hesitantly.

"Yes, hello."

"Hi, Jane, it's me, Phoebe. We're outside."

As she pressed the entry button, Jane glanced at her reflection in the heavy, gold framed mirror beside her. Her hair an unattractive tangle, there were streaks of mascara around her eyes which were puffy from sleep. She thought of the freshness and beauty, the resilient youth, now tripping its way up the stairs and cursed. She was trapped; her advancing years brutally displayed. In the light filled interior of her holiday apartment, every line and wrinkle would be visible.

Before she could even splash her face with some reviving cold water, there was a ring on the doorbell and there stood Richard's progeny; both sporting rucksacks, both in tight blue jeans, trainers and different coloured tee shirts. There was little trace on either face of the long journey endured to get to Florence at such an hour. Phoebe's eyeliner appeared recently applied, Jane noting particularly the expert flick at the edge of each eyelid. It was a skill she had never perfected.

Phoebe marched in, without even managing the civility of a greeting.

"Any news?" she said.

Cressie muttered a "Hi, Jane", which prompted Phoebe to remember her manners.

"Yeah, hi, Jane. I know it's sort of early. And we should have told you -"

Jane cut her off. "It's fine," she said. "You're both welcome. God knows I could do with the company." Tears pricked her eyes as the truth of her own words struck her. "I'll make us all some coffee. You must be shattered."

She led them into the sitting room, where the sisters flopped down on the one and only settee. Jane opened the door which led to the balcony and then stood for a few seconds, consoled by the feel of the cool air on her skin. Turning back, Phoebe and Cressie were studying her, clearly awaiting the news they were sure Jane must be bracing herself to impart.

"I've heard nothing," she said. "I was hoping that you might have done so."

Phoebe, seemingly the spokeswoman by virtue of her age, pushed back her hair from her face in a gesture of frustration.

"Christ. What the fuck is going on? I spoke to that guy yesterday, Pavesi, sent him a photo of Dad. I mean, do they know what they're doing? We've no idea."

Cressie burst into tears and Phoebe put her arm around her.

"I don't have a number for him, which is ludicrous. But if you do, we can call him in an hour or so. I think they start work quite early here," said Jane, hoping she sounded like a woman in charge – as opposed to the emotional wreck she feared she was becoming with every hour which passed.

As Jane poured the coffee, they exchanged what few facts they'd each been given. It didn't take long. Richard had been kidnapped; at some point after his meeting the night before last; it was a case of mistaken identity. That was it. Precisely when, where and how remained unanswered.

Phoebe was restless, taking only a few sips of her coffee before asking Jane if she minded her going on to the balcony to have a cigarette. Cressie scurried after her, carrying their coffee. Jane didn't join them. She told them she was going for a shower and left them alone, scrolling down their phones, a cigarette dangling from Phoebe's hand.

When she returned, refreshed, made up and properly attired, they were where she'd left them. An ashtray had been found and placed on the table, several stubs within it.

She took a wooden chair from the kitchen and squeezed it alongside them on the balcony. It was a perfect morning, no breeze. She looked out over the rooftops of the city, thinking how wonderful it might have been to be sitting there contemplating a day as a common tourist rather than embroiled in – what felt like – the over-heated plot of a depressingly bad drama.

As soon as it was nine thirty and they'd all agreed that Pavesi must be at his desk, Phoebe called him. He wasn't there; just his answer machine. She left a short message in her clipped English accent.

They sat there, for over an hour, waiting. When they'd still heard nothing, Phoebe pushed back her chair and got up.

"I can't stand this. I'm going over there. Come on, Cressie."

"Do you know where you're going?"

"No, but I've looked up the two main police stations here and I'll track him down – one way or another. Pavesi has been drafted in specially, hasn't he, so he's not listed."

Jane looked at her sceptically.

"Is there any point to that?" she asked, directly. "If he's not contacted us yet, there'll be a reason, surely? I think kidnappings are delicate operations – you know, sensitive negotiations. They don't like," she hesitated on the words she wanted to use, not wanting to insult or patronise Phoebe "well, people meddling."

"I'm sorry, Jane. He's my father. I can't just sit here, patiently, like you. I'm not meddling. I just want to know what's happening. It's not a lot to ask."

Jane nodded.

"Ok, I understand. But call me if you learn anything, won't you?"

"Of course," said Phoebe.

The door banged behind the two girls, leaving Jane alone again. She looked about her. There was nothing to keep her incarcerated within the apartment. Despite the crowds, she would feel better walking the streets of the city. While she waited for her mobile to fully charge, she searched online for somewhere which might offer her the distraction she sought.

It wasn't the reference to Elizabeth Barrett-Browning which motivated Jane to set out to find the *Piazza Donatello* and *The English Cemetery*, since all she could recall of the poet's works was the famous – "*How do I love thee?*" read at a thousand weddings and so, perhaps, diminished by its ubiquity. It was the print in the bedroom – *Island of the Dead* painted by Arnold Bocklin. It mesmerised her; sufficiently so that she googled the artist and discovered that this had been his interpretation of the English Cemetery. Under a cloud heavy sky, it showed two ghostly figures in a boat, one dressed in white robes and standing upright, transporting their dead for burial. The island they approached was made of rock and rose majestically from the sea. A further search gave her more detail about the site. It was a Protestant cemetery, opened in 1827, a final resting place for many of the English residents who had fallen in love with Florence and died there in the nineteenth century. Bocklin had clearly exercised his imagination in depicting the place as surrounded by the sea. Now it appeared to be hemmed in by the city's ring road. It may not, she concluded, offer the distraction from her ordeal which she should look for, but, in a macabre way, it matched her mood and, bringing up google maps on her phone, she set out to find it.

On her way down the stairs, emerging into the bright light of a Tuscan morning, she thought of Richard again. What would he have made of her choice? Likely, he would have described as it as 'perverse' and rattled off a number of more worthy sites to visit in the limited time available.

She later concluded that Richard would have been right. The cemetery, despite its auspicious origin, was situated on a traffic island. It was hardly the space of meditative peace and tranquillity she'd hoped for although she was able, once she'd navigated her way inside, to find some interest in the marble statues. And for the first half hour that she wandered along the gravel paths, amidst the Cypress trees, she had the place to herself. She sat for a while, feeling sleepy as the day's heat increased until she heard a ping on her phone.

From that moment on, alone, save for the dead, the silenced ones entombed beneath the ground, she knew that it was not just Richard who might be forever damaged by the experience of his abduction. There would be a cost to her too. *A reckoning*, as someone – someone she had never met, naturally – later described it.

Stella had messaged her.

There are rumours circulating about you on social media. Have you spoken to anyone? Call me when you have a minute.

CHAPTER 26

The hounds were coming for her

Although they'd started off in a coffee shop, Halina and Alicja were now walking around a local park. The proximity of noisy, excited shoppers had, eventually, driven them away from the café and Alicja, recalling a similar situation with Debbie, had suggested they walk instead of sitting. She knew that their meeting was to be a significant one. In the intervening two weeks since they'd gone shopping for her mother's trainers, they'd had more contact – texting and calling – than they'd had in the last year.

Halina had begun to talk about her relationship with Alicja's father, Arik. She was halting at first, not wanting Alicja to interpret her disclosures as an attempt to spoil Alicja's newfound relationship with Arik. Her daughter reassured her.

"It's ok, Mum. I don't feel the need to take sides. But it would be, like, useful to know a bit more about why he went back to Poland and why you stayed on. And, well, you know, why I haven't seen him until recently."

They were standing by a pond, the antics of Egyptian geese, mallards and swans providing a helpful distraction when their conversation reached a certain level of intensity. Alicja's expert knowledge of the mating habits of the Mute swan was also a useful diversion.

"The male and female swim closely with one another, curving their necks together."

She demonstrated with her hands.

"And then, after mating, they face each other, push their breasts together and rise up, paddling with their feet. It's the most magical sight. Because they mate for life, you see. Debbie told me that they stay together until one of them dies or they can't breed."

Halina looked at Alicja's animated expression and smiled. For perhaps the first time, she acknowledged to herself that although her parenting had not been without mistakes, there was good stuff in there too. Otherwise, this mature, confident, happy young woman would not be standing by her side this sunny afternoon.

"I'm not sure your father and I ever thought we were mating for life," she said. "I became pregnant with you when a condom split. We had arguments then."

"Over whether to keep me?" asked Alicja, averting her eyes away from her mother and focusing on the beautiful brown and white plumage of a goose, beak down at the edge of the water.

"Did he tell you?"

"No. He said nothing about the past, really, except that he was young and immature. I didn't ask him many questions either. I suppose I didn't want to scare him off."

Her mother made a scoffing sound, even though she'd promised herself she would try to keep her natural cynicism in check.

There was a short silence between them, interrupted only by the odd angry exchange between the geese.

"Didn't he want me?" Alicja asked, eventually.

"Actually, it was the other way round. It was me who wondered whether I should continue with the pregnancy. We were both young. There was no money. Our families were many hundreds of miles away."

Halina wasn't sure why she had felt it necessary to confess this bitter truth to Alicja when it carried such a risk to their new intimacy. But it was something to do with starting again; establishing trust between them for perhaps the first time.

"Oh, I see," said Alicja. "What changed your mind? Or did you just find it difficult to make a decision?"

"You moved inside me one day. I was further on than I'd thought and this little kick, or whatever it was –." Halina said something in Polish and shrugged. "So *he* didn't change my mind. *You* did."

Alicja didn't need to ask many more questions. Halina was happy to talk about their early family life and the problems which had precipitated their separation. It didn't seem to be about what might have been forecast – living in a cramped, damp flat with little money and no family support. It appeared they'd survived that. It was about Arik's absence of respect for her, said Halina. He would criticise her lack of education and call her names.

"At first, I just thought he was teasing me. But it became more than that. He seemed to enjoy saying cruel things to me. And anyway, once, how do you say it, our relationship wasn't new anymore, he got bored with me and our little life. But I know two sad things. One, that I loved him and two, that he didn't love me. I think he went back to Poland so that he would be rid of me for good."

"And me," added Alicja.

Halina didn't contradict her.

"After he'd left, it was a very difficult time for me – for us. I was lonely, I suppose. I should have gone home, back to Poland. But I felt a failure, perhaps a bit ashamed."

Again, she spoke some words in Polish and Alicja determined, as she stood by a duckpond in a park on a morning in May, that it was high time she learned their language, which – in the light of her mother's revelations – seemed a bizarre subject to focus on. But language connects, she thought, placing an arm around her mother's shoulders.

"Hey, Mum," she said. "How about we go back to Poland to see your family in the summer holidays? Together. Just you and me. We'll have a mother and daughter road trip!"

"I thought you had plans to see your father this summer."

"Oh, that can wait a while," said Alicja. "There's no hurry."

"Just you and me?" her mother repeated.

Alicja nodded and smiled at the look of surprise on her mother's face.

"Plans can change!" she declared.

~ ~ ~

It transpired later that it was Cressie's posts on Facebook and Twitter which had generated the media interest in Jane Sedgefield.

As soon as the news of her father's kidnap had reached her she started posting and tweeting, requesting help with finding him and putting pressure on the British authorities to assist as if he'd been missing for weeks, rather than, at that point, some thirty-six hours. Cressie hadn't liaised with Phoebe regarding her campaign, just assumed that her sister would agree that they should do whatever they could to discover his whereabouts and 'possibly save his life'.

Help me find my father Richard Marks. Missing in Florence, Italy.

Over a period of just a few hours before leaving for the airport, whoever responded, whether known to her or not, Cressie would provide every single detail she could think of. She wracked her brain to recall Jane's surname but couldn't initially. Then she remembered her father speaking briefly of how he'd met Jane. In the days before he travelled, she and Phoebe had nagged him mercilessly.

"Look, Dad, this is the first relationship you've admitted to since Mum. *And* you're going away with her. Don't you feel that we should know a teensy bit more about her?"

Eventually he'd given in and revealed that it was Jane's husband who'd been killed on that fateful new year's day. So it was easy. Cressie just googled it - *man killed in a car accident in the Cirencester area on New Year's Day* and up it popped in some online rag.

Police declare dense fog to be the cause of fatal car accident on New Year's Day, in which 53-year-old Larry Sedgefield was killed.

Cressie didn't know for sure whether Jane had taken her married name but it was worth a shot. Thus, the identity of the girlfriend of *'missing Englishman, acclaimed academic and loving father'* was revealed and Jane Sedgefield became open game for any poacher or hunter, friend or foe, in the jungle which is social media.

Cressie had taken the first call in the departure lounge of Terminal 3, Heathrow, while waiting to be called for their flight to Bologna. She'd excused herself from Phoebe, already fearing her sister's wrath when she was discovered to have acted so precipitately. And being anxious to get the call over with, she hadn't really enquired to whom she was speaking, just answered their questions and then rang off without saying goodbye.

Phoebe looked suspiciously at her when she returned to where they were sitting with their rucksacks.

"What are you up to?" she'd barked, observing the flush on Cressie's neck. Cressie had mumbled something about work.

"Likely story," said Phoebe. "It's just gone five."

Before they'd even boarded the plane, Phoebe had discovered Cressie's antics on Facebook and ordered her to delete every single post.

"How could you be so fucking stupid?" she demanded in a loud voice, arousing interest from all their fellow travellers bored to death and seeking any sort of free entertainment. "You realise you've probably put Dad in even more danger. You fucking idiot!"

They didn't speak again until Phoebe relented just as they touched down in Bologna. Cressie had cried for the first five minutes of their flight until she fell asleep, exhausted following her midnight activity. Looking at her sister's sleeping face and smudged mascara, Phoebe had extracted a facial tissue from her toilet bag and wiped Cressie's face gently as if she were a slumbering toddler. Seeing her sister's faint smile, Cressie started weeping again with relief until Phoebe told her, sharply, to 'get a fucking grip, for God's sake.'

So the posts were gone and the Tweets deleted. But it was too late for Jane. The hounds were coming for her.

CHAPTER 27

A whore – about to face her reckoning

Throughout the rest of the afternoon, as Jane waited for news from Phoebe or Pavesi or whomever about the current situation concerning Richard, she would look nervously at the posts about her cropping up intermittently on social media. A paper, proud to lead the gutter press, had already found the story and there was a small piece about it on page 7, devised to look as if it was concerned about Richard's welfare but, in reality, merely trying to initiate interest in what might just turn out to be a really salacious affair. In that short article, neither Jane nor Richard were actually named – *Police fear for British academic's wellbeing after bungled kidnapping in Florence* – but various, less cautious, pieces on some anonymous news sites demonstrated no such prudence. Their identities were already in the public domain.

Who is Jane Sedgefield?

The answer to this question was demanded by an independent news site calling itself *Res Ipsa Loquitur* ('the thing speaks for itself') declaring that *'we ONLY go with the facts!'*

Let's look at the facts here –

1. Her husband died suddenly in an accident on January 1st of this year.

2. The only witness to this accident was the missing academic, Richard Marks.

3. Richard Marks and Jane Sedgefield strike up a relationship and travel to Florence together in May of this year.

4. Richard Marks goes missing on the same night they arrive in Florence.

We think there's justification here to delve just a little bit deeper into the somewhat eventful life of Jane Sedgefield.

Facebook was splattered with posts about Jane by the early evening. Babbs, one of Jane's colleagues at the shop had heard of Richard's plight and posted a few words of sympathy on her wall. *We're all thinking of you* Babbs had finished off. Jane knew what the 'we' meant. Babbs was a blabber mouth.

Twitter had gathered apace too. Back in the apartment, wondering why Phoebe and Cressie had not bothered to update her, Jane found herself looking at her Twitter feed even though she knew that it would distress her further. And indeed, someone from the past had tweeted. At first, while she recognized the name she couldn't place her. *Ruby*. But it dawned on her as the kettle whistled on the stove, its little cap bubbling with steam. Gladys' niece – the fickle one who lived abroad.

Jane Sedgefield. Befriended my ageing, disabled aunt Gladys King shortly before her death and walked away with all her wealth. The evidence grows about this immoral witch!

Jane's heart thudded painfully in her chest as she contemplated the consequences of the interest now generated and exploding into the common domain. She imagined the messages now being exchanged between Jill and Stella and Debbie. Images of Michael came to mind; his shaking shoulders as he sat before the log burner on the night before the funeral; the expression of grief on his face when he said goodbye to her at Larry's wake. It would confirm what he'd suspected. In his eyes, she'd replaced his brother in the blink of an eye. He hadn't been honoured by her and now the whole world knew.

Alex would know too. Having better things to do and uncomfortable about gossip generally, he wouldn't linger over the Tweets. But nor would he feel any sympathy for her, merely relief that he hadn't been drawn further into her seductive web.

Jane's only consolation, at that moment, was that her parents would not be privy to the Twitter storm engulfing their daughter. They took no interest in social media. But *should* some well-wisher let them know that their daughter was being described as a witch – and, actually, in just the last few minutes *a whore – about to face her reckoning* – the shame would destroy them. Tears pricked Jane's eyes at the prospect of harming the two gentle people it was her duty to protect as they approached the end of their lives.

Jane hesitated when she heard a faint knock on the door to the apartment. Why wasn't it the buzzer? Her thoughts raced in paranoid fashion. The press had gained entry to the building. Would she open the door to some fresh-faced reporter anxious to 'help' her?

"Who is it?" she asked, injecting as much confidence into her tone as she could muster.

"Sylvano from apartment 14."

His low voice reverberated faintly against the wooden door. When she didn't immediately answer, he spoke again.

"I wondered how you were, that's all. Sorry to disturb you."

Jane opened the door and Sylvano, dressed in blue cords and a white open-necked shirt, smiled at her. In a matter of seconds his expression changed to one of concern.

"Are you not well?" he asked, hesitantly. Jane pushed her hair back from her face, wondering just how deep the dark circles beneath her eyes were. Why did this stranger care how she was?

"I'm still waiting for some news," Jane said. "It's difficult.... I'm finding the waiting difficult." It was the most honest answer she could manage.

"Come to my apartment," said Sylvano, after a brief pause. "It will distract you. We can talk of ...of other things."

Jane looked at him, trying to gauge if he was being kind, or a predatory male seeking to take advantage of her as soon as he had her locked safely in his flat.

"No," he said, holding up his palms to her, "I completely understand. It would be foolish of you to come to a strange man's apartment. Let me fix some cocktails and bring them to you. We can sit outside on this wonderful evening and you will feel safe and relaxed."

"Well," said Jane, her resolve weakening at the thought of some normality entering the day. "It would be good to have some company, thank you."

"Give me five minutes!"

Sylvano departed, the soles of his leather moccasins slapping against the stone stairs.

"I'll leave the door open," Jane called after him. She went into the bathroom and reapplied her foundation. The heat seemed to have rendered her skin a sweaty, shiny mess. It was no wonder the man had blanched at the sight of her. Plucking the new red lipstick she'd bought at the airport from her make-up bag, she smeared it over her lips, adding a touch to both cheeks. The word *whore* came into her mind as she stared at herself in the pockmarked mirror which hung over the sink.

She was brushing her hair vigorously when her reflection suddenly darkened. With a start she shifted her gaze to the two figures standing behind her.

"Expecting company?" asked Phoebe. She and Cressie were standing in the doorway to the bathroom. Neither of them looked friendly. Having gorged all afternoon on the varying accounts of Jane on social media, they were minded to be cautious in their subsequent dealings with her. 'Whatever – whoever – she is,' Phoebe had declared to her sister, 'we can't really trust her.'

Jane turned to face them.

"The door was open," said Phoebe.

Jane did not attempt an explanation.

"Oh, hi," she said. "Any news? I was hoping to have heard something by now."

"They've located him," said Phoebe. "But they won't tell us where or anything else. Just that he's alive, thank God. It's still all hush-hush while they negotiate with the gang that's holding him. Pavesi told us to –"

A male voice interrupted her.

"Here we are!"

Behind them all, Sylvano appeared holding up two cocktail glasses and a shaker.

There was a brief shocked silence before Phoebe looked pointedly at Jane, then at Sylvano and then back at Jane.

"Christ almighty. You don't waste any time, do you?"

Jane was surprised at the strength of the anger which overtook her at that moment. She decided later, when recalling the words she'd spat out at Phoebe, that she'd been like a pot of something heating up gradually and then boiling over – suddenly and disastrously – before managing to adjust the flames beneath it.

Jane leant back to place her hairbrush down on the edge of the sink and then, ignoring Sylvano, fixed a pair of glittering eyes on Phoebe.

"Don't be so *damn* rude to me," she said. "What gives you any right whatsoever to judge me and comment on what I do and don't do? It's none of your business. And, for the record, I don't give a flying fuck what either of you – or any of those *fuckwits* on social media – think of me. I'll live whatever way I feel like living and you can keep your pathetic moralising to yourself."

It wasn't strictly correct, of course – or correct at all. She cared quite a lot what Stella, Bob and Debbie thought of her. Michael and Lilly too, for that matter. Not to mention her parents. But, at that moment, it felt gloriously liberating to defend herself with such ferocity against the poisonous arrows which had been raining down on her all day.

Sylvano had disappeared from view by the time she'd finished speaking. Phoebe had taken a step backwards, clutching Cressie by the arm, as if Jane were about to launch a physical, as well as a verbal, assault on them. *Ha*, thought Jane, *no-one expects a good bit of aggression from a 50 something, menopausal woman, do they? They just expect you to cower, or smooth the waters, avoid conflict, apologise – no wait, cry!*

Then they fled. As she stood, shaking with the emotion she'd just injected into the atmosphere, Jane heard them run to the sitting room to collect their bags. The apartment door banged and she was alone.

She walked into the kitchen with the intention of extracting a bottle of wine from the fridge. There on the table were the cocktail glasses and the shaker. It appeared to be a sign.

Grabbing her keys and stuffing them into her jeans' pocket, she picked up the two glasses and the shaker and left the apartment. She ran up the stairs and knocked on the door of number 14.

A rather startled Sylvano opened the door and stared at her.

"Sorry about that," she said, accompanying her words with a brittle smile.

Sylvano stood back and ushered her over his threshold.

CHAPTER 28

The scent of a hundred roses hanging heavy in the air

Sylvano's apartment was altogether more spacious and, certainly, much plusher than Jane's rented one. Jane was mildly surprised to see the large, contemporary artwork on the walls in the living room. Given his academic background, she'd placed him in a similar pigeon-hole to Richard who was impervious to fashion. Now, looking around from her position on one of the two opulent leather sofas, an elegant marble coffee table separating them, it was evident that Sylvano Bussotti was a man of confidence and sophistication.

Jane apologised again. "Goodness knows what you must think of me," she said, trying to sip at her drink rather than knock it back in one go. "But I've been under immense pressure in the last couple of days and – well, I suppose – it just got the better of me."

"Tell me about it," Sylvano demanded.

Jane nodded. Having witnessed what he had, he was entitled to seek some explanation.

Her account covered the time she'd spent in Florence. She didn't dwell on the history which was now the subject of such hysteria on the part of strangers. She didn't mention that she'd been widowed less than six months ago – although she did say she and Richard had only known each other 'a few months.' As the Negronis slipped down during the course of that hour, Jane relaxed. Every now and again, her heart would leap as she reminded herself that *Richard is alive*, that they knew where he was, that there was every possibility – probability even – that he'd be back with her shortly. Surely, this was now just a waiting game.

"How long have you rented the apartment for?" asked Sylvano. He appeared oddly un-shocked by her story, as if such kidnappings were regular occurrences in his country.

"Until Saturday. Three nights left for him to be found."

Sylvano waved his hand.

"You can stay here if not. I have plenty of room. You have been through hell. I am not surprised that you responded so ..... so intensely to the criticism of the young lady. Perhaps, I think, that can be fixed when this nightmare is over for you all."

It was a kind gesture, Jane thought, to reassure her about the consequences of her words even though she herself had yet to feel any remorse for how viciously she'd spoken to Phoebe. There had been something cruelly casual about Phoebe's accusation, as if Jane's feelings were of slight importance in the affair, her purpose being to emphasise her dispensability.

Jane shrugged. "Yes, perhaps I was harsh. I suspect Phoebe took the brunt of the anger which had been building in me all day, seeing what extraordinarily hurtful things total strangers posted about me on Twitter and Facebook."

"I keep well away from all that," said Sylvano. "Luckily, my work does not require anything other than email."

"Yes, your work," Jane said, keen to move the conversation on to something less fraught. "Tell me about what you do."

"Oh, nothing glamorous," he said. "I run an auction house in centre of the city, specialising in Asian art and antiques. I don't do the auctions any longer. My partner deals with those. I'm on the acquisition side and do quite a bit of travelling."

He pushed a glossy brochure across the table to her. Jane picked it up, flicking through it and noting the hefty price tags which accompanied the list of items auctioned well above their reserve price.

"It seems glamorous to me!" she commented, comparing it to her own menial position at *Magnifique.*

She put the brochure down and sighed.

"You are preoccupied," said Sylvano, leaning back and surveying her.

"The thing is," said Jane, "I don't have the detective's contact details. Phoebe has those and so I've no firm idea what's going on. I'm hoping he'll think to call me but so far he hasn't."

"That should not be difficult," said Sylvano, looking thoughtful. "If you would allow me, I'll help you find him. I can make some calls first thing in the morning. Get this man – Pavesi – to make some contact with you about what is happening."

"Do you think you can achieve that?"

Sylvano nodded.

"I have my contacts," he said, somewhat darkly. "It helps to know the right people in this city."

She left shortly afterwards. After taking her mobile number and email address, together with further details about Richard, they shook hands, Sylvano assuring her that he would be in touch.

"Try to sleep," he advised. "Your friend will need you to be strong when his ordeal is over."

Later, as Jane sat in the lounge of her apartment, staring out through the balcony doors at the gathering darkness while eating a supper of cheese and crackers, she thought back to her chance meeting with her Guardian Angel, the suave Sylvano. Had she rejected his kindness, not engaged with him, doubted his motives by tainting him with all the toxic characteristics which many of her sex view the males amongst them, she would have been the poorer for it.

When had good faith ceased to be a starting point in human relations, she wondered?

~ ~ ~

"Did *you* know she'd embarked on an affair with the cyclist involved in Larry's accident?" Debbie enquired of Stella.

They were sitting in a café, a few doors down from the deli where Debbie worked. She'd asked to take a half hour break to meet up with a friend. Something 'urgent' had come up.

"Well, actually, yes," replied Stella, stirring her coffee and thinking back to her conversation with Bob after discovering the identity of Jane's companion on her trip to Florence. "I thought I'd said as much when she wasn't able to meet up with us last weekend."

Debbie frowned. "You hinted she was going with a man – you didn't say it was *that* man."

"Is it that relevant how she met him?"

Stella knew she was being hypocritical having voiced exactly the same thoughts to Bob only a matter of a week ago.

"I think it's very odd, that's all. I mean, is she so desperate to have a man in her life that she hooks up with whoever she encounters after poor Larry?"

Stella shook her head.

"I think that's very judgmental, Debbie. And let's be truthful here, there's enough judgement doing the rounds on Jane without us, supposed to be her friends, contributing to it."

"I know," conceded Debbie. "She's taking an awful battering. I suppose I'm just thinking of Larry. It doesn't seem, well, very honourable, does it?"

"Is there any point in being honourable for the sake of it?" asked Stella. "Who would she be doing it for, given that Larry is dead and can't be harmed?" This was more Bob's argument than her own but some sense of balance compelled her to make it.

"Those of us who loved Larry, I suppose. And he has a family. Replacing him with such – almost indecent – haste seems to reflect that – well, he meant very little to her."

Stella raised an eyebrow at her.

"Lord, where's all this moralising coming from? So she has to withdraw into a corner and remain celibate until we are all satisfied she has honoured her dead husband? How Victorian."

Debbie looked at her thoughtfully.

"I could understand if it was a fling – or a series of flings. But this seems to be a, well, *serious* relationship."

"So what you're saying is that it would be acceptable to do some bed-hopping but not to engage with anyone as if she truly values them? Anyway, how on earth do you know whether it's serious or not? She's not moved in with the man!"

"Ok, point made. And, yes, look at the dreadful situation she's in now. Have you heard anything further from her?"

Privately, Stella thought this should have been Debbie's first question rather than, what appeared to be, an afterthought.

"Yes. Last night she sent me a short text. Apparently they've located Richard. So he's alive which is fantastic news. She said someone she's met is helping her liaise with the police as they seem very reluctant to engage with her."

"Someone she's met?"

It was Debbie's turn to raise an eyebrow.

Stella ignored Debbie's expression and went on to talk about the texts she'd received from Jill.

"Happily ensconced in her French chalet, she messaged me endlessly about Jane last night. Repeating all the slanderous remarks, pretending she was shocked when, in reality, she was probably delighted at the scandal."

"Mmmm," said Debbie. "That figures. With their history."

In fact, they were misjudging Jill. Despite what she may have said to Stella, she'd been in contact with Jane privately, offering her support. *Our house will be empty until mid-June. If you need a bolt hole, it's yours.*

Alex Snow's attention had been drawn to Jane's plight by one of his colleagues who'd recognized Jane's name as a previous client of the firm. He'd been sitting in his room with his eyes shut when David Jackson had burst through the door, waving his phone excitedly.

"You look completely done in, Alex," he quipped. "Which of your delightful clients has brought you to this sorry state?"

Alex groaned.

He was trying to erase the image of Veronica Stern's thin twisted lips from his mind. When their meeting had ended – drawn to an end by Alex, naturally – and he was trying to steer her towards the door of his office, she had stood unnecessarily and uncomfortably close to him.

"Miss Stern. The bane of my life. She will *not* accept my advice. She will *not* negotiate. I've tried to get rid of her, suggesting another solicitor might be more in tune with her but, no, she's sticking with me whether I like it or not."

David laughed.

"Oh stop looking at me with such glee," Alex said.

"Oh what it is to be so desirable! Anyway, Jane Sedgefield. One of yours I seem to recall. She's in the news! Oh boy, is she in the news!"

After he'd got rid of David, Alex googled Jane and a few Tweets came up. There was an online tabloid article also, just published, with both Jane and Richard named.

A frolic in Florence ends in a kidnap.

Alex knew what that meant. There would be a pack of reporters sniffing around Jane's door for more details and, possibly, one or two of them already hot footing it over to Italy to track her down in Florence.

He thought back to their recent meeting, when he'd felt such promise in that May country air only to realise, later, that he'd been made a fool of. He wasn't used to making such colossal misjudgements. Try as he might, it was difficult not to indulge the gentle wave of *schadenfreude* which lapped over him as he digested the contents of the article.

But, after a few moments, the wave receded and, clicking his computer shut, he decided to go for a head-clearing walk. Surely enough time had elapsed for Victoria Stern to have left the immediate area and caught her train home. She would be sitting, rigid with fury, her legs twisted around each other, his unwanted – yet familiar advice – an irritating echo in her head.

~ ~ ~

It was another twenty-four hours before Jane received any further news.

At around midnight the following evening, just as she was dozing off, her phone vibrated on the bedside table.

"Signora Sedgefield?"

Jane murmured her response, her stomach churning, with that toxic combination of excitement and anxiety.

"It is Pierre Pavesi here from the special operations unit. Our colleagues in Bologna have Signor Marks in their care. They will interview him in the morning and then drive him over to the hotel there where his daughters are staying."

From Pavesi's tone, terse and official, Jane inferred that Sylvano had done as he'd promised. Pavesi had been tracked down and ordered to call her. He wasn't going to volunteer any more information than he had to.

"Thank you for letting me know," Jane said quickly, hoping she might placate the man. "How is he?"

"I am not sure of the details. Perhaps Mr Marks' daughters will let you know when he arrives with them."

"Wait," Jane said, "his daughters? I assumed he'd be brought back here to me."

"The arrangements have nothing to do with me, Signora."

"Well, who should I contact then?" Jane demanded.

There was a pause and then an audible sigh from Pavesi.

"His daughters, Signora. I suggest you contact his daughters."

Before Jane could enquire further, there was a click and he was gone.

There is usually a *physical* price to pay for the turmoil the mind has experienced. Jane sat up properly and swung her legs over the side of the bed. But she was unable to stand as her body started to judder from the sobs released inside her from where, during the last seventy-two hours, the tension had been incubating.

Richard was free. He was alive. It was over.

Overwhelmed with gratitude towards Sylvano, she texted him, her eyes blurring as she wiped away the tears which continued to fall; a dam broken.

Jane hadn't seen Sylvano since their evening together. He hadn't been in touch, evidently confident that whoever strings he'd pulled would do his bidding. She'd started the day with every intention of visiting the *Uffizi* and then remembered a chapel that Richard had mentioned in connection with the artist *Masaccio*, the subject of his intended second lecture. Still nervous about being door-stepped by a reporter, she'd left the apartment shortly after 7am and found a small café where she had coffee and a pastry, before making her way to the *Brancacci Chapel* near the *Piazza del Carmine*. She'd meant to cross the Arno over the *Ponte Vecchio* but ended up taking a wrong turning and crossed eventually via the *Ponte Santa Trinita*. She paused half-way across, standing for a long time in the sunshine, gazing over at the Ponte Vecchio and delighting in the view. Her lack of navigational skill had been fortuitous. She'd avoided the crowds of tourists she could see milling over and around the bridge; bypassed the couples taking selfies next to old *Benvenuti,* dodged the pedlars imploring the visitors to buy their wares.

As she tried to identify the spires and domes of the buildings in the distance, Richard's voice had sounded in her head. It was so clear, she even turned around, expecting him to materialise through a mist – not that there was one – and appear at her side.

"So what else did you see and do while I was lounging in my cave?" he would say.

She shook herself, knowing that this was just wishful thinking of the romantic variety. Richard hadn't got off at the wrong stop on the tube or been on a re-routed flight. He'd been *kidnapped.* Blindfolded and then forcibly bundled into the boot of a car, probably, and kept in God knows what conditions for the last three days; deprived of food, cold, lonely, frightened. It was unlikely he'd be quizzing her as to whether, in his absence, she'd taken proper advantage of the rich cultural treasures the city offered.

But because it seemed to represent some faith in the future and enraptured by the shimmers of light cast by the sun in the ripples of the Arno, she pressed on to the *Santa Maria del Carmine* that morning. She'd been in luck. It was still early and although it meant waiting in line for fifty minutes for the Church to open, the usual huge crowds had yet to descend.

Jane had little knowledge of the Bible so the life of St Peter, the subject of the frescoes, meant little to her. But in a little café on the *Via Porta Rossa*, she'd undertaken some research on her phone and obtained sufficient background to interpret the stories depicted on the walls of the chapel. Masaccio's most famous fresco, *The Tribute Money* – in which Jesus instructs disciple Peter to extract a coin from the mouth of a fish to pay the tax man – had attracted numerous theories as to why this particular subject had been chosen. Now, standing in front of the six-hundred-year-old fresco, absorbing the artist's use of colour and perspective, she gained some understanding of the reverence it aroused. But her dominant emotion that morning was of sadness; sadness that Richard was not there too and that their plans had gone so terribly awry.

Since she was already on the south bank, Jane decided to have a picnic lunch in Boboli Gardens, even though she knew it might stir up memories of Larry and their honeymoon. They had both found the gardens to be a haven of comparative peace in that hot and over-crowded city. Finding a bench not occupied, she ate her mozzarella and tomato wrap and then dozed in the afternoon sun, occasionally checking her phone to see if there was any news of Richard. There were messages of support from Debbie, Stella and Jill and several posts on her Facebook page. Her boss had emailed her, asking her to confirm that she'd be back in the shop as originally planned.

Sorry to hear of your trouble, hope all works out for you had been tagged on the end of the email. It would have been better had she said nothing, Jane thought, given the lack of sincerity in those, carelessly chosen, words. She got up from her bench and wandered into the rose garden where she gazed across at the rooftops and the view of the distant hills. The scent of a hundred roses hanging heavy in the air, she was decisive.

Sorry, Fran, circumstances don't permit me to return to work as planned. I think it's best you replace me. Regards, Jane.

As she pressed *send*, she wondered how she'd found any satisfaction in selling over-priced fabrics and talking about matching cushions. Similar thoughts occurred to her. What did she need the house for? Why did she think staying on had been a good idea? *Just supposing I don't go back?* she asked herself as she dodged and weaved her way through the crowds, now so much denser than on her outward journey. The question both distracted and amused her. She answered it first in the affirmative and proceeded to examine how she felt. And then tried the opposite answer, before discarding the inner dialogue for when things might become clearer.

But later, after that brief, unsatisfactory telephone conversation with Pavesi, once she'd recovered her balance, once the texts she sent Phoebe – asking if it were indeed the case that Richard was being 'delivered' to her and Cressie, rather than Jane – remained unanswered far into the night, the question came back to her. It was a starker one this time.

What am I going back for?

In the ensuing hours, there would be even further justification to ask such a question of herself.

CHAPTER 29

Hanging around like a jilted bride

Sylvano drove Jane the sixty-five miles from Florence to Bologna.

He'd insisted, despite her protestations. He travelled frequently on business around the country and parked his Volvo – with its spacious boot in which he stored his various purchases – in a reserved spot outside the auction rooms.

"But aren't I interrupting your working day?" Jane asked, trying to disguise the relief she felt at having someone who wanted to help her, considered her worthy of help.

"My work is very flexible," Sylvano assured her, bestowing his most charming smile as he uttered the words. "It will save you so much time."

Phoebe had maintained her cruel silence with regard to Richard's welfare and whereabouts. Jane had had to call yet again on Sylvano to establish where Richard was. He'd called round to the apartment very early on the Saturday morning to deliver the news in person.

"Your friend is in the hospital in Bologna. He's been there since yesterday. I couldn't find out exactly when he was taken there."

Jane walked into the sitting room and gestured to Sylvano to sit down. Anger pulsated through her. How could Phoebe and Cressie be so cruel as to not let her know that Richard was now free and in hospital?

Sylvano didn't sit. He paced in front of her, aware that to furnish more details would upset her even more.

"He... he, Signor Marks, was not in a good way. He'd been beaten, I was informed, and was also discovered in a dehydrated condition. So he's being treated for his injuries but...but I was assured he will recover, Jane."

Jane blinked away her tears, keen to know the worst.

"Beaten? How badly?"

Sylvano shrugged.

"The call was brief. They wouldn't answer any of my questions even though I made it clear I was calling on your behalf. I'm afraid I got annoyed. It didn't help."

"Thank you for trying," said Jane, trying to smile. "I don't know what I'd have done without you."

It had been a mistake to arrive at the hospital ward with him. Jane had sensed it might be even as they arrived in the hospital car park. She'd considered saying – "look, it might be better if I went in without you." But she'd waited for Sylvano to say it first and he hadn't and, anyway, she reminded herself, he was invaluable as an interpreter. She might need him. Still, she hoped he might disappear off to the café when they got inside but he didn't. She was certain that he was simply being gallant although having previously witnessed Phoebe's anger he should have been aware his presence might elicit yet another venomous outburst from the overprotective daughter.

The nurse on duty at the desk had asked them to wait in the wating room while she enquired whether it was an appropriate time to visit Richard. She was gone for some time. *Go and get some coffee*, Jane inwardly entreated Sylvano, as they sat awkwardly side by side – like a married couple. Her attempt at telepathy didn't work.

Perhaps if he hadn't been there when Phoebe eventually emerged from her place by her father's bedside, she might have taken pity on Jane and relented. Jane would never know as once Phoebe had clapped eyes on Sylvano, reconciliation was a distant dream.

Jane didn't need to see the narrowing of Phoebe's beautiful eyes and the pursing of her full, red lips to know her thoughts.

"Look, Phoebe, Sylvano just drove me here. He's been helping me during these last few days. That's all," she pleaded. "Please believe me. I'm anxious to see Richard. Please let me see him. *Please.*" She wanted to add that if Phoebe hadn't shut her out in such a loathsome manner, she wouldn't have needed Sylvano's assistance but she confined herself to a simple appeal to Phoebe's better nature.

Sylvano joined in, suddenly realising his mistake in being there at all. They spoke over each other for a few seconds, voices raised, until the same nurse came over and, according to Sylvano, told them to take their arguments *'outside'*.

"He's very weak," said Phoebe, into the silence which had descended after the telling off. "And he doesn't want to see anybody but me and Cressie. He doesn't want *non-family members* seeing him like he is at the moment."

Jane tried to keep an even tone to her voice.

"Just tell him I'm here, Phoebe, and ask him – *ask* him if he wants to see me. Please."

"He's asleep."

"Then I'll wait," Jane snapped back.

Phoebe turned and went back in the direction of a side ward a few yards away. Jane followed her, determined now to see Richard.

At the door, Phoebe became aware that Jane was right behind her and tried to shut the door in her face. There was a brief, undignified tussle before Jane surrendered and retreated. But not before she caught a glimpse of Richard, lying in his hospital bed, his face a sea of bruises so as to make him almost unrecognizable. In fact, it was this image, seared into her memory like no other she could recall, which shocked her enough to let go of the door handle and to stop hissing invectives at Phoebe.

"Let's go," she said to Sylvano. "There's no point to this. I'm not wanted."

She was as sure as she could be that Richard had not seen her. His eyes had been closed. Whether he'd heard her voice, she was less certain of. Whatever the reality, she needed to accept, she told herself, that his current condition did not allow him to make demands or even ask where she was. So it served no purpose to remain there, hanging around like a jilted bride, waiting for him to come to his senses and call out her name.

But despite her attempts, on the journey back to Florence Jane struggled to contain her fury at the manner in which she had been treated. Larry would have said, she conceded, that her explosive behaviour towards Phoebe in the apartment had set the tone of their relationship and she should not have been surprised. Try as she might, she could not accept this. Phoebe and Cressie had been influenced by what they had read about her on social media. They hadn't spoken to their father; they were arrogant enough to feel they were speaking *for* him and the more she examined the facts, the less she believed that Richard would side with them. Richard was his own man. Jane had been with him long enough to know that much. As far as the rumours and speculation were concerned, he wasn't likely to let the 'great unwashed' with time on their hands – time spent idly, time spent thoughtlessly – dictate his views on any subject.

By the time she and Sylvano had arrived back at the apartment block, Jane's determination had hardened. She was not going to retreat, mouse-like, into the shadows or fly home the following morning, dodging the press at Heathrow. Nor did the prospect of throwing herself onto the mercy of Bob and Stella appeal, holed up in that spare room of theirs until the furore abated.

She would bide her time, await Richard's recovery and then take her cue from him, not his daughters or, indeed, anyone else.

"You can stay, Jane," said Sylvano, unsurprised when she informed him clear-eyed, that she was going to persist in her quest to see Richard and was thus staying on in Florence. He'd just ordered another bottle of Chianti. Following the debacle at the hospital, she'd agreed to have dinner out with him and they were now at a restaurant on the *Via della Oche.* Jane had blanched at the sight of the cuts of raw meat in the cabinet at the entrance to the place, hoping there was fish on the menu

"You can live in my apartment until he is on his feet, as they say. Wait until he asks – no, demands – to see you!"

Sylvano nodded at the waitress as he tasted the wine.

"Are you absolutely sure?" Jane asked, as she watched her glass being refilled.

"Really," Sylvano persisted. "It is no trouble."

He surveyed her face and then leant on his elbow, his head tilted.

"I would like to see this thing end well for you, Jane. And – if I am honest –" he started laughing before completing his confession. "I want to be around for the grand finale – or at least *know* the ending."

Jane smiled at his honesty.

"Are you expecting fireworks and drama?"

"At the very least!"

They ate and drank in silence for a few minutes.

"So," said Sylvano, leaning back, holding his wine glass. "What is your plan?"

"I'm going to go back to the hospital tomorrow afternoon, I think. And, no," she held up her hand. "You do not need to be involved. I can take the fast train to Bologna. I will ask to see him again, and, if refused, I'll leave a note for him with one of the nurses or a doctor."

She shrugged.

"And then see what happens."

Sylvano nodded and then beckoned the waiter, requesting another jug of, much needed, water.

CHAPTER 30

Grief didn't work like that

Jane awoke with a severe hangover. When she tried to recall the last hour of her evening with Sylvano, she found she couldn't. She didn't even remember entering her apartment although, clearly, she had arrived back safely as she was now in her bed and her phone was vibrating noisily on the bedside table. It was gone 8am and she needed to shower, pack and vacate by the allotted 10am.

Gulping down two glasses of water, accompanied by some pain relievers, she then made a black coffee before slinging her case onto the bed. A wave of nausea overtook her every time she lowered her head and she was forced to take regular breaks between the various stages of packing. It was hardly the wisest start to what was likely to be a challenging – and emotional – day.

Richard's case had not been emptied. After she'd ransacked it, concluding that he'd taken all his important documents with him on that fateful night, the case had been left it to sit, balefully, in the corner of the room. Even his toilet bag remained inside. Picking it up, she placed it in the hall by the front door, just in case, in her weakened condition, she forgot about it.

At a few minutes to ten, the apartment doorbell rang. It was Sylvano, seemingly in a rush, as he thrust his keys at Jane and said he needed to be at a meeting on the other side of the city in ten minutes.

"I am late," he gasped, dragging a hand through his hair.

"You look like I feel," quipped Jane. This remark was not understood by Sylvano, who simply smiled politely and apologised for not being there earlier as had, apparently, been arranged when they'd parted the previous evening.

"You will manage your luggage?" he asked, unable to entirely abandon his manners.

"Of course," said Jane. "I'm so grateful to you. Go! I'll be fine. I'll keep in touch about everything, I promise."

"Those are my spare keys. Take them with you," he instructed, before disappearing in the direction of the stairs, the clattering of his shoes echoing around the building as he sped down them.

"Thanks!" she called after him.

Keen to avoid any conversation about Richard, or indeed any conversation whatsoever, Jane didn't wait to hand over the keys to Signora Greco, the lady with the fake face and flamboyant jewellery, just left them on the hall stand. She felt a surge of relief as the door slammed shut behind her.

Sylvano's flat was light and airy and smelt of fresh coffee. He'd left the balcony windows open, the duck-egg blue drapes flapping gently in the breeze. She spent a minute looking at one of the large original abstract paintings hanging in the living room, wondering if he'd hung it upside down, before locating her room and depositing the bags. Sylvano had told her that the trains to Bologna were fast and frequent and she should be able to pick up a taxi easily from outside the station. Tempting though it was to take advantage of Sylvano's generosity and to linger in that quiet safe place – to make herself yet another espresso and sit on the balcony amidst the herbs and blooms – Jane didn't. She ensured she had a fully charged phone and pen and paper and left within ten minutes of her arrival.

On the train, she mused over what she should say in the note to Richard, assuming the necessity for one. There was something poignant, she thought, in considering its contents. Their relationship had begun with a note. Was it to end with one too? As the train rattled its way through the numerous tunnels between the two cities, she felt no surprise at the ambivalence growing inside her.

She was seeking a dénouement if only because, she reasoned, this chapter of her life required one.

~ ~ ~

In the event, no note was needed. Nor were explanations required at the door of Richard's ward. The nurse asked Jane to wait while she spoke to Richard whom – as she understood – was much brighter that morning. There was no sign of Phoebe or Cressie either. No doubt they hadn't anticipated such a speedy return visit from Jane and thus had abandoned their twenty-four-hour vigil at his bedside.

Within minutes, she was staring at Richard's battered face, one of his eyes completely closed, the other so bloodshot it was difficult to know whether he could see her at all. He hauled himself up to a semi-sitting position and then, still slumped sideways, he smiled weakly at her and murmured something. Jane took his hand, noticing the scabs on his knuckles.

"God, Richard," she said gently. "You have been in the wars, haven't you? I'm so sorry."

"I'm not as bad as I look," he said, attempting another brief smile. She glanced at his mouth, anxious to check he still had his teeth. There was a small cut on his lower lip but, otherwise, his smile was intact.

"Have you seen the girls?" he asked.

It was a question she should have anticipated.

She nodded.

"I'm not sure I was entirely welcome." *What an understatement*, she thought.

"Why?" asked Richard, his bloodshot eye flickering over her face.

"It doesn't matter," she said. "I'm here now. I....I wanted to see you. Christ, I wanted to see you." Her last words caught in her throat as the tears sprang into her eyes. If she'd had one solid intention that afternoon, it was that she would not cry.

"I'm not being helpful," she gulped. "I'm sorry. It's just been a very difficult few days not knowing if you were dead or alive. It's the relief. The tears I mean."

Richard nodded and she felt him squeeze her hand.

"I'll be fine," he said. "Were you able to stay on in the apartment? Weren't we supposed to be leaving today? I've lost track, actually."

"No but I managed to store our bags this morning before I headed over here to see you. I wanted to talk to you before making any decisions."

She wasn't going to mention Sylvano. It was a gamble of course. If the girls were determined to do her damage, they would make capital of the fact she hadn't told their father of his existence. On the other hand, if she went into detail about him there and then, at Richard's bedside, it might sound like a confession. *He's just a friend. There's nothing between us.*

She leant over and kissed him lightly on the lips. His hands come up to clasp her face and she felt the wetness of his tears on her own face as they cradled each other.

"I kept thinking about you," he whispered. "It's so good to be back with you. To touch you."

His words surprised her. She had expected some faux stoicism from him, his pride too great to admit that, after all his suffering, his greatest need was to be held by her. But, she supposed, his ordeal had been more than the usual reminders of our mortality; the mangled vehicle by the side of the road, the floating wreckage of a plane. He *looked* as though he'd fought for his life. He *talked* as if he no longer needed to be reminded of what mattered. He'd expected to be killed and he'd survived.

"Do you want me to stay?" she asked.

"Of course," he said, huskily.

"Then I'll stay," she said, smiling.

A trolley came into the room bearing lunch and a tray was slotted in front of Richard, it being assumed he would be partaking of the lasagne and salad in front of him. The lady involved, large and smiling, spoke some rapid Italian to him. Richard smiled and muttered his thanks.

"I think she said I was looking much better this morning," he said. "They appear to have forgotten that I'm supposed to be careful about consuming too much food too quickly."

As Richard picked his way through his meal and Jane watched him, she learned about his experience little by little. He'd been smashed in the face more than once when they'd first captured him a couple of hundred yards from the University. They'd beckoned him over and "like a fool, I went" and then he was dragged into the back of the van and given a couple of vicious punches to stop him shouting. He'd struggled so he got a couple more before realising there was no purpose to his protests.

"They realised their mistake once we got back to the cellar in Bologna. They took my bag and went through everything. I begged them to drive me back and just dump me on the street but they wouldn't. From what I gather, they'd already made the phone call to the tycoon's family and had no idea what to do. I heard a lot of argument and although I understood very little of what they said, it was obvious they were panicking."

"Were you given food?"

"Some, a little, and just cups of water twice a day. I can tell you now that being thirsty is torture. I was really dehydrated by the time I was rescued. And I didn't sleep either. It was impossible, despite the dark."

"Eat," said Jane. "Can you manage a few more mouthfuls?"

Richard shook his head and leant back into his pillow. He closed his bloodshot eye.

"Sorry," he said. "I'm just so tired."

"Look," said Jane, taking the fork from his hand and placing it back on the tray. "Why don't I go back to Florence, pick up our bags and come back. Find a hotel. Until you're discharged."

"I think I'll be out tomorrow," said Richard, opening his one good eye and looking at her. "There's nothing wrong with me. No broken bones. Just fatigue. I think I have to stick around in the city to speak to the police before we can head home. Is that a problem for you? With work?"

Jane laughed.

"Not anymore. I quit. I had a moment of enlightenment in the Boboli gardens."

She left a few minutes later, telling the nurses that she'd be back that evening.

At the exit to the hospital, she saw Phoebe and Cressie walking towards her. There would be no escaping the confrontation.

"What are *you* doing here?" barked Phoebe. She looked exquisite in a short white dress and high-heeled strappy white sandals.

Fighting the impulse to walk on and ignore them, Jane stopped. She knew she needed to *behave*.

"I've seen your father. He wanted to see me. We agreed I'd come back this evening. So just to be clear, I'm looking for a hotel here in Bologna where we can go when he's discharged. So for his sake, Phoebe, can we please abandon this ridiculous charade. He's safe with me. I'm not sure why you think otherwise."

Phoebe raised one of her over-plucked eyebrows.

"I think," she said, turning to Cressie who was looking mildly uncomfortable, "*We* think you're a schemer, Jane."

"Well, there's nothing I can do about that," responded Jane. "I don't need to *scheme,* as you put it. But hey, I've got an idea. Why don't you allow your father to make his own decision about me? He's not a fool. In fact, he's about as far from a fool as any man I've ever met. I'm surprised that neither of you seem to recognize that."

"He doesn't know the truth about you," chipped in Cressie, taking advantage of Phoebe's failure to spit back an immediate rejoinder.

"Well I can depend on you two to enlighten him," Jane replied, as she walked away. As she did so, it occurred to her that Richard's interests were in danger of being eclipsed in their continuing spat. But it was too late. The darling daughters were already marching purposefully towards the hospital entrance.

Back on the train, Jane messaged Sylvano to update him, saying she might not be able to thank him in person as she needed to travel back that same evening. There appeared to be lots of vacant hotel rooms in Bologna so booking something for her and Richard did not appear to be a problem. Knowing how long their stay might last was more of one.

Sylvano, I am truly grateful for the friendship and support you have shown me during the last few days. Thank you.

Sylvano texted back that he was unlikely to be at the apartment when she collected her luggage and she should let him know when she and Richard were finally reunited.

I'm sure this horrible experience will mean you stay lovers forever! My best wishes to both of you!

~ ~ ~

Jane was both surprised and relieved when, the following morning, Richard was discharged into her clutches without – seemingly – any further objection from Phoebe and Cressie. Later, she was to conclude that they'd allowed themselves such dereliction of daughterly duty by injecting a healthy dollop of poison into their father's heart. And, Jane reluctantly reminded herself, while she had positively invited the girls to share what 'dirt' they had on her with Richard, she had not anticipated that they would do quite such a thorough job. Having previously adopted an almost disconcerting lack of interest in Jane's past life and loves, Richard was now keen to make up for his neglect. It prompted him, it appeared, to begin his interrogation of her with a question concerning Gladys King.

"Exactly what happened between you and this old biddy, Gladys whatsit, which persuaded her to leave you her fortune? I understand foul play was alleged."

After Ruby King's tweets, there had been other exchanges #Gladys King which – in the last 24 hours – Jane had not bothered reading.

My sister and I never got the explanation we were due. But we were diddled out of our inheritance without doubt. A woman without morals, Jane Sedgefield.

The method by which Jane and Larry had come to acquire the necessary monies to purchase *The Old Byre* had never been discussed between them.

"So you weren't related to her at all, then?" Richard continued.

He was lying in the king-sized bed in the suite Jane had booked for them in a fashionable part of the city. The hotel staff had been given prior warning of his condition and had been suitably attentive to their needs. At that very moment they were awaiting some coffee and sandwiches courtesy of room service. Jane was standing at one of the sets of French windows looking out over the city's red tiled rooftops to the soft green hills beyond and recalling *Masaccio's* frescoes. She'd been looking forward to impressing Richard with details of her visit to the Chapel.

She turned away from the window to face him.

"Are you ok with this window being open?" she asked. "The sun's not yet come over to this side."

"Well, were you?"

"Related to her? No, I wasn't. She took a shine to me, that's all. I was as surprised as anyone, I can tell you."

"So how long did you know her?" Richard persisted.

Jane sighed and sat down at the foot of the bed, rubbing Richard's feet with both her hands.

"Why are you interested? What does it matter? Is this about all the rumours going round on Twitter? It's not like you to be bothered by gossip."

"Are you being deliberately evasive?"

"What if I said I didn't think it was anyone's business but mine and I didn't want to discuss it? It's water under the bridge."

"Lawyers were involved, weren't they?"

Jane stood up and moved back to the window.

"We need to get your passport sorted out, don't we? That's what we should be focusing on, Richard."

"Sure. Phoebe did something about cancelling my bank cards after a lot of yelling down the phone at the bank. She's given me one of her credit cards for the time being."

Jane smiled. "There was no need. I can settle the bills. When are you likely to be interviewed by the police?"

"Tomorrow, I think. I assume Phoebe has passed on my new mobile number to Pavesi. She said she would."

"Well, you'd better contact the Embassy or whoever it is you need to help with the missing passport. Although I don't mind hanging on here for a while. What I've seen of the city so far, it seems really interesting. I went into the Cathedral earlier. It's vast. Lots of beautiful marble columns."

"I need to get home as soon as I can, actually," said Richard. "I've a lot of work to catch up on. I was hoping we could look at flights home as soon as I've satisfied the authorities."

That same night, they went to the small restaurant in the basement of the hotel for dinner. Richard seemed brighter. His closed eye was gradually opening although the bruises on his face were still in the process of changing colour, even as Jane looked at him from the other side of the dinner table.

She'd asked him whether it would help to talk about his ordeal at the hands of the kidnappers but he'd been very clear that it wasn't 'necessary'. Since those first few hours when he'd let down his guard and allowed Jane to comfort him, she had watched him gradually rebuild the barrier to the intimacy which she'd glimpsed. Except that now she knew that he was capable of showing such affection but preferred to withhold it, she began to question whether there was any real future for them. These thoughts, disturbingly clear, kept popping up throughout the meal. Neither of them had much of an appetite. Jane's had diminished from almost the moment they'd sat down. She kept reminding herself of Richard's experience and how unfair it might be to him to be so critical of the emotional straitjacket he seemed intent on wriggling back into.

"You know, Richard," she said, putting down her fork even though she'd only just picked it up to attack the salmon dish she'd ordered. "It is ok to admit to how frightened you've been and what a relief it is to be back. Safely."

Richard nodded and smiled; briefly, insincerely.

"And there's no need to patronise me, Jane," he said a few moments later.

Jane's eyes widened in disbelief.

"I wasn't. I'm actually trying to help you."

"Well, I'm fine. I'll talk if I need to. You don't need to try to *cajole* me into doing so."

"Ok," said Jane, after a minute's awkward silence. "What would you like to talk about – assuming you do, of course?"

Richard looked up from his plate of lamb and vegetables.

"What did you get up to while I was whiling away the time in that vile basement? This man who the girls mentioned for a start. Did you sleep with him?"

"Is that a serious question?"

Richard nodded although Jane detected that he wasn't truly comfortable with the direction their conversation was taking. Was he, after all, displaying some newly acquired vulnerability?

But, even if this were the case, Jane could not help herself from going on the attack.

"Gosh, your dear daughters really have gone to work on you, haven't they?" she snapped, bringing the wine glass to her lips so fiercely that the red liquid spilled out, seeping into the white linen tablecloth like blood.

"I know things have been difficult between the three of you. But I can't believe they've reached these conclusions without some... some justification. I suspect that's difficult for you to hear."

"What conclusions, Richard? Spell them out. You don't usually have difficulty in saying precisely what you mean."

"You know, about you and this Italian guy. Hanging around our apartment, drinking cocktails with him. It reminds me of the easy way you flirted with that man at the airport."

Jane surveyed him.

"He was helping me, Richard."

She started to explain how they'd met at the door of the apartment block, how Sylvano had been concerned for her.

"I would not have heard anything about your release had it not been for Sylvano. Phoebe was determined to exclude me, believing everything she read on Facebook and the like, jumping to conclusions without the courtesy of asking me for an explanation."

"Both she and Cressie said you were incredibly rude to them and made it very clear that you didn't want them staying at the apartment."

"Oh, nonsense!" exploded Jane. "They seemed keen to believe the worst of me. I responded in anger. Yes, perhaps unwisely. But it wasn't exactly an easy time for me, either. Do forgive me for seeking out a friendly face."

"It hurt me when they told me how badly you'd behaved towards them. Cressie was in tears. And, anyway, even now you don't seem to want to answer any questions directly," said Richard. "It's not surprising that people think the worst of you."

It was Larry she wanted then, wanted him with such intensity that the urge to throw back her head and howl with misery became almost overwhelming. She looked about her, trying to disassociate herself from the situation developing at such speed between her and Richard; their unravelling. It had taken only a matter of a day for them to become, what felt like now, virtual strangers.

That night, they slept fitfully together, each keeping to their side of the bed. There was no attempt at affection, just a polite exchange when necessary. Unable to keep her memories of Larry at bay, she eventually gave in and allowed herself to be submerged in regret and longing. She made a confession too. She had many, many miles to travel before she came to terms with his loss. Until then, she'd employed, quite cleverly, a number of distractions to avoid being dragged into the pit of grief which awaited her. It was no use pretending that she wouldn't enter this smoking cavern until she'd been told how and where to exit it. Grief didn't work like that. Once you reached its edge, a claw would catch your ankle and pull you down into the gloom. And there were no companions in there.

Most definitely, you were on your own.

CHAPTER 31

The sleepy tiger and the strange-faced arhat

Debbie was helping Alicja pack her bag. It was half term and Alicja was moving out, returning to live with her mother in the new flat which wasn't a patch on the old one and about as far removed from the wildness and beauty of the nature reserve as it could be. But Debbie had assured her that she could visit at any time and enjoy the bird hide. A pair of willow warblers had been spotted the previous weekend by an enthusiastic twitcher and chalked up on the board. Others were sceptical and had added a couple of question marks to the entry.

Alicja had not wanted to leave Debbie's but Halina's newfound respectability had prodded her conscience regarding her new flat. She now worried she'd have to pay the extra – the infamous bedroom tax – or she would lose the property in the fullness of time. She pleaded with Alicja and Alicja had given in.

"And my room is small," she complained to Debbie. "Half the size of my old one."

Debbie took her by the shoulders. "Look, you can always come back here for weekends. I'm not going to let the room out if that's what you're worried about. It's yours whenever you want it."

Alicja hugged her tightly. "You have been so good to me, Debbie. Thank you."

"Things are very different now. Your mum's got a regular job and is making a fresh start. That's fantastic. Compare your circumstances to a year ago. And you've got Matthew too!"

"And the trip to Poland in the summer," added Alicja. "I am pleased about that. It will be so good to meet my family. To know my roots. See their faces." She blushed a little, wondering if she was giving too much of herself away. Debbie nodded and kissed her lightly on the cheek. *Christ, if you can't have dreams at 15 years old, what hope is there for any of us,* she thought as she stuffed the last jumper into the side of Alicja's sports bag.

Alicja had yet to tell Arik that her plans had changed. Matthew had suggested she tell him she'd postponed them for the time being, that she would visit sometime in the future, just not that summer. She'd learned more about the struggles Halina had faced as a young single mother, her resentment leaking away as she noted what it cost her mother to own her past mistakes.

"And how's the Polish going?" asked Debbie.

"Mum is teaching me the odd phrase. I'm still looking for a course although with GCSEs on the horizon, I need to be realistic."

"Very sensible," Debbie commented, looking around the room. "I think that's it, and I suppose we ought to get going before the traffic builds up."

Alicja went over to the window and Debbie joined her. There was some distant honking and then five Canada geese appeared in graceful formation and crash landed, gracelessly, in the water. A nearby moorhen took offence and paddled away quickly, its little head bobbing up and down. Pure white clouds chased each other across a blue sky.

"I will so miss this, Debbie."

~ ~ ~

. Alex Snow was in celebration mode. Veronica Stern had called him and said that 'with a heavy heart' she was prepared to negotiate with Bradley Blake. Her capitulation was late but 'not too late' he advised, attempting to keep his elation in check.

"I will soon be rid of that wretched woman," he told David Evans, whose head had appeared from around the door saying he had some gossip to impart.

David interpreted Alex's remark as an invitation to invade the sanctuary of his office.

"Oh yes," he drawled. "And this was the case that was about as watertight as it could be?" He clicked his teeth and shook his head. "Losing your touch, Alex, if you ask me."

Alex looked at him.

"Actually, I've been wondering if it's not time I parted company with the law. Retired, to be blunt."

He was surprised at the thrill which surged through him as he spoke his thoughts out loud. *Freedom.*

"What? Are you serious?"

Alex smiled at the look of shock on David's plump face.

"Deadly. But I'll take the weekend to crystalise my plans."

"Well, keep me posted. And oh yes, the gossip."

Alex emitted an audible sigh but David continued.

"I just got a call from the father of our former client – June Sedgefield."

"Jane."

"Whatever. Well, she's selling her house. You know, the one she bought at the end of last year."

"Her father called?"

"Yes, she's still in Italy and apparently, not sure when she's returning – if at all. But, in any event, if she does it won't be to that converted pile in Cirencester. Have you read much about what she went through in Italy with that bloke of hers? He was found in the end. His daughters have been spilling the beans to the tabloids. Actually, one of them is a model – quite a looker."

Alex cut him off, standing up and pulling his jacket off the back of his chair.

"Fascinating, David. But I'm off to lunch. See you later."

As he left the room, David called after him.

"Let me know if we need to call a partners' meeting, won't you?"

Alex put his hand up in the air and waved, acknowledging David's request – but he didn't turn around.

~ ~ ~

Jane's telephone conversation with her father had been difficult.

The tentacles of social media had not reached her parents or their little body of friends. But the tabloids had. By the time Jane had worked out what she would reveal to them – and what she would not – her story was out, in all its sordid detail. Her parents knew the salient facts: she'd gone to Florence with her 'new man' – *yes, would you believe it, the very man whom Larry had swerved to avoid when he'd been killed!* – who'd been kidnapped, possibly tortured but eventually rescued from a cellar in Bologna by the Italian Special Operations Unit.

Kidnapped Brit found beaten but alive in bunker in Bologna

"Sounds like a crossword clue," quipped her father, despite his disappointment at the exposure of his daughter's morals to the entire world.

"At least you're ok," he concluded, after many awkward gaps in their conversation. "But your mother is heartbroken, Jane, I can tell you. So she won't be coming to the phone just now. You'll need to give her a bit more time."

Jane muttered her apologies, more than once, guilt-ridden as she recalled their sweet, kind faces when they'd stayed with her after Larry's funeral. She didn't bother with any justifications or explanations. She was no longer sure she had any.

Her father had argued with her over her insistence that he *immediately* organise the sale of *The Old Byre*, saying she was making a momentous decision in the worst circumstances possible.

"What's the harm in waiting, love? The dust will settle. You know what they say – today's news is tomorrow's fish and chip paper!"

But Jane was adamant and begged him to speak to David Jackson on her behalf. She'd forward an address in due course where the documentation could be sent.

"Just do this one thing for me, *please* Dad," she implored and her father, hearing the desperation in her far-away voice, relented and promised to do her bidding.

"But where are you going now, Jane? Are you with this... this same man. Richard? What are your plans?"

"No, I'm not with him, Dad. His daughters are looking after him. I think it unlikely I'll see him again."

Her parting from Richard had been a low-key affair. If either of them had thought that a good night's rest, if not sleep, might rebalance them, it had not come to pass. Once Jane had established that Phoebe and Cressie had yet to fly back to the UK and remained in Bologna, she had little conscience about her decision to abandon him. The following morning, after breakfast had been delivered to their room, they embraced briefly and with little further discussion – "I'll settle the bill for last night and tonight, don't worry. I hope things work out for you, Richard." She'd turned to look at him as she left the room and was momentarily struck by the pathos of the man, sitting on the side of the bed, his face still an almost vibrant display of blues and blacks. But he didn't say 'don't go, Jane' or 'I'm sorry.' He didn't try to stop her from leaving.

Jane's father was a practical man. His daughter's vague intentions were just not good enough.

"Jane, please! You must have formed some idea of where you'll go. Or are you staying in Bologna for the time being? Why not come home and stay with us for a while?"

Home? She didn't know what that meant any more. The concept of home had disappeared with Larry.

There was a long pause before Jane answered him.

"I'm going to look for a mountain," she said. "Although I doubt there'll be any tigers there."

She thought of adding context to this declaration; about seeking a place where she would be alone. Perhaps by a lake or on an island, she might have said, where her memories could come and go as they pleased – like the surf in the sea or the clouds in the wind.

"So I won't be coming back," were her final words to her father that afternoon.

And, in that moment, the sleepy tiger and the strange-faced *arhat* having appeared with startling clarity in her mind's eye, she was surprised to discover that the prospect of being alone with her grief no longer daunted her.

> *Living in the mountain,*
> *just let the year advance*
> *entirely as it likes.*

THE END

Acknowledgements

The exhibition of Japanese *surimono* poetry prints at the Ashmolean Museum in Oxford took place between October 2018 and March 2019. The book accompanying the exhibition *Plum Blossom & Green Willow* can be purchased online from the museum itself or from other outlets.

The print which so fascinated Jane – *An arhat with a tiger* – is on page 43 of that book (although a search on the web should also bring up the print).

Finally...

If you have enjoyed this sequel, please check out the rest of my list:

Putney Bridge
A Crack in the Door (long listed for the Bridport Prize 2017)
The Contagion of Loss
The Back Room

And – if you're in the mood for romance – *Hedgeman!*

All are available on Amazon Kindle.